BIA'S BLADE

A RELIC HUNTERS NOVEL

KERI ARTHUR

With thanks to:

The Lulus
Indigo Chick Designs
The lovely ladies at Hot Tree Editing
Jason Nuhrung Editing Services
The ladies from Central Vic Writers
Julie from Cover Craft for gorgeous cover

CHAPTER

ONE

The man who stood in front of me was tall and thickset, with long silver hair, eyes that swirled with clouds of gray, and an aura that resonated with the power of storms. His face was lean, and his skin almost translucent. He was certainly a handsome man—not elven perfect, perhaps, but damn close to it.

Except he wasn't a man.

He was a god of thunder and lightning.

One who had been bound to Earth in the form of a curmudgeon—the male version of a hag. Unlike their female counterparts, however, curmudgeons were able to shift into a more pleasing countenance, and I couldn't help but wonder if this was the form he'd used when he'd seduced my mother and begat me.

For several minutes, neither of us moved. He simply studied me, his gaze scanning my length, as if searching for something. When his eyes finally rose to mine again, a flicker of... not so much disappointment, though that was definitely there, but rather annoyance, ran through them.

"You know," I said, never one to keep quiet even when

that was probably the best option, "if you're disappointed in how I turned out, you've only yourself to blame."

Amusement lurked briefly in his expression then fell away. "And how do you come to that conclusion?"

His voice was filled with gravitas and warmth and resonated through every inch of my being, oddly connecting with something deep within. What that something was, I couldn't say, but I wasn't sure I liked the sensation.

"Well," I said evenly, despite the belated stirring of trepidation, "aside from the initial few minutes of involvement at my conception, you've basically had nothing to do with me in my sixty-odd years of existence."

A dark silver eyebrow rose at that, and once again the amusement flared. I wasn't sure what reaction I'd expected from my godly parent, but this definitely wasn't it.

"Is not sixty-two considered to be little more than a sapling in terms of pixie development?"

"Well, yes, but if you were expecting me to be something other than what I am, then you should have come forward earlier and had a little fatherly input in how I was raised." I paused. "Which leads to the question, why appear now? And why here? Liadon's realm is considered neutral ground by those who play this bout of godly games, and this meeting jeopardizes that neutrality, does it not?"

Liadon was the guardian of what Deva's Fae Council—who I now rather reluctantly worked for—called the Cavern of the Gods. It was basically a world between worlds—an access point, if you will, for gods and who knew what else to enter or leave our world. But it was also a library that not only held all council records from their inception, but also the records of all earthly races and their histories. *That* was what I was after. Somewhere in those records might be the name of the man—or woman—who had killed my mother.

As for the fucking games... the old gods considered testing humanity in various cataclysmic ways a sport and, in the past, had chosen their players and thrown chaos their way just to see what eventuated. According to Liadon, what the gods found so fascinating was the fact not even *they* could predict how those within any active game would react to the stimuli provided.

Unfortunately, after a few pleasant centuries without such input on their part, a new game was afoot—one that was, by all accounts, started by my father, with me the "Queen" on his side of the playing board. Which meant, of course, I had a counterpart running about somewhere. I had no idea who that person might be, though if this game involved the rat god's—or Ninkil, to give him his proper moniker—rising into our world, then it might well be Carla Wilson, a multi-shifter who could take on any human form she wished, and who we believed had her claws in multiple council members. And I knew—because I'd seen in a vision —that she was sexually involved with the man who was the Ninkilim's current leader. A man whose name we didn' t yet know.

"Did you not bid Liadon to fetch me less than a week ago?" he asked. "In fact, did you not say you were unimpressed with my efforts so far?"

Despite the flares of amusement, the clouds in his eyes were darkening, and a chill that was part trepidation, part recognition stirred. Because those same shadows moved within me, and I had a bad feeling that was what he intended, what he wanted to draw out.

"Well, yes, but it wasn't like either of us actually expected you to hear me say that, let alone respond."

"There are no secrets in this place, other than the scriptures and memories Liadon guards. These"—he waved a hand toward the small chamber's brown-streaked black walls, which held none of the smooth luminosity that was a feature in the other tunnels and chambers—"are here to protect you from sights and sound beyond your ken."

"And no doubt also protect me from those who would destroy your queen in the current godly game."

His expression remained pleasant, but the storm around his form was intensifying, matching the intensity gathering in his eyes. "You are not my queen. You are more... a knight."

My gaze was drawn to the briefest movement beyond the chamber's thin walls, and I clenched my fingers against the desire to grab my knives. Liadon would not have allowed this meeting to take place without it being safe for both of us, but I couldn't escape the notion that what lurked beyond the oddly streaked walls was no friend to either of us.

Which might well be the whole point of this meeting. Maybe in being here, talking to me, he was announcing to the opposition that he was stepping fully into the fray.

If he *was*, then that could only be bad news for me.

"Why is that?" I said, somehow dragging my gaze away from the movement. "Isn't a queen the most powerful piece on any chess board?"

"Situationally yes, but the knight is the only piece on the board that moves completely different to every other piece. And that, I believe, is an apt description of yourself."

As summations went, I couldn't argue that it wasn't on point. "Then was Beira wrong when she said you were not one to play these games?"

"No."

I waited several beats, but when he didn't continue, added, "Does that mean Liadon was wrong when she said you started these games?"

"No."

"Then, as I said only a few minutes ago, why the fuck are you here? What is the point of all this?"

He took a step forward, bringing me into the circle of his aura; electricity danced across my skin and lightning flared through my being, once again drawing on the deeper darkness that lurked within.

A darkness I'd been fighting for weeks now.

I clenched my fists tighter still and stepped away. The dangerous brush of energy eased, but I still felt it deep within.

"What are you doing?" I growled, fear, anger, and perhaps even a touch of... avarice?... running through me. I might not *like* the feel of the lightning's caress, but that inner darkness wanted it.

Bad.

"*I* am doing nothing."

"Bullshit."

One eyebrow rose. "You have your mother's straightforwardness."

"Well, I certainly didn't get it from you, as you seem to be doing everything *but* giving me answers."

"I needed to see if you are worthy, child. Needed to know if you are capable of withstanding the darkness that rises."

"What darkness are we talking about here? Ninkil? Or the one you're trying to draw out of me?"

"Both."

"To repeat—why?"

"Because to defeat darkness, you sometimes have to embrace it."

"Then we are doomed."

"There *are* degrees of darkness," he commented. "Ask the man who would be king."

My heart skipped several beats. There was only one man in my life about to be crowned, and while he'd been an integral part of the hunt for the missing Éadrom Hoard up until his father had passed, it was doubtful he would remain so now.

"Cynwrig?" I replied, unable to keep the edge out of my voice. "What the fuck has he got to do with anything?"

"Did you not ask who the king to your queen was?"

"Yes, but you've already said I'm not your queen, and I will certainly never be *his*."

"Perhaps not, but remember, chaos is the point of our games."

Meaning he'd been placed in my path to cause problems? That he was never meant to be an end game? Which, rationally, I already knew. Trouble was, when it came to Cynwrig, rational and me weren't often on speaking terms.

"Is the refusal to harbor darkness the reason your first child failed?"

"In truth, she neither failed nor won. Ninkil was not unleashed on this world, but he was not ended either. The game stalemated."

My eyebrows rose. "How can a god be ended? Don't you just leave this world permanently?"

"All things can be ended—it just takes the right weapon and motivation." He motioned to my purse. "You carry two such weapons."

He was referring to my silver knives, which had been gifted to the females of my line back in the days when we—

alongside the Taliesin pixies—had been the guardians of godly treasures. Both had been blessed by multiple goddesses and were capable of protecting me against all sorts of magic. His comment did at least confirm the family rumor they were an effective weapon against male gods, but in reality, there was little likelihood of me ever being able to use them that way. Said male god would simply smite me long before I ever got within stabbing or throwing distance.

"Did your firstborn carry such a weapon?"

"No, though she was an Aodhán such as yourself. Just not of your line, and definitely holding none of your mother's seeress abilities."

Suggesting those abilities—which had made her one of the preeminent relic hunters in the UK—had factored into his seduction. Though if I knew Mom, she'd probably been aware of his plans. After all, she'd worked with the hags for a very long time, was familiar with their very different energies, and likely would have known who and what Ambisagrus was the minute he'd come to her. If she'd allowed the pregnancy—could you actually stop a god impregnating you?—perhaps she'd foreseen that the daughter she'd give birth to would one day walk amongst the gods and do their bidding. And yet, if that *was* the case, then why hadn't she done all she could to prepare me? Why had she refused to train me until it was all too late?

There were so many damn things I just didn't know. So many answers I would never get, at least not from her.

"And the darkness you mentioned?" I growled. "How did that play into your first child's death?"

"In the end, it did not, because she failed to embrace it."

"Which is why you're trying to force its emergence in me."

"It already emerges in you, as you are well aware."

"Then why does your power still run through me? What lies behind it, if not an effort to bring the darkness to the fore?"

"That, I cannot say."

Frustration sharpened, once again overriding caution. "Seriously, what is it with you gods avoiding direct answers? Is that part of the game's rules or something?"

"If the road is without obstacles, where is the fun?" He held up a hand to stop my retort. "There are rules that cannot be broken. However, they can be bent, which is why I am here. Please, let us sit."

It was on the tip of my tongue to say "let us not" but I resisted the urge. The clouds still lurked, and while the dangerous energy had retreated, lightning still flickered around his body, a sharp reminder of what he was, what he could do. I'd been told that as a godling, I could not be undone or otherwise altered, but did that statement apply when the undoer was my father?

I seriously hoped I never got an answer to *that* particular question.

I turned and discovered two rather plush-looking chairs now sitting where seconds ago there had been only emptiness. I walked over to the nearest one and sat. I might as well have been sitting on a cloud rather than anything resembling a common old chair.

He sat opposite me and crossed one leg over the other, the movement elegance itself.

"To answer one of your questions, Beira was right in that I am generally not a player of these games. Aside from the fact I am a curmudgeon, which makes participation a trifle harder, I find them tedious. In fact, the only other time I participated was the last time Ninkil attempted to rise."

"You're not a fan of the chaos he creates?"

"Indeed no, though if that was all he brought to the table, I would let him be. He is not, after all, the only god who delights in the taste of chaos—the games are proof enough of that. It is his insistence that our artifacts be released unfettered into this world that I and others oppose. Humanity was never meant for such objects, and few can truly understand or control them."

"And yet they do find their way into our hands."

"Only those whose destructive nature is not world destroying."

"Agrona's claws could have destroyed our world."

Thankfully, the man who'd claimed those claws had wanted to destroy Annwfyn—a world that exists alongside and yet apart from ours, accessible by bridges of darkness and inhabited by an elf-like people who considered humans and fae damn fine eating—in retribution for their attack and erasure of his entire family.

"Indeed," my father was saying, "though I doubt it was Ninkil or his followers who unleashed those particular artifacts. It would be pointless rising into a world in which chaos and destruction has already been unleashed."

"But he *was* behind the theft of the hoard from the Ljósálfar?"

There were two elven lines in the United Kingdom—the Ljósálfar, otherwise known as light elves, and the Myrkálfar, who were dark elves. Most humans believed Myrkálfar to be the more dangerous of the two, and while it was true they ruled the black market with an iron fist, the wise knew it was the golden-haired, golden-skinned Ljósálfar you truly had to fear.

"His earthly followers were, that is a certainty. And before you ask, no, I can provide no names. That would break rather than bend the rules and be dangerous for us both."

"Because the game itself doesn't hold *any* danger to me at all, does it?"

My tone was dry, and a smile flirted with his lips again before receding back into coldness. "You have already foreseen one possible end this quest holds, as that fate is the same as the one that claimed my first seed's life."

His words had the vision I'd had via Castell—the blind light elf oracle who sent me a message from him—rising. It had started with shadows and fire that gave way to a cowled figure standing over a sacrificial stone darkly stained with eons of bloodshed, and a knife that gleamed with an unearthly light raised high. Words had filled the air with darkness and intent. Words meant to take life and gift it to another. Words designed to restore Ninkil's place in this world. The knife had flashed down, finally revealing the sacrifice—a red-haired and green-eyed woman whose features could not be seen.

"If your first child was sacrificed on Ninkil's altar, how did she stop his rise?"

"I'm afraid—"

"It's not within the rules to tell me," I finished for him. "But if you're hoping I'll willingly sacrifice my life for the greater good of the world, I'm afraid you will be disappointed."

"I would hope so. Sacrifice worked once, but it will not do so again. Ninkil is many things, but he is not stupid."

"Then why say sacrifice might yet be my future?"

"Because it is a possibility that remains in play. Your bloodline—that of a god and a seeress of extraordinary strength—holds the necessary power to bring forth a banished god."

Suggesting his first daughter had been powerful in her own right—and that Liadon had been right. The darkness he was still attempting to bring to the fore in *me* was very much a part of *his* line.

"Then how do I stop him *without* ending up as a sacrifice?"

"He has a relic—"

"The Harpē? Yeah, we know."

"Find it and destroy it."

"You don't think we've been trying?"

"To the degree that's necessary, no, and it emboldens our enemies."

"Those enemies watch every step I take, and until I can uncover how, slow progress is the better option." The clouds in his eyes darkened, an obvious indication he disagreed. Tough, I wanted to say, but resisted. "Once I *do* find it, what am I meant to do with it?"

"Destroy it, of course."

"In the forge of the gods?"

"For normal artifacts that is an ideal solution, but the Ninkilim will feel the moment you lay a hand—be it flesh or wind—on the Harpē, and they will swarm your location to claim it. You must destroy it with the power my blood has given you."

"Drawing down that much lightning could kill me."

"Indeed." He paused. "In fact, your death is a necessity for the game to be won."

CHAPTER
TWO

For several seconds, his words echoed around me, gaining no traction or comprehension in my mind. He simply sat there, watching me, judging me.

I swallowed the instinct to rage against his proclamation and said, as calmly as I could, "And why might my death be necessary?"

"Because that is the rules of the game—the key players on either side must die for a winner to be declared."

"*That* is an utterly stupid rule."

He shrugged, as if it was of no matter to him. And I guess it wasn't. I was a player in a game, nothing more, nothing less.

At least to him.

"But... how can any side consider themselves a winner if their main protagonist dies?"

"In this particular case, while winning is vital for both sides, so too is a fitting tribute to the vanquished. Is not the blood of the strongest fighter considered such by many in your world?"

Only by the psychos, I wanted to say, but once again resisted. "So why did your first daughter fail?"

"She killed the key, but she did not destroy the Harpē and therefore left open the ability for him to rise. Death found her because she had not the strength to fight the Ninkilim, who believed her blood would sustain their god until the Harpē was found."

"But even if she *had* destroyed the Harpē, death would have found her, true?"

"As I said, it is a requirement."

I got up to pace. I couldn't help it, because if I just sat there, staring at him, anger would get the better of me. Or, worse still, the inner darkness, which continued to roil deep inside, fighting restrictions I was barely keeping in place, would break free and attack. I rather suspected that was what he wanted, what he was waiting for.

Because we both knew that once the darkness had truly seen the light of day, it would not be put back into its box.

"Is there any way of breaking said rule?"

"Breaking, no. Bending? Possibly."

"What if I simply refused to play the game?"

"Such a refusal will lead to unwanted consequences for all those you care about. I might prefer to play within the rules, but our opponents often walk deep in the gray."

I dropped back into the chair and wearily rubbed a hand across my eyes. A migraine was brewing, and I wasn't sure if it was this place, this situation, or the fact that I'd only gotten out of the hospital a few hours ago after being at death's door for several days.

"Then what if I find and kill the opposition's key, as well as all the other major players? Would that be enough?"

"No, because chopping off the head of the Hydra rarely

results in the whole beast dying. It simply results in more heads being produced."

"But it *is* possible?"

"Anything is possible, but do not think you can avoid finding the Harpē. That was my first child's option, and it is not a road that will be allowed this time."

"Have you got any good news to impart?" I growled. "Or did you just come here to completely wreck all my dreams and hopes for the future?"

Amusement lurked briefly again. "You must accept that which brews within you. You must also trust the instincts inherited from your mother, especially when it comes to those around you. You must remember that sometimes control cannot be taught. Sometimes it comes from letting yourself be overwhelmed."

"And once again we're back to statements that hold nothing but meaningless platitudes."

"Nothing I have said here is mere platitudes, child. I have given you a path forward, and a means of survival, and that is more information than my first child had. What happens next is completely up to you."

And with that, he rose and walked away.

I thrust to my feet. "Wait!"

He didn't. The door closed behind him and the cloud chairs disappeared, leaving me alone with the shadows that still lurked beyond the brown-streaked black walls.

I swore softly but vehemently, then turned as pale green light speared across the darkness behind me.

Liadon's orb bobbed midair several yards away. I'd initially believed it was nothing more than a sphere of light through which she spoke and which she used as a guide for those of us not of this place. I now suspected it had some sentience. Not a ghost, as such, more an otherworldly will-of-the-wisp.

"How much of all that did you hear?" I asked her.

"This is my world and my sanctuary," she replied, her soft voice warm and yet as otherworldly as her domain. "I hear and see all."

"Any opinions?"

"Plenty, but I must remain neutral in the games of god and man. My orb will lead you out."

"Then Borrhás considers our business done?"

Borrhás was a god of the cold north wind and the bringer of winter, and my aunt had used his relic—a horn capable of encasing people, buildings, or even entire cities in ice—in an attempt to claim vengeance on all those she deemed responsible for killing her daughter. She'd come damn close to succeeding with me. Unfortunately for her, Borrhás had been rather annoyed that his relic was being used in such a manner, and my aunt—along with the witch who had wielded the horn for her—were now forever entombed in Borrhás's ice somewhere in this underground labyrinth.

"Indeed," Liadon murmured. "He thanks you for your swift action."

"I dare say anyone threatened with having their entire city encased in ice would also have acted in a similarly swift manner."

Liadon laughed, the sound surprisingly warm. "Indeed yes. Now please, you should go. You have been too long in this place, and it will take its toll on you, godling or not."

Her words had the intensity of the migraine increasing, and I quickly rummaged through my purse to find some painkillers. I swallowed them dry, grimacing at the taste, then followed the orb through a different exit door back into the familiar black walls of a corridor. *Which* corridor was the question of the hour, because I had a feeling the paths in this place were far from static.

"Would it be too bold of me to ask if a search can be done for any mention of my mother in the more recent council files?" I asked after a few minutes of twists and turns.

"Bold? Yes, definitely, but I shall see what can be done. No promises."

Which is more than what I'd gotten the last time I'd mentioned it. "Thank you."

"Welcome."

The light continued to lead me through a number of glassy black tunnels, eventually depositing me at the forbidding metal door that would take me back into the real world.

I glanced at the orb. "Thank you for your assistance."

It spun briefly, then winked out of existence. I took a deeper breath and continued on. The door slid open to reveal a lone figure leaning back against the metal railing, a large paper cup in one hand and his phone in the other.

Mathi Dhār-Val—who was not only a former lover but also the liaison between me and Deva's Fae Council—was a Ljósálfar elf, and like all of them, he was lean in build but absolutely divine to look at, blessed with golden skin and hair, fine, almost angelic features, and eyes the color of summer skies. We'd been lovers for nearly ten years before splitting eight or so months ago, and although I'd always known he was not my one true love—and could never be, in fact, given he was a highborn light elf, and they only married their own kind and rank—I'd always enjoyed his company. In fact, he was one of only two people who would fit into the category of a "best" friend. Darby Riagáin—a light elf I'd met during our school years and who was now dating my brother—was the other.

He glanced up as I approached and put his phone away. "I was beginning to think I'd have to break into Liadon's domain and rescue you."

His tone was coolly distant—a trait all light elves had, as they tended to present an emotionless façade to the world in general—but warm amusement danced through his eyes.

"Why? How long was I in there?"

"Three hours."

"*Three?* You jest."

"I," he said severely, "am a Ljósálfar elf. We never jest."

A laugh escaped, but it was quickly followed by a wince. I resisted the urge to rub my forehead, not wanting to give him cause for alarm. "What in the hell have you been doing for three hours? You and boredom are not great companions."

"Indeed, we are not." He handed me the cup and fell in step beside me as I headed for the stairs. "Which is why I was on the phone. I finalized one deal, and made an initial offer on another."

Which explained his upbeat mood. Closing a deal was an aphrodisiac to light elves. I took a sip of the drink, immediately discovering it was not only tea, but *damn* hot. "Given the temperature of this drink, I take it you also sent poor Henrick on multiple runs?"

Henrick was his chauffeur, and one of two he used regularly. While Mathi was quite capable of driving, he—like many elves who lived and worked within the somewhat crowded boundaries of Deva's old town—preferred to be driven rather than dealing with the daily hassle of traffic themselves.

"*Poor* Henrick is extremely well paid to do my bidding and offer no opinion." He pulled a block of chocolate out of his jacket pocket and handed it to me. "We also acquired this."

I dropped a quick kiss on his cheek. "You are a darling."

A smile tugged at his lips. "We do have a meeting with the council at three—which, I may point out, is now a mere five minutes away—so I thought it a prudent step after your recent hospital stay and your tendency to overdo it. Which you obviously have, given the current squinty nature of your eyes. You've taken pain relief?"

"Yes, and since when did we have a council meeting booked?"

"As of about two hours ago."

"That's all rather sudden, isn't it?" I handed him the tea, broke off a row of chocolate, then tucked the rest into my purse and retrieved my drink. "Has something happened?"

He shrugged, the movement elegance itself, and motioned me ahead of him as we reached the top of the circular staircase. "Perhaps, but I've been doing business rather than scanning social media. It's totally possible that now you're deemed fully recovered, they've decided it's time for another relic hunt."

"They usually give a bit more notice than that, though." I bit into the chocolate, then added, "And surely they're aware that we both have businesses to run?"

"You know they are, and you also know they do not care. You are at their beck and call as punishment for your actions with your cousin, and they all know I am never one to let the perfect opportunity to overcharge expenses pass me by."

I snorted and clattered down to the second level as fast

as I could without upsetting my headache or spilling my tea —the latter being the more important of the two. The guards at the double doors leading into the council's chambers opened them as we approached, but the minute I stepped inside, the magic woven into the antechamber's fabric to protect those in the main room from both regular and magically enhanced weapons detected my knives and sounded the alarm.

Of course, it was no longer necessary for me to carry them—these days, I could simply imagine them in my hand, and they appeared—but I still preferred to keep them close. That aside, the alarm going off every time I entered this room annoyed the hell out of the councilors in the room beyond and, as petty as it may be, that always made me happy.

Mathi switched the noise off, then motioned me on through the next set of doors. The meeting chamber was the size of a grand hall, without any of the usual decorations—no wall hangings, no crests, no paintings. Basically, there was nothing here that could be manipulated in any way by the elves or pixies present. Even the furniture was plastic. In normal circumstances, this would have given the shifters a serious advantage, thanks to their greater strength, but aside from the chamber being an electronic null zone designed to block listening and recording devices, it was also wrapped in magic so strong it actually prevented shapeshifting.

There were only five people in the room, which was very unusual. Two were light elves, two were shifters—one being the rat shifter who never seemed to miss a meeting and who also seemed to have taken a great dislike of me— and the fifth was a dark elf. That there were no Malloyei pixies here surprised me, because they were the most political branch of us all and always had a representative present. But given Mathi had only received notification two hours ago, maybe the notice had simply gone out too late for them—and everyone else—to get here. Very few Malloyei lived in Deva, be it the old section or the new.

My gaze was drawn to the far end of the table and the Myrkálfar sitting in Cynwrig's usual position. Recognition stirred. It was Bodhrán, a thickset dark elf who'd accompanied Cynwrig to a previous meeting. His gaze met mine, and he nodded politely, but there was no instantaneous, hungry response from deep within me. Dark elves were renowned for their seductive nature and their ability to render even the stoniest maiden into a puddle of wanton desire, but this elf's energy held none of the magnetism of the one who was about to become his king. That might be nothing more than my hormones remaining determinedly —*stupidly*—fixated on the man I could never have, but, given my father's comment, it could also be due to the fact that he'd been deliberately set in my path by the opposition to cause chaos.

Game wise, it was a very good move, because chaotic was certainly an apt description of my feelings and responses to Cynwrig.

Mathi seated me at the head of the table then walked around to the right and claimed a chair not far from the convener, who, if his golden brown hair and sharply hooked nose were anything to go by, was some kind of hawk shifter.

He banged the gavel and said in a voice that held a sharpish edge, "Thank you for being so prompt, Ms. Aodhán."

"Always eager to be of service," I said blandly.

Mathi was too controlled to snort in such company, but

I could nevertheless feel the deep amusement practically oozing from him.

The shifter raised an eyebrow, obviously sensing the insincerity, but simply pushed a red folder toward me. "Your next mission."

I stopped the folder's slide with my fingers but didn't bother opening it. "Which is?"

"Aamon's Pectoral. It gifts the wearer with invisibility."

A pectoral, I knew from Lugh—who was not only my older brother, but an antiquarian with the National Fae Museum—was a pendant or ornament worn as a brooch or attached to a necklace. They often had iconography carved or painted on them, and while they generally had nothing more than symbolic importance, Lugh had told me there were some that had been blessed by the gods with certain "attributes" in return for the wearer's devotion.

"I take it there's a reason behind the sudden urgency to find this thing?"

"Indeed," Bodhrán replied, his tone dry. "It appears that someone wearing the pectoral walked into the Tylwyth Teg bank just before opening this morning, rummaged through the safe deposit boxes, and then presumably left with whatever they were there to find."

Which definitely explained it. The Tylwyth Teg Banking Group was the largest fae banking group in the UK, and was used by a good portion of fae, who generally had little faith in human banks. I had never banked with Tylwyth Teg, even though it was just up the road from my tavern, and if his unconcerned expression was anything to go by, neither had Mathi.

"Whether gifted with invisibility or not," I commented, "that should not have been possible. Not with the amount of alarms, heat sensors, and indeed all the security measures placed around and within the vault itself."

"As we have noted in the file," the shifter said, "it appears the brooch shifts the wearer's being from flesh to vapor."

His tone suggested we should read the file first before asking inane questions, which only made me determined to continue asking them. I was, as previously noted, nothing if not petty, especially when I had a booming fucking headache.

"While a vaporous form would certainly allow them to bypass security and even breach the vault's defenses," I said, "it's unlikely they'd be able to *physically* interact with our world in any meaningful manner. They certainly wouldn't be able to carry anything solid through either the building's walls or the thickly constructed nature of a vault."

"Unless, of course," the rat man said, his voice as sharp and as unpleasant as his face, "the brooch's gift extends to whatever the wearer was holding or has on their person, which we believe is the case here."

I instinctively wanted to say that wasn't possible, but we were dealing with a godly relic and impossible wasn't a word in their vocabulary.

"The security cams didn't catch anything unusual?" Mathi asked.

"I believe the IIT are still in the process of acquiring and examining the tapes, and have said they will brief us if and when they get anything solid," the convener said. "In that regard, it's likely your joint connections will give you more complete information far faster than whatever they decided to provide us with."

Given Mathi's father was the day commander of the IIT

—or the Interspecies Investigation Team, as it was more properly known—that was a certainty, because Ruadhán had basically given him full access to IIT's computers and records. The few restrictions he did have had been placed there by Sgott Bruhn—who was not only the night commander, but the man who'd been my mother's lover for nigh on sixty years, and the only real father I'd ever known.

"Are we allowed to visit the crime scene?" I said.

The convener raised an eyebrow. "Again, it would probably be faster if you requested that directly yourselves, but I have to ask, why would you need to do so?"

"I might catch something they missed."

The rat shifter sniffed. "I think it *very* unlikely the IIT will miss anything."

"The IIT do not have goddess-blessed knives sensitive to not only all forms of *human* magic, but also godly," Mathi commented. "While it may be unlikely, we cannot discount the possibility of Bethany's knives uncovering a thread or clue that has otherwise been missed by the IIT's consultants."

"Do you truly think they can find clues that the best witches in Deva cannot?" Bodhrán asked.

I met his gaze evenly. "I can't guarantee it, but if a godly artifact is indeed behind—"

"What makes you think it isn't?" the convener cut in.

"What evidence is there that it *is*?" I countered.

"If you would just read the files—"

"Gentlemen, I've been in Liadon's realm the last three hours delivering my aunt to Borrhás, and I have the biggest fucking migraine as a result. It *hurts* to read. So please, do me a goddamn favor and just tell me."

The convener looked briefly startled, then hastily said,

"We were in the midst of a ratification meeting when we received an anonymous call—"

"The council did?" Mathi said, straightening a little. "That's rather unusual, don't you think?"

"Yes. And no, we have no idea whether it was male or female, because they were using a voice modulator."

"But the call was traced?"

"Indeed—to the café down the end of the street. Phone was left on the chair."

"Too early for fingerprints then," I said.

Mathi glanced at me. "If it's been left, then it's been wiped clean and means it's likely a burner anyway."

True, but that didn't stop me from living in hope that just this once we might get lucky. "What time did you get the call?"

"Five minutes past nine. It took an additional five minutes for the message to be passed on to us. We, of course, called the IIT immediately."

And *they* would have responded in the same manner. "What did the message actually say?"

"That the Tylwyth Teg would be robbed at ten past nine and they will be using Aamon's Pectoral to get in and out."

"They were all but daring you to stop them," Mathi said.

"That is also our impression," the shifter replied. "There are some who get a rush from cutting their escape time down to the wire."

I frowned. "It would have taken the IIT only a few minutes to get there, so our thief was likely still in the vault at that point."

"Indeed," Mathi commented. "But aside from all the usual bank security measures, there are two separate time locks securing that vault, and a backup power system that prevents the possibility of someone cutting the power and using the keycode to get in. All of which means the manager would not have had access until nine thirty, opening time."

I raised an eyebrow, wondering how he knew that. He merely smiled.

"Even so, that still means he only had at most twenty minutes inside that vault, and I wouldn't have thought that enough time to pry open all the security boxes, let alone rummage through all the assets contained within them." I paused. "Unless, of course, he was after cash."

"They do not keep cash in that particular vault," Mathi said. "But I agree that he—or she—was likely after something specific, and was well aware of its location."

"Whether that something was in the form of contracts or business papers, bond certificates, or family heirlooms," the convener said, "we won't know until all the owners have been contacted and an assessment done."

I nodded. "Is there anything else we need to know?"

"No, but just remember, a good portion of Deva's elite had property stored in the bank's safe deposit boxes, so there is a major push to find the culprit *and* the items he stole."

My gaze found Bodhrán's again. "I take it the Myrkálfar are already monitoring the black market?"

Amusement flickered through his expression. "Constantly, but we've placed a notification alert for any unusual activity and are monitoring all services brokers."

A fact that would no doubt thrill them, given many had a booming business brokering off-the-books and often illegal services.

"We have asked for a summary list of stolen items," the convener said. "But I suspect many will not be forthcoming about all that their boxes contained."

Undoubtedly those who were storing illegal goods or blackmailing information. Both branches of elves did enjoy the odd bit of extortion.

"You'll pass that on—along with anything else we might need to know—when you get it?"

"Indeed, though to repeat what was said earlier, I dare say you two will be able to gain that sort of information far quicker than any of us."

I pushed to my feet. "You have met Sgott Bruhn, have you not?"

The convener frowned. "Yes, of—"

"Then you'll be well aware he is a stickler for rules and not one to discuss ongoing investigations with anyone outside the investigative team, even if that person is considered family."

Ruadhán was a different matter entirely, at least when it came to his son, but I refrained from adding that. I doubted anyone beyond Sgott knew just how complete Mathi's access was. I picked up my tea, gave them a polite nod, and left. A chair scraped as Mathi rose and followed me out.

"Thoughts?" I asked, as we clattered down the austere concrete stairs to the ground floor foyer.

"I have several."

"Color me unsurprised," I replied, amused. "There's generally a whole lot happening under that inscrutable façade you present to the world."

The security guard opened the front door as we approached, and Mathi touched my back lightly, guiding me through and then around to the left. His car—a silver Mercedes—was parked just in front of a delivery van. Henrick was studiously ignoring the van driver's verbal rampage about illegal parking as he stood beside the vehicle's rear door and waited for us to arrive.

I climbed in and scooted across to the driver's side, but Mathi paused, got out his wallet, and handed the van driver a couple of notes. I had no idea how much, but the abuse instantly stopped.

"Devious," I said dryly as he climbed in.

"My middle name," he replied. "Are you up to heading over to the bank? Or do you need to go home and hide in a dark room for a few hours?"

"I need the latter, but we'd best do the former if we want any chance of finding whatever magical residue remains."

"I'll ring my father and inform him we're on the way and why. Henrick, could you please drive over to the Tylwyth Teg Bank."

"Immediately, sir," he replied implacably, then raised the noise barrier between us and him.

Mathi took out his phone and made his call. I placed my cup in the center console, then leaned my head back and closed my eyes. I didn't sleep, as such, but I certainly lost any real awareness of my surrounds for the short time it took us to get over to the bank, which was located on the corner of Eastgate and St Werburgh Street, and only a few buildings down from the tavern I called home.

The two streets were taped off either side of the building, and there were double yellow lines for a good distance in both directions, so Henrick stopped in a delivery bay, then opened my door and offered me a hand. I accepted the assistance gratefully, then stepped away from the car and drew in a deeper breath of air. There was a storm coming, and its electricity was sharp and vibrant, dancing enticingly across my skin. But that storm didn't just come in the form of weather threat. It was deeper, more dangerous, and far more encompassing than that. It was coming for me, for my life, and it was going to turn everything I knew upside down. Prescience? Or simply the fear of knowing what now lay ahead of me and how little room to maneuver I truly had.

But maneuver I would. I didn't want to die.

And if there really is no other choice? an inner voice whispered.

I shivered and rubbed my arms. Mathi immediately took off his coat and draped it around my shoulders. "Do you need more tea? I can ask Henrick—"

"I'm fine, Mathi, but thanks."

"Knowing you as well as I do, I recognize the lie, but I will ignore it for the moment. Shall we continue?"

"The sooner we get it over with, the sooner we can both get home."

"And, more importantly, the sooner we can start the evening activities."

He kept close as we walked down to the bank, obviously meaning to catch me should the migraine overwhelm me. I didn't often get them, but he'd seen the consequences often enough in the ten years we were a couple. It was tempting to tell him that wasn't going to happen today, but in all honesty, between the light hurting my eyes and the growing wash of weariness, it was better to be safe than sorry.

"I intend to do nothing more than climb into my bed and sleep for ten hours, but I take it you have a hot date?"

"Indeed. Several new prospects have arisen, and I'm seeing one of them tonight."

I laughed softly. "I do love the oh-so-romantic way you refer to a woman who might one day become your wife."

"Marriage is a business rather than romantic transaction for us, as you well know."

"I know, I just—" I stopped and shrugged. "As much as I wish you a beneficial betrothal contract, Mathi, I also want you to be happy. I'd hate for you to discover you can't stand the woman when it's all too damn late."

"That won't happen, because I have a devious plan."

I glanced at him, my eyebrows raised. "And am I allowed to know this devious plan?"

"Indeed, you are a vital part of it." His smile flashed, warm and bright in the afternoon's gathering gloom. "But more on that when we have the time."

I harrumphed. He laughed and guided me around the corner. Eastgate Street was filled with all manner of law enforcement, with the regular police doing the more menial tasks such as crowd control while the IIT—whose purview was to deal with all police events involving nonhumans—handled the actual investigations. I couldn't see any familiar faces amongst the officers here, but that made sense given day division would have the operational lead on this, not the night. The copper manning the tape gave Mathi an acknowledging nod—meaning he'd been advised of our arrival—and lifted the tape for us.

The bank was built in a Neoclassical style, which meant not only was it grand in scale, but possessed rather dramatic-looking Corinthian columns, gloriously arched windows at street level, and smaller sashed windows in the upper two floors. The main entrance was situated in St Werburgh Street and was, unfortunately, of a modern design, totally out of keeping with the rest of the building, but likely far more secure than the original wooden doors.

The officer guarding the entrance requested our IDs and then opened the door and motioned us around to the right. The main banking area was again modern in design, with very little of the original architecture visible. Hopefully, those features had simply been boarded over rather than destroyed, especially given the upper two floors apparently retained the features missing here, including a hall that had lovely old oak paneling and Ionic columns.

Ruadhán stood with three other officers toward the end of the long, featureless room, but turned as we approached. He was basically an older version of Mathi—though his eyes were much colder than his son's and lacked the mirth that often flitted through Mathi's—with age lines creasing his forehead and frown furrows near his mouth. Mom always said such furrows were a sign of deep-set unhappiness, though if she'd known what lay at its cause here, she'd never let on.

I stopped a respectful few feet away. He didn't like me, I didn't like him, and we tended not to get within each other's personal space unless it was absolutely necessary.

"Let's be clear, Bethany," he said. "I believe this to be a fool's errand, but given your recent success hunting for the council, I am willing to give in to their request and allow you access."

The council hadn't made that request, which meant Mathi had stretched the truth a tad when he'd called his father. "Then let's hope such generosity results in me finding something worthwhile."

His blue gaze darkened a fraction, but all he said was, "Please, follow me, and remember, you are not to touch anything without first clearing it with me."

"Understood, but please tell your people not to react when I draw my knives, as I'll need them to find whatever magic remains." Had it been Mathi or even Cynwrig I was speaking to, I would have added, "I promise not to stab you," but Ruadhán would not have appreciated the humor.

"They have already been warned. This way."

He turned and led us to the left and then down a set of stairs that, though now concrete, still retained the lovely old oak handrail. I ran my fingers down it, listening to the wood's muted song, hearing the sadness in it thanks to the disconnect with the rest of the building. All pixie lines had some sort of rapport with nature, be it controlling water, plants, insects, or bending trees to their will. Aodhán pixies could hear the song of, and manipulate, any sort of wood, whether it was alive or dead, in the forest or in furniture.

Of course, the females of our line also had one other skill the others didn't—while all pixie women had received the blessing of the goddesses, giving them the so-called six virtues of womanhood, we Aodhán had a rather handy variation on one of them—we could control people's actions with voice and touch. Unfortunately, it worked on everyone except elves, which was a pain in the ass because I'd really love to know why Ruadhán disliked me so much. Had it been any other Ljósálfar of royal blood, I would have said it stemmed from me being a part of what they consider a lower- or working-class family, and therefore a far from suitable partner for his son, but he'd always been aware our relationship had been based on friendship and sex rather than anything truly emotional. In some ways, his dislike felt almost instinctive. It was as if he couldn't help it, thanks to what he was and what I was.

Which had never made any fucking sense, especially

since he had seemed to like—or at least, respect—my mother.

We continued on until we hit the basement, then walked down a long concrete corridor interspersed with several sets of heavily barred metal doors. The vault room lay at the far end. The vault's door was not only massive but also surprisingly opulent. Its surrounds were Neoclassical in style, with stone—marble?—a textured golden color that gleamed in the muted lighting. In the half arch above the doorway was a mosaic tile flower decoration that almost looked Roman in style and was, again, simply gorgeous. The only modern part of the whole vault lay on the wall to the right of its frame, where there were a couple of small, linked metal boxes and a slightly larger but separate one. I had no idea what any of them were for, but presumably they had something to do with the multiple number of locks and thick metal pins that radiated around the inside of the door. Just beyond the vault's frame, on the inside of the vault itself, was another barred door that was no doubt meant as a final line of defense if the two timed locks and the backup generator went down, and a would-be thief had the lock combination.

We stepped through the thick metal door frame into the main vault area. The room was narrow but long, with safety deposit boxes stacked ceiling high on either side—the higher ones being accessible via antique-looking rolling ladders—and three privacy booths down the end. There was also a rather untidy pile of about twenty boxes sitting in a middle of the tiled floor midway down the room. Money, jewelry, and a number of rolled-up parchments lay scattered around them, which lent credence to our suspicions the thief had been after something specific.

"Anything?" Ruadhán asked.

"I only just got in the door. Give me time."

He didn't say anything, but I sure as hell felt the roll of his annoyance. I dragged one of the knives out of my purse, then handed the bag and my tea to Mathi and walked on, being careful to avoid anything that looked like evidence. A woman squatted a foot or so away from the pile of metal boxes, and it took me a second to realize it was Marjorlaine Blackguard, the head of the spellcasters' guild here in Deva.

She glanced around as I neared, and her eyebrows rose. She was a well-dressed woman in her mid-forties with spiky silver hair, silvery eyes, and dark brown skin. A thick veil of energy surrounded her that, while it didn't fizz with lightning, still felt electric.

"You do pop up in the strangest places, Bethany Aodhán."

Her voice was dry and amused, but then, I had the feeling she saw me as nothing—as an untrained joke. Could be doing her an injustice, of course, but I doubted it.

"When it comes to godly relics, I'm apparently the latest go-to girl."

I stopped beside her and scanned the pile. I couldn't see anything that suggested magic had been used, but given none of the boxes had been opened, our thief had obviously just used his vaporous state to reach in and draw out whatever lay inside. "I'm just as surprised to see you here, Marjorlaine, given your talent leans towards weather manipulation."

"That's my primary ability, certainly, but I am also sensitive to the detritus that remains after the casting of a spell."

"Did you find anything here?"

"I didn't expect to, given we are dealing with a godly relic, but surprisingly, there are lingering remnants of a leash spell around each of these." She motioned to the boxes. "Our thief presumably created it to drag them from their positions at the same time rather than retrieve each one separately."

"It would certainly have saved him a whole lot of time and effort." I scanned the rows of boxes for a second. The boxes had come from all over the place, high and low, so it did make sense that they'd all been ripped free at the same time. "Will you be able to trace the practitioner through the remnants of magic he or she left behind?"

She wrinkled her nose. "That would normally be our next step, but in all honesty, a leash spell is simple enough and can be formed by anyone with the barest minimum of magical talent. There's a good chance he is not even registered."

"So we are dealing with a male?"

She glanced up. "The detritus feels male. I take it from the questions you are not sensing anything?"

"Haven't tried yet."

"Then perhaps you should do so." Ruadhán's voice held a colder, sharper edge that hinted at deepening impatience. "We do have a crime scene to finish documenting."

I bit back the instinctive need to make a tart comment, squatted beside Marjorlaine, and lightly touched the tip of the knife to the nearest box. Purple lightning flared down its fuller and danced briefly across the pile before fading. There was something here, but its pulse or presence was neither dangerous nor traceable. At least, that was what instinct was telling me. It wasn't like I had a how-to book when it came to using the knives or indeed the triune as a whole.

"Does that flash mean the knives *have* detected something?" Marjorlaine asked, in unsuppressed surprise.

But then, she'd never actually seen the knives in action; the only other time I'd drawn them in her presence was when the witch controlling the Horn for my aunt had been icing over the Fae Museum, but she'd retreated before I had a chance to use them.

"Seems like it." I rose and scanned the vault again. Instinct twitched as my gaze fell on the privacy booths at the far end. I turned and pointed. "Am I okay to approach those? I won't mess with any evidence collecting, will I?"

"If there is information down there to be gathered, then probably. Daniel, go with her and record everything."

Daniel was a thin stick of a fellow, with grayish, scaly-looking skin, red eyes, and pupils that had a distinctly oval shape. He moved toward me, and I had to stop the instinctive need to step back. While it was extremely rare for snakes to be seen around these parts—they were generally found in the warmer south coast areas—it was even rarer to see a snake *shifter*. This was certainly the first time I'd come across either, and to be honest, I hoped it was the last. There was something about the way he walked that was decidedly... unnerving.

I spun and went down to the end of the room and the three privacy booths. Each one was three sided, with the vault's rear wall providing the fourth, with a small walkway separating them. They were constructed and paneled with oak which was so darkly stained with usage it was almost black, and the doors were worn with age.

A faint pulse of lightning once again ran down the edge of the blade I was holding, but this time it echoed through the Eye—which was not only the second part of the triune, but was in fact the actual eye of the goddess Ethine, who'd been turned to stone long ago and who'd gifted her eyes in the form of black seeing stones to both an ancestor of mine and the hags. Mom had used it to amplify her second sight when relic hunting, and to keep in contact with Beira and the other hags when she was undertaking tasks for them. The triune had supposedly been designed to gift the women of my line with foresight, knowledge, and protection, thereby providing all the tools we needed to fight those seeking the rebirth of the dark gods in the tangible world, but by the time I'd come into possession of it, the triune's true power had not been used or even remembered for centuries. Which meant that between the lack of directions and my own inexperience, my ability to use it to its full capacity was currently somewhat limited. However, the fact that the Eye had echoed the knife's reaction meant that not only was there magic to be found here, but quite possibly a vision to chase.

I glanced back at snake man. "I need to touch the external wood with the knife—is that okay?"

"Yes, but please keep your contact to a minimum. We've not dusted the outside, only the inside and doors." His voice was soft and whispery, and while not unpleasant, it still had those goose bumps running again.

I moved over to the left booth. The song emanating from the oak was slightly stronger here than on the banister, but it still ran with loneliness. These booths had been constructed *after* the main vault area, and as such, had no physical connection to the building's greater network. To both Aodhán and Tàileachs pixies, that network was something of a superhighway—living, breathing rivers of golden energy that allowed us to follow the various connections throughout a building, seeing the locations of rooms, furniture, and even people without ever having to physically enter. In the very distant past, many pixies had a secondary line in thievery—and indeed, it was a light-fingered distant ancestor that had gotten us kicked out of the relic guarding business—but the invention of metal door and window furnishings had ended all that.

This booth, however, couldn't really tell me anything. Processed wood, unlike trees, didn't hold much in the way of memories—not when it came to people, anyway. The oak here did whisper of the earth in which it had rooted, but its memories were growing ever distant as every year passed. I switched the knife to my left hand, then dug the Eye out from under my sweater and wrapped my hands around the lovely metal "cage" Lugh had made me so I could wear it as a pendant without having to risk it constantly hitting my skin. That tended to have unfortunate consequences, such as being hit by unwanted visions at inconvenient times.

I warily touched the knife's tip to the edge of the wood. Light flickered faintly down its fuller, then died, indicating that whatever they were sensing, it wasn't emanating from here. I turned to the next booth and again touched the knife tip to the wood. This time, lightning shot down the blade and danced across the wood toward the door, and the Eye pulsed in time to the movement.

I glanced at snake man, discovering he was recording what I was doing on his phone. "I need to step inside."

He reached into his pocket with his free hand and dragged out a set of silicone gloves, handing them to me. "Put these on then."

I tucked the knife under my armpit, pulled on the gloves, then stepped left and opened the door. Both the knife and the Eye flared to life again, spinning dark lightning through the room's golden light. I moved inside warily. The booth was pretty basic in design, holding nothing more than a comfortable-looking chair, an oak table attached to the side walls, and a smaller shelf sitting above it. I took a step toward it, and the pulse of lightning immediately eased. I frowned and turned, pointing the knife at the rear wall. The pulse sharpened once again. Did that mean our thief had come into the bank from the building next door? If so, why? A vaporous form could move through walls unimpeded, so why wouldn't he have simply slipped in from the street frontage and then come down into the basement? Why take such a roundabout route?

He wouldn't have. Not when he'd given himself so little time to find what he needed. Leaving this way, however, was a different matter entirely.

He had, after all, called in a warning about his intentions, so it made sense for him to leave in the opposite direction from which the IIT was entering. A vaporous form wasn't the same as an invisible form, and what could be seen could be caught.

I glanced at Daniel again; he was now filming my actions from the doorway. "My second sight is twitching, so I need to sit."

"Did he use the chair?" Ruadhán asked before snake man could answer.

"I don't believe so. I think he left the vault via the back wall, but to be sure, I need to—" I stopped. With my aunt and cousin dead, there were probably only five people—aside from the gods themselves—who knew about the triune and its power, and I really wanted to keep it that way. Especially when we were damn sure the IIT was riddled with people working for the other side. "To use my focus stone to see what second sight is trying to tell me."

"Do you think it wise when you've spent three hours in Liadon's domain and are still suffering the side effects?" Mathi said.

"Wise? No. Necessary? I think it is."

He half shrugged, as if it was of no matter, despite the fact that even from where I was standing I could feel his disagreement. He didn't show it, of course, but I'd known the man for a long time now, and could generally read him pretty well.

I sat on the chair, drew the second knife, and placed both on my lap. I took off my glove then pressed that hand on top of them and wrapped the other around the Eye. I didn't have the Codex—the third part of the triune and basically a doorway through which I could access a godly library holding all manner of information about all manner of relics—with me, but unless I was intending to visit said library, I generally didn't need its physical presence.

With a bright flare of purple, the knives and the Eye combined, and my mind's eye was swept away so damn fast, it was briefly disorientating.

For several seconds, there was nothing more than darkness, then light speared through it, so bright it made me blink. The shadows lifted, revealing the vault's innards and a dark figure standing in the middle of it. The vision shifted position, giving me a view from above and to the front of the figure. He was almost fully cloaked in black, wearing thick gloves, a ski mask that covered his face, and ski goggles over his eyes. It was hard to see the shape of his body because his clothing seemed overly large, but the bottom part of his pants was black and crisply ironed, and he was wearing dress shoes. They definitely weren't the type of shoes I'd have thought ideal for thievery—unless, of course, our thief believed it was only proper to dress well when you were targeting the security boxes of Deva's upper echelon.

He pulled off a glove, revealing dark skin, and began to

murmur softly, making quick gestures with a hand that was free of lines or spots or anything suggesting age. A heartbeat later, the security boxes ripped free from their places and formed a line in the air in front of him. He touched something at his neck with his right hand and briefly closed his eyes; his left hand and arm became invisible. One by one, he reached into the boxes, withdrew their contents and examined them, then dropped both the items and the box to the floor and continued on. He was three quarters of the way through the line when he found what he was obviously looking for—an old-fashioned and rather ornate key, and several rolled up scrolls. My view shifted again, this time giving me a direct look down the line of boxes, allowing me to catch the number of the one he'd just raided as it bounced onto the pile and was covered by the remainder. He tucked the key and scrolls into his pocket, placed both hands on the pectoral, and became black smoke. The light went out and I was torn from the vision.

I gasped and leaned over the knives, my body trembling as I sucked in air and fought the blackness that threatened to sweep me into unconsciousness. When my pulsed rate eased, I dragged the chocolate out of my pocket and broke off another row.

Daniel frowned at me, something I felt more than saw. "I do not think that—"

"If you want fucking answers then you'll let me consume this slab of chocolate," I growled without looking up. "Otherwise, you'll be taking me to the hospital and talking to me there."

He sucked in a breath, as if to argue further, but another figure pushed him out of the way then knelt in front of me. "Here," Mathi said softly. "Drink this."

"This" was my tea. I handed him my knives and

accepted it gratefully, but my fingers were shaking so badly, bits of tea splashed up through the lid. I quickly sipped it, not wanting to waste a drop, and alternated between it and the chocolate. It still took a good five minutes before the threatening blackness retreated.

"Better?" Mathi said eventually.

I nodded. He rose, offered me his hand, and helped me up. The room spun briefly, and pain stabbed through my brain, dragging tears to my eyes. I really had overdone it this time.

"Did you uncover anything?" Ruadhán said from the doorway.

I squinted at him. "The thief unveiled himself in the vault but was covered from head to foot in bulky black clothing. He did take off his left glove to spell, which revealed dark skin. He pocketed the contents of Box 369. The rest he simply threw onto the floor."

"Any identifying features aside from dark skin?"

I shook my head and winced. "I did get the impression he was young though."

"Define young?"

"Looked to be in his twenties rather than fifties. It was impossible to tell if he was human or not."

"Most of those who are magically gifted tend to be," Marjorlaine commented from behind me.

"The Myrkálfar can spell," I replied. "It's part of the reason they guard the Annwfyn gateways."

"I doubt the Myrkálfar would stoop so low as to raid a bank," she said, "especially when a good portion of them use it."

"If you think that," Mathi murmured, "then you do not know the Myrkálfar."

Ruadhán cast him a warning look before returning his

gaze to me. "And our thief left through the rear wall, as you said?"

I nodded, though I hadn't actually seen that thanks to the plunge back into darkness. "Can I go now? Because unless you want me to vomit all over your pristine crime scene…"

Ruadhán immediately stepped back. Mathi wrapped an arm around my waist and helped me out of the vault, but once we reached the stairs, swept me into his arms and carried me up. He didn't set me back on my feet once we reached the street, but continued on.

I leaned my head against his chest and wished I could let go, but there were lots of little questions buzzing around my brain and I just had to ask a couple of them.

"Tell me," I said, "was there any particular reason the council meeting was attended by so few people?"

His amusement swum around me. "Is there any particular reason you ask that question?"

"Given the hawk shifter—"

"Marlan Nash."

"—said they were ratifying some decisions, I'd have thought they'd want more people there. They didn't even have a quorum—or doesn't that matter?"

"Only for major decisions, and having seen the agenda for today's meeting last night, there was only routine issues to be dealt with. I dare say a good portion of the absenteeism was because they were attending Jarvil Maehdon's funeral."

"Who's he when he's home?"

"A long-term councilor and a dark elf of some importance."

"Did you know him at all?"

"I didn't like him, if that's what you're asking."

"You never liked Cynwrig, but that hasn't stopped the two of you working together."

"Because we now have something—some*one*—in common," he drawled. "Besides, while I might not have liked him in times past, I did always respect him. There is a difference."

Meaning if I did want to know more about Jarvil, I'd have to ask Cynwrig. While their rules of grieving meant he couldn't socially interact with anyone outside his own people during the set three-month period of mourning, I did have a means of talking to him without him risking a face-to-face meeting. But up until now I hadn't had the courage or indeed a proper reason to use the Bruadar bracelet he'd gifted me.

Missing him was *not* a proper reason, no matter how much my stupid hormones might attempt to convince me otherwise, especially when I had another lover in my life deserving attention.

"What time was the funeral?"

"Eleven, but it was being held at Dorcha Dearg, and there are formalities that must be followed before any outsiders can enter that place."

Dorcha Dearg was the main Myrkálfar encampment in the area, and was situated on—and in—the Peckfort Ridges to the west of Deva. Though I'd never been there—and never would go there—I'd seen plenty of photos of the weighty but wondrously exotic buildings that ran the length of the ridge. It had become something of a tourist attraction over the centuries, although most folk were constrained to viewing platforms some distance away. And, of course, tourists also needed facilities like public conveniences, cafés, and souvenir shops, all of which the

Myrkálfar ran and which, by all accounts, were making serious coin.

"I take it," he continued, as he moved out of the building and turned toward Eastgate Street, "that you believe there is a connection between Jarvil's death and today's events?"

"The timing of it all just seems suspicious."

"And the vision? Did that provide any gravitas to support said suspicion?"

"Under the bulky coat, I think he was wearing a suit. He was certainly wearing dress pants and shoes. Maybe we're dealing with a fashion-conscious thief, but I think it worth looking at the funeral's guest list and checking backgrounds."

"You should have mentioned this to my father."

"I wasn't sure if I could mention the council connection. I mean, you've all sworn an oath not to discuss business with anyone *not* on the council."

"We have," he drawled. "You haven't."

I sighed dramatically. "Then I am forced to admit it was my insane desire to get the hell out of his presence as soon as possible."

"He does not hate you, Bethany, no matter what you think."

"Hmm," was all I said to that. We turned into Eastgate and headed down toward the tavern. I took a deeper breath that didn't help ease the continuing ache in my head, then said, "You can put me down. I can walk the rest of the way."

"You lie, Bethany Aodhán."

"And you, Mathi Dhār-Val, have an exciting date with the latest prospect to get to. You don't need to be babysitting me."

"Pixie sitting would be a more apt description," he

mused. "But let's be honest here, you have developed an alarming tendency of late of getting kidnapped, so it behooves me to ensure you get home safely."

"No one has any reason to kidnap me right now. Besides, it's not like you can't find me when it happens. You did last time."

"Cynwrig found you, and I can assure you, that journey underground is not an experience I wish to repeat. We Ljósálfar are not meant to be in such realms for long."

I smiled but didn't say anything as we arrived at the tavern. Ye Olde Pixie Boots—the name Mom had given it when she'd taken over the business from Gran umpteen decades ago—had stood here for hundreds of years and, aside from a few changes here and there, was basically the same late medieval building that had been rebuilt on this spot after fires destroyed it and much of the old city in the late 1400s. Like the other buildings that made up Deva's famous row, it was listed, and consisted of a small bar in the undercroft at street level, another at row level, and my living area on the top floor.

Mathi stopped to the side of the time-worn front door and finally placed me on my feet, though he kept hold of my elbow until he was sure I wasn't going to collapse before handing me my purse.

"Thank you. Enjoy your date." I paused, but curiosity got the better of me. "Is this woman the statuesque blonde with largish breasts—for an elf—that was hanging off your arm at the memorial?"

"No, but she is in consideration."

"How many have you got in consideration right now?"

"Three, though one has a voice that could shatter glass, which is a shame because she is rather delightful in bed."

I laughed and shook my head. "And you, of course, are

perfection. She'd have nothing to complain about to her friends now, would she?"

"Nothing at all," he said solemnly, though his eyes twinkled. "I'll be in contact tomorrow morning about our next step."

"Make that the evening," I called after him. "I intend to sleep well into the afternoon."

He waved an acknowledgement over his shoulder. I turned and opened the old door, letting my fingers run across its stained wood, listening to its joyous song and briefly losing myself in the network of gold that enveloped the whole building, then stepped inside. The main tavern area was intimate—no surprise there, given that, like many along the row, it was long and narrow—with five larger tables in the front half of the room, and the bar and four small tables on the far side of the stairs. Stairs to the upper floor divided the two areas, and bright pixie boots of various sizes hung from the exposed floor joists and beams, some of them real, some of them not, but all of them a nod to tourist expectations that a tavern bearing the name "Pixie Boots" would have said boots displayed. Beyond the door at the far end of the bar was a warren of rooms that included the kitchen, a furniture store, fridges, stock stores, staff changing rooms, and toilets.

It wasn't yet five o'clock, so the evening rush hadn't started—though to be honest, during the winter months, the so-called "rush" generally consisted of nothing more than a half dozen regulars and a couple of hardy tourists willing to brave the often harsh weather. Right now, aside from Kitty and Jonnie, who were polishing glasses down near the bar, there was only one other person here.

That person was not a stranger, and she certainly wasn't a customer, even if she did enjoy a good glass or two of our whisky every time she came here. It said a lot about my current state of fitness that I hadn't felt her presence before now. I certainly should have, given the thunderous energy that surrounded her.

She was also absolutely the last person I needed or wanted to see right now.

Especially when, yet again, she looked fucking furious.

CHAPTER

THREE

Of course, Beira and unhappiness seemed to be constant companions, but then, she was a very old, very powerful goddess now confined to what she labeled as an "unsatisfactory and inconvenient meat suit."

It could also be due to the fact that she was just a short-tempered old woman with little patience for those she was forced to work with.

Which didn't mean I didn't like her. I actually did. I just wasn't sure my migraine could cope with her presence right now.

"It's about fucking time you got here," she growled, in a voice so grating fingernails down a blackboard were sweet by comparison. "I've been sitting here for nigh on three hours. I've other things to do than wait for your ass to appear."

"Said ass has been in Liadon's domain for the last three hours talking to my father, and I now have the mother of all migraines," I snapped back, "so if you could lower your fucking tone several octaves, I would really appreciate it."

She blinked. "Ambisagrus *met* you? Now that is an interesting development."

"Yeah, it certainly was."

I motioned to Kitty for a glass, then plonked down on the chair opposite Beira's. I'd given standing orders that she be provided with a bottle of whatever whisky was on special when I wasn't here and she decided to wait, simply because it did help mitigate her temper. Today, it was a particularly fine single malt from The Lakes being sacrificed.

"What did he say?" she asked.

"That in order for this particular game to be won, I would have to die."

She sniffed. A disparaging sound if ever I'd heard one. "Death is not always final, child, as you are well aware."

Meaning the situation with my aunt, no doubt. She'd "died" to escape the magical restraints that had been placed on her by the pixie council via the red knife, but had ensured there were medics close by to bring her back to life. "I'm thinking that is not an option when it comes to this round of godly games."

"Perhaps. Perhaps not." She tapped a yellowed nail against the old wooden table, and though it didn't seem to affect the wood's song, it annoyed the hell out of me. I bit my tongue against the urge to say anything, however, because she had at least modulated her tone. "Did he say anything else of import?"

I glanced up as Kitty arrived with my glass; I thanked her and poured myself a double. "Apparently the only way I can destroy the Harpē is via my storm powers."

"Did he enhance said powers?"

"If that's what he was doing when he tried to draw out

the darkness in me, yes. He claimed it was the only way we could win."

"That darkness is a power that comes via anger through his line. I dare say embracing it will not be a choice in the end."

"Where life remains, so does choice." I had to believe that. Had to believe that my path and my death weren't already set in stone. After all, did not the gods start these games because they enjoyed humanity's unpredictability? I took a large drink and felt it burn all the way down; it didn't, unfortunately, do much for the pain battering my brain cells. "Why are you here, Beira? What's happened?"

"I gained some interesting information that could help our quest."

That quest being stopping the Ninkilim from raising their god, though this was, I thought, the first time she'd said "our" quest. It suggested she'd stepped things up a level. "I thought you were more an interested spectator rather than an active participant."

She hesitated. "You could define me as a spectator with a deep interest in seeing particular players succeed."

"And spectator participation isn't banned?"

She cackled; the sound was as sharp as the energy that crackled around her. "Oh, it is. There is a reason I landed in this meat suit, child."

I snorted, winced, and drained the whisky. It might not be helping the headache, but I suspected it would help me sleep. I poured another glass, topped up hers, and then said, "So, what have you found?"

"The means by which the Ninkilim might have taken control of the council. Or, at least, some of it."

"We already know Carla Wilson—"

"She hasn't, in and of herself, the power to force her will

on others, though I suspect she is indeed the wielder of the weapon."

"She's a shifter who uses her sexual wiles to very, *very* successfully get what she wants," I said. "She doesn't need godly help in the form of a weapon."

"Using sex is an approach that has worked for eons, and one that will no doubt continue to do so for at least as long as men can be led by their dicks. However, sexual wiles can only do so much, especially when it comes to the Ljósálfar."

"Why particularly light elves?"

"They are cold, unemotional creatures at their core, and while they might enjoy sex, it would not be enough in and of itself to convince them onto paths they would not have otherwise taken." She pursed her lips. "That aside, I've nothing more than a suspicion that the rat god's latest attempt at rising centers around the Ljósálfar more than the Myrkálfar."

And I suspected her suspicions might be anyone else's truths. "What sort of godly weapon is she using to control people, then?"

"It's called Bia's Blade—"

"And Bia is?"

"The goddess of force and compulsion. Her blade allows the wielder to enforce his or her will onto others."

"How? Do you press the blade against the skin or stab it in?"

"The latter, of course."

I stared at her for a second, horrified and yet not entirely surprised. She grinned in response, revealing surprisingly straight, white teeth. "We goddesses do have a bloody bent."

It wasn't just the goddesses in my experience. "How could Carla or whoever else might be wielding this blade repeatedly stab someone and get away with it? Being knifed isn't something you'd easily forget."

"It is a goddess-gifted blade, remember, so the target's memory is adjusted, and the wound heals as the blade is withdrawn from flesh."

"That latter gift was mighty generous of her."

It was sarcastically said but Beira nodded in agreement. "It was indeed. Most would not have provided the healing."

I snorted softly. "You're a charming lot at heart, aren't you?"

"But you love us."

I harrumphed and took another drink. "Am I immune to the blade? Or will it affect me the same as anyone else?"

She waved a hand. "That is unknown, but your godly blood will protect you from at least some relics even if doesn't protect you from all of them."

Fabulous. *Not.* "I take it you're here to demand I find the blade, without telling me how to do so?"

"In part. The blade has an unusual resonance that should allow you—through the wind—to find its location when in use."

"How do you know this?"

"I asked Bia."

I just about choked on my drink. "She's a player?"

"Sort of. She's what we call a sideliner—a semi-active participant that works to impede."

"Both sides?"

Beira nodded. "The uncertainty caused by sideliners does add an extra zing to the games."

I snorted. "I take it that means she wasn't willing to give up the name of the current wielder?"

"Of course not, but given she is one of the ancients, the Codex should hold some information on her blade." She drained her glass and pushed to her feet. "And now, I should go. I have spent too long here already."

She picked up the whisky and tucked the bottle into the voluminous folds of her rather ratty-looking coat. The bird's nest that had for ages been in her matted hair seemed to have migrated to the inside of the coat, if brief but outraged tweeting was anything to go by.

"If I find anything, I'll contact you," I said.

"Sooner would be better than later."

"And the blade itself? What do I do with it once I've found it?"

"Take it to Liadon."

My eyebrows rose. "Really? What is the damn point of finding these things if they're just going to be handed over and released again?"

"The point is godly pleasure, as you are well aware, but items returned rather than destroyed cannot be used again in the current game."

"There are rules? Color me shocked."

"There are always rules; whether most are actually followed is another matter entirely."

I rolled my eyes, and she cackled, a harsh sound that seemed to linger long after she'd left. I gulped down the rest of my drink, walked the glass back down to the bar, then clattered up the stairs, my hand on the railing so I could feel the wood's warmth.

The next floor was larger, as there was no kitchen up here to take up space, and contained a mix of booths of varying sizes, a few tables, and the doors leading out onto the covered row area. The only customers up here were Jack and Phil. They'd been coming to the tavern as long as anyone could remember and, like many of the elders in the pixie community who lived permanently here in Deva rather than one of the widely scattered enclaves, basically treated the Boot as a second home. The fierce joy that radiated off the old oak beams in the tavern was undoubtedly one reason for that; it was as close as they could come to communing with nature in the old city without having to take public transport out to a public park or even an enclave. But I suspected the real reason was the fact that the Boot provided a deep discount on food to all the older fae—except elves—to ensure they had at least one decent meal a day. The only reason we excluded elves was because there were two large encampments sitting outside city limits, and elves generally did a good job of looking after their own.

I ducked into the office to get an update from Ingrid, the short but take-no-shit pixie I'd recently promoted to full-time manager, then headed around to the narrow stairs tucked away behind the bar and deactivated the alarm on the door. It had been installed after a break-in, and while it wouldn't stop a determined thief or thug for very long, it would make a hell of a noise and send an alert to both my phone and Sgott's.

I relocked the door, then padded up stairs worn down by centuries of foot traffic. As a pixie, I could have restored them, but their song was rich and warm, and I really didn't want to alter it. Mom and Gran had obviously agreed with me.

The living area was very confined, even though the roof had been illegally raised by Gran years ago, and contained a combined kitchen-living area and two bedrooms—one had been Mom's and was now mine, while the one Lugh and I had shared as kids was now a spare. The bathroom was the second-biggest room in the flat and with good reason—it had at one point needed to cope with four oversized pixies using it. Gran had moved out of the tavern when she'd handed the reins over to Mom, but before then, she'd slept in the loft.

I threw my purse on the sofa and walked over to light the fire, saying a prayer of thanks to the wood for its sacrifice, then placed the grate across and headed into the kitchen to grab the sleeping potion Darby had made me specifically for moments like this. Once I'd taken it, I headed into my bedroom, stripped off, and fell into bed. I was asleep almost before my head hit the pillow.

It was who-knew-how-many hours later when the Eye burning against my skin woke me. I had no sense of danger, and the building's song was bright and happy, but I remained still, pretending sleep as I fought my way toward full consciousness. It didn't take all that long to realize why the Eye had lit up, and heat of a very different kind stirred, right along with my hormones.

Eljin lay pressed against my spine.

"I thought you were heading to London for the weekend to meet your sister?" I murmured.

"I was. I am."

His voice was softly accented, sending shivers of delight down my spine. Or maybe they were caused by the finger that was ever so slowly tracing its way down to my hip. "But we did arrange to meet here for breakfast before I left, remember."

I didn't remember, but it wasn't like I'd really had time to think since I'd left the hospital. "And we both know 'breakfast' is your code for hot sex."

"Only if my breakfast partner is willing."

She definitely was. "What time is it?"

"Ten o'clock, or thereabouts."

Meaning I'd slept for a *very* long time. I turned to face

him. He was a typical Tàileach pixie in looks, with wide shoulders, slim hips, and thick mahogany hair. Though his face was probably a little too sharp to be called handsome, his lips were full and definitely made to give pleasure, and his body was well muscled.

"Hey," he said softly, and kissed me, a warm but intense prelude to what was to come.

"That," I said, when I could, "is quite a lovely way to wake up."

The burnished gold flecks in his buttery brown eyes gleamed in the room's shadowy light. "Your pendant would seem to disagree. One of these days, that lightning is going to strike."

I laughed, tugged it off, and placed it on the bedside table, where she continued to throw little jabs of energy into the air. She did this every time we shared a bed, though not, strangely enough, at other times. I wasn't sure why it was happening, and I really needed to ask Beira about it, given she'd known the goddess who had gifted the Eye to my family and could likely tell me if this was a warning or something else.

I really, *really* didn't want it to be a warning.

I pushed the concern aside and ran a hand down the chiseled length of his body, letting my fingers play lightly across his erection. He made a low sound deep in his throat and wrapped his hand around my neck, pulling me closer, kissing me almost savagely. From that moment on, there was no talking; we explored, kissed, caressed, until desire burned as hotly as the Eye and all I could think about, all I wanted, was him inside.

Then he was, and we moved as one, slowly at first but with increasing urgency, until need and desire combined, becoming a force so fierce I couldn't think, couldn't breathe, couldn't do anything more than simply *want*. My orgasm hit hard and fast, and I gasped, shuddering and shaking as pleasure consumed me. He came a heartbeat later, his body stiffening against mine, his deep groan echoing.

For several long minutes after, neither of us moved, then his lips brushed mine and he slid to one side.

"Now that," he murmured, "is an even better way to wake up."

"Agree. But now, I need a proper breakfast."

I flung off the blanket, grabbed the still-pulsing Eye and put it on, then picked up my knickers and a T-shirt from the floor, pulling them on as I headed into the kitchenette.

"Tea or coffee?" I called. "Toast or cereal?"

"Is there no bacon on offer? I'm mortified."

I laughed. "So am I, but I forgot to go shopping after getting out of the hospital yesterday."

"*That* is what I call a very good excuse. Coffee would be perfect." He came out of the bedroom barefoot, wearing jeans but no T-shirt—a look I'd always approved of when it came to a good-looking man. "Did you ever find out how Mathi and Cynwrig found you?"

I shrugged and filled the kettle, then dragged the coffee machine from the under-bench cupboard, blew away the dust, and reached for the bag of beans I kept in the upper cupboard. I had no idea how fresh they were, given how rarely I made myself bean coffee up here, but if he didn't like it, well, there was always tea.

"Mathi said it was something to do with the resonance of my weight on the earth."

"A Myrkálfar can pick one resonance from another? That is indeed a talent."

"Well, we've been bed buddies for a while. I daresay that helps. Toast?"

He shook his head. "I'll grab something at the airport if I get hungry."

I shoved a couple of slices into the toaster for me, then made his coffee and handed it to him. "What's the plan for the weekend? Are you taking your sister and her children anywhere special?"

"Children?" he said, looking at me blankly for a second. Then he laughed. "Sorry, no, the children are staying home with their father. She had some business in London and thought it the perfect opportunity to catch up with her big brother."

My eyebrows rose. "I thought she'd retired to raise her babies?"

"She stopped helping me, but she never retired from her business. She's a designer."

"Clothing?"

He shook his head. "Interior stylist."

The toast popped, so I dropped it onto the plate then slathered it in butter. "Unusual business for a Tàileach."

"She is an unusual woman."

Admiration laced his reply, which was totally natural given said woman was his sister. I certainly admired the hell out of my brother. And yet... suspicion stirred, even though it had absolutely no reason to. None other than the Eye's continuing pulse, anyway. I grabbed the jam out of the cupboard above my head, spread it over the still-melting butter, then picked up a slice and faced him again.

"You want me to pick you up at the airport?"

He shook his head. "I'm not coming back until late Sunday, and I daresay that now you're out of hospital, the council has you hunting again."

"Yeah, they do." I gave him a brief rundown about the

bank then added, "You didn't have an account there, did you?"

"No, I remain with Paribus." He glanced at his watch, then drained his coffee. "I should get going, given the traffic to the airport is usually dreadful."

"You don't want a shower first?"

He hesitated, then shook his head. "I'll grab one in the airport lounge. I'd risk missing my plane if I had it here."

"You're presuming I'd deign to join you in said shower."

"I am indeed."

"Mighty bold of you."

He laughed. "I'm French. Boldness is second nature."

"That is definitely a truth," I said dryly. "You'll call Monday?"

"I will." He placed his cup in the sink, wrapped an arm around my waist to draw me close, kissed me soundly, then headed back into the bedroom to finish getting dressed and collect his things.

While he did all that, I ate my toast, sipped my tea, and contemplated why the fuck the Eye seemed to have a hate-on for him. After bidding him goodbye, I listened to the building's song until I was sure he had left, then rang my brother.

"Bethany," Lugh said, his deep voice filled with warmth. "How are you this fine morning?"

My eyebrows shot upward. "You're in a particularly good mood this morning, aren't you?"

"We won the bid on a relic we've been after for a decade."

"From a private collector?"

"Estate auction. Three other museums were after it."

"Well, congrats, brother. I hope you're taking Darby out somewhere nice to celebrate."

"I am indeed. Viridis, in fact."

Viridis was one of five "dining sensations" within Deva, and one of only twenty-three restaurants in the UK to be given a Michelin green star for high levels of gastronomy and sustainability. I'd been there twice now, once with Cynwrig and once with Eljin, and it had indeed been a divine experience.

"Who'd you bribe to get a table there at short notice?"

He laughed. "No bribery needed when you know the maître d'."

"You do?"

"One of them, yes."

"And you've never thought to mention this and thereby allow me to abuse said friendship to get a regular table at that piece of gastronomic heaven?"

He laughed again. "I take it you're not ringing to simply say hello?"

"Well, no, but hello."

"What is it you want this time?"

He sounded resigned, and I couldn't help smiling. "Did you ever get in touch with your friend Frank to ask him about the people in that newspaper article Treasa gave me?"

Said article had been about an archeological site in Portugal and the unusual number of accidents that had occurred during the dig, which had eventually led to the site being closed and subsequent rumors that the area was cursed. It had been accompanied by a somewhat grainy picture of the dig team standing in the middle of what looked to be an Iron Age hill fort, but no names had been listed. When I'd shown it to Lugh, he'd known two of them, though only one remained alive.

"No, because thanks to everything that happened over

the last few days, I totally forgot all about it." The rustling of papers echoed down the line, suggesting he was now searching for it. "Why?"

"Could you push it to the top of your priority list? I think we need to know why Treasa thought it important we get that."

"Will do." He paused. "Thing is, I seem to have misplaced it."

I frowned. "Really? Where are you?"

"At the office. I'm sure I put it in the in-tray."

"Would anyone have taken it?" Would Eljin? If so, why? He wasn't in that picture; hell, he was only a couple of years older than me and would have been in his mid-twenties at the time that article was written, and likely to have still been in university.

"I can't see why anyone would," Lugh was saying. "Besides, I'm the only one with a key into the office. Even the cleaners don't come in here."

"Well, that explains the rubbish everywhere," I said with a laugh.

"I'll have you know there is no rubbish in my office." It was said with mock haughtiness. "They are all vital pieces of information."

"Yeah. Right, brother."

He chuckled. "I do put the bins outside the door for the cleaners every night, so there is in truth no actual rubbish in here. That does make it even odder it's disappeared, however."

"Luckily, I did take a photo of it, so I'll shoot it across to you."

"Ah, excellent." He paused. "How did things go yesterday? I meant to call but—"

"You forgot, not only because all the prep for the

auction took precedence, but because you knew I was safe, well, and with Mathi," I finished dryly.

"Well, yes," he admitted, amusement evident. "But don't tell Darby all that. She wouldn't understand."

Darby understood him far better than he realized. I quickly updated him on everything that had happened yesterday, then added, "I don't suppose you've heard of either relic?"

"No, sorry. I'll search the archives for the pectoral, but I'm loath to do a search for the blade, given we've probably at least one Ninkilim working for the museum, keeping tabs on me."

"Probably, though if they did take the article for whatever reason, it's all the more reason for us to find out why."

"I agree. I'll ring Frank this afternoon. He won't be up at this hour, as he habitually sleeps in. We used to have a devil of a time getting him to a dig before noon."

I snorted. "It's a wonder he was ever employed."

"He's considered one of the preeminent professors in the antiquities field, even now that he's semi-retired. That gives his behavior a pass for many, especially given he is otherwise a studious archeologist. You want to come around for dinner tomorrow night? I should have something from him by then."

"Love to—just remember to warn Darby."

"You, dear sister, would make anyone think I had the memory of a fish."

"Well, it is a truth universally known that, when it comes to your brain, day to day events have little memory traction in comparison to relics."

He laughed. "Okay, I'll give you that one. See you tomorrow night."

"I shall bring wine and champers."

"Excellent."

I smiled, hung up, and sent the image across to him before I forgot, then finished my tea and contemplated my next step. Before I could decide what that should be, Mathi rang.

"When I said afternoon, I meant late afternoon, not a few minutes after noon," I drawled by way of hello.

"Yes, sorry, but there's been another break-in, this time in Handbridge."

Handbridge was one of Deva's more upmarket districts, located on the southside of the river. "Same M.O.?"

"Almost exactly. I thought we could go around there to see if you can pick anything up."

"And your father?" I said, amused. "He made it pretty clear yesterday he thought I was a hindrance rather than a help."

"He respects your abilities, Bethany, and to repeat what I've already said, he does not hate you. But you're a pixie, and a middle class one at that, and he is, above all else, a Ljósálfar of royal blood in his middle years. He cannot help his manner."

Which didn't excuse it. At all. Still, it wasn't like a leopard could change its spots this late in the game.

"I take it you're on the way now to pick me up?"

"No, you have half an hour. I need to finish a few things here at the office first."

"That at least gives me time to shower."

"You don't need someone to scrub your back? Happy to volunteer, dearest Bethany."

"The days of you, me, and adventures in the shower are well and truly over, as you well know."

His sigh was more than a little on the dramatic side. "Indeed, I do, but I continue to live in hope."

"You already have three prospects to share a shower with," I said, amused. "You don't need a fourth."

"I'm Ljósálfar," he drawled. "It's *never* about needing, it's *always* about wanting."

I rolled my eyes, said, "I'll wait at the top of the lane for you," and then hung up.

After finishing my tea, I headed into the bathroom for a quick shower, then got dressed. The wind whipped around me, coming in from the window I'd locked open about an inch almost a week ago now, chilling my skin even as it stirred an idea.

I grabbed my coat, phone, and handbag, and clattered down the stairs, heading out the back of the building and down the old lane that led into St Werburgh Street. Almost directly across the road was my target—a lovely red sandstone cathedral.

As I waited for a gap in the traffic, I dragged out my phone and sent Mathi a text, letting him know where I'd be, then ran across the road to the wrought-iron gates. They squeaked as I opened them, but the sound was lost to the sudden rumble of thunder overhead. A storm was coming... not just weatherwise, but also life wise. I shivered but shoved the sliver of foresight aside and continued on.

The gardens that surrounded the cathedral were lovely, even in the middle of winter when there was a decided lack of color and foliage, but my target was down in the memorial section of the church grounds, where the freestanding bell tower stood. It was a far younger construct than the cathedral, having been commissioned in the early seventies after the original tower was deemed no longer safe to house the bells, and was a modern interpretation of the old Roman watchtowers that had once guarded Deva's stone walls. Directly in front of it was a circular rose garden bed that almost completely surrounded a large seating plat-form. In the summer months it was usually claimed by parents resting up while their kids ran wild through the gardens, but right now the whole area was empty.

There were undoubtedly a myriad of other more comfortable places to commune with the wind, but they weren't likely to be much safer—outside of a protective circle of magic, anyway. It might be mainly humans who considered church grounds sacrosanct, but there were very few other races who'd risk spilling blood on such holy ground. Karma, and all that.

Of course, I could now form a variation of a protective circle when gripping my knives, but it did take a toll on my energy, and I needed all that and every scrap of concentra-tion to commune with the wind, at least until I was more practiced at this whole thing.

Overhead, the thunder cracked again. I silently counted —a childhood habit that I really had no need for now, given how easily I could read the power and locations of storms these days—but had barely reached three when lightning speared the heavy skies. While it never came close to striking me, its power shot through my body, making the tiny hairs on my arms and the back of my neck stand on end. The storm felt impatient. Felt like it was ready and waiting for me to be one with it again.

I shivered yet again, briefly wondering at the advis-ability of this, especially when I had no real idea what my father had been trying to do when it came to the inner darkness. Still... it was the easiest way I knew of uncovering truths without being seen or involving someone else, and I basically had nothing to lose by trying. I sat down on the platform, crossed my legs and then tugged my coat over my knees. After a deep breath that did little to calm the nerves

—though they came from the task I was about to assign the wind and the answers it might bring me more than anything else—I reached for the power and fury that raged above me.

Connection was instant, but for several seconds, I did nothing more than revel in its chaotic beauty, letting it flow through me, around me, empowering and somehow cleansing me, though I wasn't sure I could ever define what the latter meant.

A car horn sounded in the distance, making me start, drawing me back to my task. I closed my eyes and got down to the business of crafting my request. Beira had told me that the wind was a weapon and a gatherer of locations, but she could never reveal deeper information such as identity, because wind and storms were of land and trees, cities and seas, and had no care for those who dwelled in any of them. And yet, I had already done what she said couldn't be done. If luck was with me, I'd do it again.

I might not get a truly clear picture of what Eljin was doing, but I could certainly see who he was with. If it *wasn't* his sister, that in and of itself was no big deal. He and I weren't exclusive and, up until very recently, I'd spent my time between his bed and Cynwrig's. It was the lie that mattered.

That, and the Eye's response.

Once I'd given the wind her orders and streamed her toward London, I sighed and opened my eyes... to see Mathi leaning against the trunk of a nearby ash tree. He was wearing a black trench coat that emphasized his slim figure, crisp black pants, shiny black shoes, and looked rather dapper.

"Is there a reason you're dressed so formally?" I asked, accepting the hand he offered me.

"Had a business meeting this morning, and the client expects a certain look." He released my hand and fell in step beside me. "What did the wind have to say?"

"Nothing. I just sent it on a little scouting mission."

"For the pectoral?"

"No, as we haven't yet got any information about what it looks like."

"Then what did you ask it to do? Or shouldn't I ask?"

"Probably the latter, but I asked it to follow Eljin to see if he is doing what he says he's doing this weekend."

He glanced at me, his eyebrows raised. "That's a little stalkerish, isn't it? It's not like you're in a committed relationship with the man."

"It's not that."

"Then what is it?"

"The Eye. It reacts badly to him. I'm not sure why, but I intend to find out."

"Surely the museum would have done a background on him before he started."

"They did, and it didn't reveal anything untoward." I shrugged. "In truth, the Eye's reaction might be nothing more than my own uncertainty about our relationship but—"

"Instinct is niggling, and that is never a good thing, as I well know. It did end a wonderful relationship."

I nudged him. "Only our sexual one."

"Indeed, but I did rather enjoy sex with you." He paused. "There are easier—and definitely more reliable—ways to check what he is doing than using the wind."

I glanced at him. "We can't risk running a trace on him through the IIT system; the system is likely compromised, and there's a chance such a search would tip off whoever stole the hoard."

He stopped and stared at me. "Your instinct is suggesting he's a plant? Why have you never said anything?"

"Because instinct has had very little to say about him until very recently, and besides, I'm not sure he is. I just…" I shrugged. "I guess I just need to be sure one way or another, especially when I have the gods telling me to be wary of letting new people into my life."

"I would suggest that if the gods are saying *that*, then we definitely need to check him out more thoroughly." He walked on. "I'll contact a friend in London who specializes in this sort of thing and get him onto the case immediately. Where is Eljin staying, do you know?"

"Montcalm Royal." My eyebrows rose. "What if your friend is busy?"

"He owes me several favors. He will not be busy."

"Spoken as only a royal-blood Ljósálfar could."

"Said royal Ljósálfar elf will do serious damage to Eljin if he does turn out to be a plant. And then he will be handed over to Cynwrig, who will ensure what life he has left will be spent in agony."

"And why would Cynwrig do that? He and I—"

"—are lovers, yes, and you do not ever mess with the lover of a dark elf lord. They tend to get a little touchy about that sort of thing." Amusement teased his lips. "To be honest, I am utterly surprised he allowed you to even *have* other lovers."

I rolled my eyes. "He doesn't own me, Mathi. He has no say in who I date or bed."

Although he very definitely had *not* been happy when I'd told him that if he wasn't exclusive, then neither was I.

"In case it has escaped your notice," he said, tone dry, "we elves have somewhat backward—some might say caveman-like—views when it comes to certain things. For us Ljósálfar, it's never double cross us; for the Myrkálfar, it's do not mess with those they consider dear to them, be it family, friend, or lover."

"But we don't even know each other that well, Mathi. Outside of the bedroom, anyway."

"He knows you well enough to hear your resonance on the earth and unerringly lead me to you, and trust me when I say my finest bit of work that day was convincing him your aunt's body needed to be returned to Liadon's cave and Borrhás."

My eyebrows shot upward. "He threatened to *bury* her?"

"Her, her people, the building, everything. The man was *not* happy."

And wasn't my stupid little heart happy to hear *that* little tidbit.

Henrick opened the rear passenger door as we approached. I nodded my thanks, then scooted across to save him from having to run around the car for Mathi. As we drove off, Mathi made the call to his friend; said friend did not refuse the commission.

In very little time, we were crossing over the river and heading into the genteel area that was Handbridge. I'd thought we'd be going to one of the many grand old manors that littered this area, but instead we stopped at a simple, end-of-terrace, red-brick cottage a stone's throw away from the river with the park at its back.

Just as we stopped, the storm finally unleashed. I clambered out of the car before Henrick could run around and open the door for me, then hastily zipped up my coat and tugged on my hood. The rain was fierce enough that it still felt like hail through the coat's thick padding. But it wasn't the rain or the storm itself that had goose bumps skipping across my skin. It was the odd note in the air. Music that was distant and jarring. Or maybe the problem was me; maybe my ears weren't quite attuned to the music that played within the wind.

Why it felt like that, or where it was originating from, I couldn't yet say.

I fell in step beside Mathi, my hands in my pockets and my gaze searching the buildings around us for the source of the wind song. But she was swirling about recklessly, tugging at hair and clothes with abandon, making any sort of seeking nigh on impossible.

Well, at least impossible on the fly for someone like me. I dared say I could do it given time to frame the question and a safe spot to do it in.

The officer guarding the tape blocking the street was the same poor soul who'd gotten the task yesterday, and he looked utterly miserable, but he nevertheless greeted us with a pleasant nod and lifted the tape so we could go under.

"Is the commander inside?" Mathi asked.

"Indeed, sir," he replied.

Mathi nodded, and we moved on briskly, but as we neared the front door, the knives burned to life, their heat once again echoing in the Eye.

In that same instant, the odd, scratchy music riding the wind disappeared. I stopped abruptly, my gaze searching the area.

"What?" Mathi immediately said.

"The thief is still here. Not in the house, but close."

"Our man definitely likes flirting with danger, doesn't he?"

"Either that, or he's waiting or watching for something."

Some*one*, instinct whispered.

"I'll inform my father—"

"You inform; I'll walk on and see if I can find anything."

He hesitated. "Fine, but promise you won't go far. I don't want to be rescuing you again."

"I promise. And don't worry, I have my knives and can call down the lightning if anything untoward happens."

"You had both those options the last time you were kidnapped, and neither did anything to help. So please, be careful."

I rolled my eyes but didn't reply, instead continuing on as he hurried inside. The gap between our terrace and the next one was big enough to allow two cars to park, but at the back of the area, sitting in the middle of a fence that was more brambles than wire or wood, was a homemade gate. Obviously, those living in the street did not like having to walk the few extra yards around the corner to get into the park. The knives were pointing me in its direction, so I walked up to the gate, pushed it open with some effort, and stepped through. The path sloped upward and was a mix of stone and dirt that had multiple rivulets running down into rapidly filling potholes. About halfway up the slope, just on the edge of one of those puddles, was a set of boots. Safety type boots. With no body attached. Even as I watched, the boots dissolved into the rain.

He was here. *Right* here, and had obviously been unconcealed until I'd come through the gate. The fact that he'd chosen to fade rather than run said a whole lot about his character. Or more likely perhaps, his overconfidence. Either that, or he didn't realize his disappearing trick wasn't instantaneous.

I grabbed the wind and spun her toward him. While it was unlikely vapor could be leashed, surely at least *some* laws of physics had to apply. In this case, I was hoping to disperse his body and save us the trouble of incarceration.

Unfortunately, it seemed the laws of physics did *not* apply.

He did, however, laugh at the attempt. Then he ran—something I felt through the wind more than heard or saw. She might not be able to disperse him, but she could still feel his presence and location.

I ripped a knife free from my purse and bolted up the path after him, the wind at my back, pressing me on even as she spun information around me.

I raised the knife and threw it, as hard as I could, at the man I couldn't see, using the wind's directions as a guide. The knife flew straight and true, then abruptly stopped, hanging midair about shoulder height. Lightning spun out from the blade in all directions, and vapor became human. He stumbled, then reached back with a gloved hand and ripped the knife from his left shoulder blade. He ran on a few more yards and jumped—dove—into the ground and disappeared.

Or maybe *that* was just an illusion. Maybe he was simply using the pectoral to make it appear he'd disappeared into the earth.

I recalled the knife and listened to the wind as I continued on, trying to figure out where he'd gone. She had no answers. The blade thudded into my hand, and I gripped it tight, closing in on the spot where he'd disappeared.

And discovered his disappearance *wasn't* an illusion.

It *was* a hole in the ground.

One I fell into head fucking first.

FOUR

I hastily wrapped the air around me but had little time to do anything more than right myself. I hit the ground, bounced, and was flung into a wall so hard my air bubble burst and a jagged strip of stone scraped the left side of my face.

I dropped the remaining few inches to the ground and swore, long and hard. From deeper within the darkness that lay ahead of me came another laugh.

"Do not come after me, young pixie, or I will entomb you."

His voice was soft, earthy, but held a brash edge that spoke of youth.

"And you, young Myrkálfar, have a lot to learn about us pixies and orders."

I charged after him, using the fierce lightning emanating from the blade to light my way, but had barely gone a dozen yards when the ground under my feet began to shift, shudder, *move*.

Oh, fuck...

I turned and ran, as hard as I could, back toward the

hole, which was already beginning to close over. I swore again, wrapped a leash of wind around my wrist and gripped it tight as I ordered it to haul me out. It obeyed so damn fast my head spun. As I broke back into the storm, I glanced down... just in time to see the earth lunge at me, a darkly liquid serpent desperate to drag me back. Then it fell away, and the hole closed over.

I released my leash and dropped back to the ground, staggering a few feet forward before catching my balance.

"I thought you promised to be careful," came a rather dry comment.

I looked up and saw Mathi and his father striding toward me. "Well, no, I promised I wouldn't go far. I never responded to the whole 'be careful' suggestion."

He stopped in front of me, tugged a crisply ironed handkerchief from his pocket, and handed it to me.

"What happened?" Ruadhán asked.

I gently pressed the handkerchief against the wound. It stung like blazes, but it obviously wasn't too bad, otherwise Mathi would have insisted I be taken to the fae hospital. "Our thief was watching from that pathway. When I shoved through the gate he started disappearing, then ran."

"And you, of course, chased after him rather than call for backup," Mathi commented.

"I would have lost him completely if I'd done that."

"It would appear you have lost him anyway." Ruadhán's voice held the slightest edge of contempt. Which, for him, was showing extreme control.

"Yeah, but I discovered two things. One, his vapor form is not immune to being knifed. And two, he's definitely a Myrkálfar, and a youngish one at that, if his voice is anything to go by."

Ruadhán's eyebrows rose. "You spoke to him?"

"He told me not to follow him. I told him he has a lot to learn about us pixies."

"Or at the very least," Mathi murmured, "*this* pixie."

I glanced at him. His expression dared me to disagree. I didn't. Couldn't, really, though it was a family trait rather than just mine.

"Just to confirm, you did wound him?" Ruadhán said, dragging my attention back to him.

I nodded. "Left shoulder blade."

"Then I shall contact the Myrkálfar immediately. If he is one of theirs, they will find and hand him over."

I wasn't so damn sure about that, because from the little I'd learned about them from Cynwrig, they had their own, rather gruesome, methods of dealing with those who betrayed them. But Ruadhán undoubtedly knew that better than me, so I didn't say anything.

I watched him walk away then glanced at Mathi. "What did he take this time?"

"They're not sure yet." He stepped to one side and motioned me forward. "The place was ransacked, and the owner wasn't home. They're currently trying to contact her."

"I wonder how this event is connected to the bank robbery?" I went through the gate, then stepped to the side as a number of officers rushed past us and headed up the slope. What Ruadhán expected them to find, I had no idea.

"It might not be."

"You don't believe that any more than I do." I watched the officers for a moment, then added, "He's obviously searching for something specific, so do we know if there was a safe or lockbox in the cottage?"

"They haven't found either as yet."

I wrinkled my nose. "He's obviously got a plan, but going from a bank to a cottage is rather... odd."

"I daresay when we uncover who he is, we will also uncover his intent."

I glanced at him. "That's a big leap of logic right there, because one does not by necessity lead to the other."

"In my experience, it often does."

And he had a whole lot more experience than me when it came to dealing with unsavory types. "Are we going to be allowed inside the cottage to have a look around?"

"No. My father has the description of the items taken at the bank, and for the moment would rather forensics be given the time and space to do their thing."

I resisted the urge to say "I told you so." "I'm betting he didn't exactly use that wording."

"Well, no, but the sentiment is the same."

Henrick stepped out of the car as we approached and held the rear passenger door open. I scooted across to the other side so Mathi could get in and poor Henrick didn't have to be in the rain any longer than necessary.

He had, goddess love him, purchased a tea and coffee for us both and placed them in the center console. Beside the tea was a small tube of numbing antiseptic gel—though how he'd known it would be necessary, I had no idea.

I thanked him profusely and dabbed on the gel, then picked up the tea, wrapping two hands around the container to warm them up.

"Are you going to have a chat to the godly library some-time today or tomorrow?" Mathi asked as the privacy screen went up and we got underway.

I nodded. "I have some paperwork that needs to be done, but I've nothing on tonight, so I'll do it then."

"Let me know what you discover, and we can plot our next move."

"I shall." I took a sip of tea. "You out with another of the prospects tonight?"

"I am indeed."

"And when are you intending to let me in on this secret plan you have?"

"Once I've dated all three several times and have formed an opinion on them all."

I rolled my eyes. "Stop being so secretive—just tell me where I come into it."

His smile flashed, bright and amused. "I want you to have dinner with each of them. And me, of course."

"To what end?"

"To help me choose the most suitable prospect."

I just about choked on my tea. "You want *me* to help *you* choose your *wife*? Mathi, that's insane."

"No, it is in fact brilliant, even if I say so myself."

"I don't think—"

"Then perhaps you should." His eyes gleamed with warmth, but deep in those blue depths, seriousness lurked. "You are my best friend, Bethany, and we highborn Ljósálfar elves are very rarely gifted such a thing. It is important to me that the woman I choose gets along with you, because I do not intend to ever lose our friendship. If that means stepping away from a contract that is very beneficial to my family, then so be it."

I reached out and briefly caught his hand, squeezing it lightly. "Thank you."

Surprise flitted briefly through his expression. "For what?"

"For saying all that. For being in my life. For trusting me to help with such an important decision."

"Then you *will* help?"

"Of course." I couldn't help my sudden grin. "But you are aware that I am by nature somewhat chaotic and will likely choose the least suitable candidate."

He laughed. "Yes, I am well aware of that factor, which is why all three are being screened beforehand. I want to ensure suitability and compatibility no matter who you choose."

"Then let me know when you're ready."

"I will. Thank you."

"Welcome—though I dare say you had better not mention this deal to your father. He's unlikely to be pleased."

"That would be a very definite understatement."

We cruised back over the river and wound our way back to St Werburgh Street, where Henrick parked as close as he could to the rear lane. I jumped out and, as they drove away, ran down the lane, tossing the now empty takeaway cup in the nearby dumpster before punching in the door code and dripping into the back corridor. Once I'd stripped off my coat and boots, I padded down the corridor, listening to the building's song and finding nothing untoward.

After checking that everything was fine in the kitchen, I quickly headed upstairs to the bathroom to check my face. I'd been expecting a minor scrape, but the wound basically stretched from the side of my cheek to my chin, and while it wasn't particularly deep, it did look rather ugly. Thank goddess for Henrick's numbing gel, because I rather suspected it'd be a painful mess without it. I searched the first-aid kit for a similar tube, then carefully cleaned away all the bits of grit and stone that were lodged in my skin before carefully reapplying more numbing salve. The end result was a wound that at least looked less red and sore.

With that done, I made myself a cup of tea then headed back down to the office. After shoving my feet into the spare pair of runners I kept under the desk, I booted up the computer to do the few bits and pieces Ingrid couldn't.

It was close to five by the time I stopped—and only did so then because my stomach was giving me a loud reminder that I hadn't eaten lunch. I arched my back to work out the kinks, then rose and went upstairs. After investigating the fridge and the pantry for anything resembling a decent meal, I made up a couple of ham and cheese toasties, shoved them in the maker, then made myself another pot of tea as I waited for them to cook. I caught up on the news—most of which involved yesterday's heist—as I ate, then after doing the dishes, I grabbed the chocolate Mathi had given me yesterday and headed up the loft ladder. When Gran had moved out, Mom had converted this area into a chill-out zone where she and I could read our books in peace. Even though she was now dead, and this place was mine to do with as I wished, I didn't ever intend to change it. Her soul might not haunt the building or this space, but echoes of her presence nevertheless lingered. It helped ease the ache of missing her and somehow made me feel closer to her, as impossible as that sounded.

Tears stung my eyes, but I determinedly blinked them away. After placing my tea and the chocolate on the small table beside the cushion-adorned sofa, I walked toward the wood heater at the back of the room to retrieve the Codex, which was safely hidden in a special storage pocket in the back of the mesh surrounding the flue. It was one of the first things Gran had done when she'd lived up here, though she'd simply created the space by slicing the mesh open and bending it inward to form the small shelf she'd used to hide her smaller valuables. While it had been large enough to hold the Codex and the Eye, my knives were far too big to fit. Cynwrig had solved that problem by not only replacing the entire length of decorative mesh but had widened the gap between the mesh and the flue and made an inner "pocket" between them that was big enough to hold everything. He'd also added a door that, unless you knew it existed, wasn't visible. I hooked a finger into the hole that served as a handle, opened the door, then reached down for the Codex. When I'd first found it, it had been nothing more than a worn and very plain-looking leather notebook, but the blood-bonding ceremony had changed its appearance, turning the old leather a glassy black. The light that rolled across its surface at my touch echoed that in the Eye but generally held none of its dangerous electricity, though that didn't mean it wasn't dangerous. The cost of using it was strength—linger too long in the library's godly realm, and you could be drained unto death.

I made myself comfortable on the sofa, then called the knives to me. Once they'd thudded into my hands, I placed them on top of the Codex, then undid the Eye and put it on top of the knives. I closed my eyes, pressed all three items together, and said, "What can you tell me about Aamon's Pectoral?"

For the briefest of seconds, nothing happened. Then light erupted from the triune, forming a whirlpool that was so dizzyingly bright I could see it through closed eyelids; it swept me up and then swept me away, though it wasn't a physical departure but rather a mental—spiritual?—one. I could still feel the old leather sofa under my butt, could still hear the building's gentle song, and the rattle of noise from staff and customers echoing up from the floors below, but it all paled in comparison to the howling wind being generated by my descent through the colorful maelstrom now surrounding me.

I finally came to a halt in a bright, open space filled with a multitude of different shapes. Long and tall, thin, or thick, some round, but most square or rectangular. They weren't shelves. They were books that hovered in orderly rows in the nothingness of this place and glowed with an unearthly energy.

It is such a pleasure to see you again so soon, Bethany. What do you wish to know about Aamon's Pectoral?

The voice was neither male nor female, and it not only exuded a deep sense of wisdom and knowledge, but also a hell of a lot more friendliness than the first time I'd stepped into this place—though the librarian had never, in anyway, been hostile toward me.

As per usual, Aasym, I'm after anything you can tell me about it.

Pleasure rippled through the brightness around me. From what I had gathered the last time I was here, few had ever even bothered asking its name. Which, to be honest, just seemed rude to me.

Aamon is a minor god of air and was most revered in humanity's Egyptian period. He has long fallen out of favor and indeed moved on from this world.

And his pectoral?

Allows the wearer to attain invisibility via a vaporous form.

Is that all it gives?

Its amusement spun around me, as bright as the area in which I stood. *It is ever part of human nature to want more, so yes, it also gifts the wearer the ability to use the wind to spy on others.*

Which explained why our thief had been standing on that path rather than in the street itself. He hadn't needed to risk going any closer, even in vaporous form, because he could hear everything that was going on, both outside and inside, thanks to the fact the front door had been propped open.

It didn't explain why I hadn't sensed his use of the wind though. Technically, I should have. Unless, of course, the pectoral used the wind in a manner way different to what the gods of storms and their by-blows did.

Have you got a picture of it?

As had happened on the previous occasions, the librarian didn't answer, but the book blocks around me spun with dizzying speed for a few seconds, then one popped out of the rotation and floated toward me. It hovered in the air several feet in front of me while the pages flipped open.

There were no words in any of these books—or at least, in any of the ones I'd seen so far—only images. I suspected Aasym believed me incapable of reading anything that might be written within them, and given I couldn't even read Latin, let alone a language as old as the gods themselves, it was undoubtedly right.

The pages stopped flipping. The pectoral was made of gold, and had cloisonné inlays—an ancient technique for decorating metalwork objects with colored material held in place or separated by metal strips or wire, which in this case, was gold—of red and blue stones. It was shaped like an eagle, its wings spread wide, and was clutching two cloudy white stones that glowed luminously in its claws. It was absolutely gorgeous.

I glanced up from the book. *When Aamon departed, did he store his artifact in any particular place?*

The pages flipped over again, this time revealing some sort of altar. It was made of the same white stone that the eagle clutched in his claws, and held a moon-like glow against the darkness in which it was held.

I don't suppose you know where that altar is, do you?

This is a library of information, not maps. However, in this case, you are fortunate, because Aamon did provide a footnote to his book.

I take it most gods don't bother?

Not when it comes to location details. Chaos, as you well know, child, is a pet project of many.

And don't we appreciate it, I replied darkly.

Its amusement slipped around me again. The pages flipped some more, finally stopping near the end. What it revealed were two rivers that flowed into one, a crumbling castle on a riverbank, and a doorway set in a dry stone wall, which would only open if you twisted a vaguely cross-shaped stone that was barely visible even in the drawing. The book snapped shut and spun back into its spot. *That is all the information we have written down.*

But not all the information you have?

You are quick, young pixie. Find the altar and you find the means by which to find the pectoral.

If our thief didn't take it when he stole the pectoral.

Humanity cannot take what is little more than air. Only a god—or godling—can do that.

At least that was something. I hesitated, and heard in the brief silence the inner beat of weariness. I needed to be quick before the strength draining began in earnest. *What about Bia's Blade? Have you got information on that?*

Bia is the goddess of force and compulsion. Her blade allows the holder to enforce his or her will onto others.

Which was what Beira had said. *Do you have a picture of it?*

The shelves once again did their spin thing, then popped out a book that sped toward me, its pages flipping open even before it had stopped. The blade was an unadorned silver that looked translucent, but the guard was shaped like a snake, the grip was scaled, and the pommel was the head of a viper, its mouth open and eyes rubies that gleamed with a bloody fire.

I glanced up. *Is Bia capable of taking other forms?*

The snake is her preferred form, but she can take others.

Mythically, snakes were seen as deceitful, vengeful, vindictive, or sly creatures, so it was somewhat appropriate that a goddess of force and compulsion would take that form. *Can anyone use her artifact, or is it restricted to those with an unscrupulous nature?*

Few gods restrict the usage of their artifacts. It lessens the chance of chaos.

The fucking gods and their fucking chaos... *I don't suppose you have any record that would help us find her dagger?*

Your supposition is correct—I do not.

I snorted softly, the sound running like laughter through the brightness. *Then I thank you for time, Aasym.*

It has been a pleasure, as usual, Bethany.

With a nod, I stepped back into the maelstrom, and then into my body. By that time, my heart raced, my breathing was rapid and shallow, and my chest burned so badly it was hard to breathe. I released the triune and leaned back against the sofa's headrest, closing my eyes against the suddenly overbright light in the room and taking deep, slow breaths in an effort to control the fierce ache in brain and body.

It took nearly ten minutes for the pain to start subsiding. I leaned sideways, carefully picked up my tea and the chocolate, and alternated between the two until I felt normal. Or as normal as I was ever likely to get.

After a few more minutes, I became aware of the noise drifting up from the lower floors. We obviously had a good crowd in tonight, which was surprising. It might be a Friday night, but it was also mid-February, and the entire month was usually pretty slow thanks to generally horrid winter conditions.

I climbed to my feet, walked back to the flue to hide the triune, then collected my cup and the chocolate wrapper and headed back down the loft ladder. After locking it back up, I dumped the cup in the sink, the rubbish in the bin, then walked into my bedroom to change into the tavern's uniform. Mom had decided when she'd taken over that not only should a tavern bearing the name Ye Olde Pixie Boots have said boots hanging from the ceilings, but all staff manning the public areas should be appropriately attired, which was why we women now wore leather shorts, a leather-and-lace corset-type shirt, thick woolen leggings, and pointed leather boots. While the outfit did not reveal a whole lot of flesh, it was form-fitting, and the corset did enhance what was already there—which, if you already had larger breasts, as I did, certainly did put a sexier spin on things. The men had it a little easier—while they wore the same boots, their uniform was form-fitting leather pants and shirt.

I clattered down the stairs and helped out wherever I was needed, be it serving behind one of the bars or clearing tables, freeing other staff to help carry the meals out. My scraped face did get a lot of sympathy and comments, especially from the regulars, who offered all manner of weird and sometimes amusing advice on how to speed up the healing or what to do when I found the bastard who ran into me.

"Now that," Ingrid said as she locked the door out onto the row then turned the Open sign around to Closed, "was a damn good night. You want help with the tills?"

I shook my head. "Grab an early night while you can. Who knows when I'll be able to help out like that again."

"That being the case, we might be needing to employ more casuals, especially now we're rolling toward shoulder season."

"If you've anyone in mind, set up an interview."

She nodded. "I'll let you know."

Once she and the other staff had left, I checked all the doors were locked then began the odious task of doing the tills and checking the stock. It was close to one by the time I stumbled upstairs, but as tired as I was, I just couldn't sleep.

There was a restlessness within that just wouldn't shut up.

A restlessness that was based in foresight but also held undeniable flickers of need. Of desire.

The former was insisting I talk to Cynwrig. The latter just wanted him.

I swore softly at the way my pulse leapt at the mere thought of seeing him again, even if only on the dreaming plane, then I threw the blankets off and padded across to the wardrobe to reclaim the gorgeous black velvet box I'd hidden at the very back of the top shelf. I had better hiding places in the bedroom, of course, but at least a couple of thieves now knew about them, and I had no idea if the pair of them were in jail or out on bail. I doubted they'd risk Sgott's wrath by breaking into the tavern again, but neither had seemed to be the brightest tool in the box.

I walked back to the bed and crossed my legs as I examined the jewelry box. It was roughly five inches square and had the Lùtair shield emblazoned in silver on the top. I ran my finger lightly over the hammer and anvil crest, then pressed the small button on the side. The lid sprang open, revealing the bracelet sitting in a bed of black silk. It was made of a polished stone the color of midnight, and its surface was alive with tiny stars. I hesitated, then ran one finger across it. The stone was warm against my skin, and the stars pulsed, as if in recognition of my touch. The urge to slide it over my wrist was once again so strong I'd lifted the bracelet from the silk before caution reasserted itself. I had no idea what might happen once I put this thing on, but one thing was certain—I wasn't going to step onto *any* type of field, dreaming or not, sans clothes, even if my hormones and my heart wanted nothing more than to get naked and madly passionate with the man I was about to see.

I slipped off the bed again and tugged on knickers, sweatpants, and a T-shirt. Not exactly the sexiest of outfits, but I doubted Cynwrig would care. He was very familiar with every curve of my body, and knew, all too well, how easy it was to remove my layers. The flimsy barrier was more for my sake than his.

I made myself comfortable again, but for several seconds, did nothing more than stare at the bracelet sitting so snugly in its bed of silk. If I did this, there would be no going back. I knew that. If I was wrong about Eljin, if the Eye's reaction was nothing more than an echo of my own insecurities about a relationship with him, then taking this step would put an end to any hope I might hold for a future with him. Because I couldn't live a lie. I couldn't let him believe that Cynwrig was out of the picture for the next three months. Couldn't allow the narrative that we had the time to explore our relationship and possibly develop it into something stronger to continue when I knew it could never, ever, be as strong as the connection I felt with the man who would never be mine.

I liked Eljin, I really did, and I'd definitely continue to sleep with him as long as he didn't, in fact, turn out to be a bad guy. But ours was a relationship that wasn't destined to move beyond a "friend with benefits" scenario, no matter how much I might have hoped otherwise.

Perhaps *that* was what the Eye was trying to tell me.

And yet, given my father had stated Cynwrig had been placed in my path to cause chaos, dare I take the bait any more than I had?

I wanted to. Goddess only knew how badly I wanted to.

But was it advisable?

Probably not.

Would that stop me?

Hell, no.

I plucked the bracelet from its silken bed and slipped it over my wrist, before any second thoughts could intrude, and said, "Take me to him." I had no idea what to expect, because the note Cynwrig had sent with the bracelet simply said to wear it if I wished a continuation of what we share in a non-physical manner. Which, considering it was a means by which two compatible people could meet and fuck on the dreaming plane, was something of a misnomer. Unless, of course, he really did intend to do nothing more than talk.

A large part of me would be *very* disappointed if that were the case.

For several seconds, nothing happened. The stars on the bracelet spun around, weirdly reminding me of one of those old-fashioned dial-up phones so often found in antique stores. In some ways, it did make sense they'd be "dialing" the person on the other end of what was normally a booty call, just in case they were in no position to receive it.

When the stars stopped spinning, their light bloomed around me, encompassing my entire body. Then, in a maneuver that reminded me of the kaleidoscope I ventured into every time I journeyed to the godly library, it swept me up, swept me away, and then dumped me not into a place of warmth and light, but rather cool darkness.

There was nothing here. Nothing but me, this darkness, and complete and utter silence.

Gradually, though, a soft sound intruded.

A heartbeat. Not mine: another's.

It got stronger, louder. Anticipation, and perhaps a little uncertainty, swept through me. Then, from out of the shadows, walked a figure. A figure who moved with all the fluid grace and perfection of a predator.

Cynwrig.

My heart skipped more than a few beats and a sigh of pleasure escaped, but I didn't say anything else, and I didn't move. I simply watched him approach.

Unlike their golden kin, dark elves were neither slender nor delicate, and this man's powerful body was nothing short of magnificent. His chiseled features were sublime, and his body ebony perfection, from the width of his shoulders, the well-muscled planes of his chest, to his washboard abs and the happy trail of dark hair that drew the eye down to the waistband of the jeans he was wearing and the impressive mound they covered. Those same jeans hugged the long magnificence of his legs, which held the muscular strength of a runner rather than a weightlifter.

My gaze rose and met his. His eyes were a smoky silver

filled with heat—the kind of heat that urged me to rip off my clothes and have hot and sweaty sex with him right here and now.

You need to talk first, I reminded myself fiercely. *You need to understand what this place is, what it means.*

But most of all, I needed to understand why he'd taken this step, if only because Darby had said the Bruadar bracelets were rare.

He stopped just beyond touching distance, his face impassive, but his hands clenched, as if he were fighting the urge to reach for me.

"Bethany," he said softly, "it is a pleasure to see you here. I was beginning to think I never would."

His voice was smooth, velvety smoke that spun around me like a caress, sending delight skittering down my spine.

"I did debate the sanity of doing this, but I needed to talk to you about the current relic hunt."

A somewhat rueful smile touched his full lips. "Whatever the reason, I am—" He cut the rest off abruptly. "What happened to your face?"

I instinctively raised a hand; the wound felt real rather than imaginary, and pain skittered lightly away from my fingertips. Weird. "I was chasing a dark elf thief down a tunnel and got thrown into a wall. Not his fault, though the bastard did try to bury me not long after that."

His anger surged around me, through me, a heated wave of such ferocity that it briefly stole my breath... and warmed my heart.

My heart was *stupid*.

"Who?" he growled. "Do you know his name? Or is this what you came here for?"

"The latter." I flexed my fingers and grimly fought the urge to let them play across the field of ebony perfection standing so close, and yet so far away. "I'm surprised Ruadhán hasn't spoken to you. He said he was going to."

"It is possible the call was taken by my sister. I have not spoken to her for a few hours." He paused, his expression briefly suggesting he was about to add something else but changed his mind. "Has this anything to do with the robbery at Tylwyth Teg?"

"Yes. The same thief robbed a cottage this morning, which is where I was injured."

Again, the fury rolled around me.

"And where was Mathi?" he growled. "He is supposed to be protecting you."

"Since when?"

He didn't answer, but something within suspected it was likely suggested after they'd rescued me from my aunt's clutches. It would also explain Mathi's sudden insistence on me being careful, though I had no doubt most of that came from my near-death encounter and his wish not to lose me as a friend.

"He's my liaison, *not* my protector," I added. "And that aside, I'm more than capable of protecting myself."

"I was not suggesting otherwise," he replied evenly. "But it is also undeniable that you, trouble, and injuries seem to have a fatal attraction."

"I'd rather label it 'unwanted' rather than 'fatal'. The latter has connotations I do not want to put out there in the ether when the gods are playing their games."

And I certainly didn't want to *think* about it, especially after my father's declaration that no matter what I did, death would be my end point.

"Describe this dark elf to me."

"Aside from the fact he's youngish and has very good control over the earth, I really can't." I did give him the little information I'd seen in the vault and described the earthen snake he'd sent after me when I extricated myself from his trap. "Given his formal attire when he was robbing the bank, I thought it possible he was going to Jarvil Maehdon's funeral after he'd finished his thieving."

"If that is true, then we at least have a starting point."

He seemed to be a little closer, even though he hadn't physically moved. If I extended my arm, I could touch him now without effort... and I really *did* want to touch. I dug my nails into my palm, but the pain did little to erase the desire.

"Why?" I said, a little confused. "I was under the impression the funeral was very well-attended."

"Both human and fae dignitaries were there in bulk, but only the heads of the main seven dark elf lines and their families attended." He paused, and his fingers twitched ever so briefly. "How did he get in and out of that vault? It's well secured against the likes of us dark elves."

"Via a god-gifted relic." Amusement twitched my lips. "And, how, exactly do you know that fact about the vault? Or shouldn't I ask?"

"My father was a consultant when the bank was built."

"Did he build in backdoor access, by chance?"

A smile briefly touched his lovely lips. "He did not. We might rule the black market, but we do not steal from the financial institutions many of our people use."

"Do you? Use it, I mean."

"I do have a safe deposit box there, as well as several other places. As the saying goes, it is never wise to place all your eggs in the one basket."

"Did your mother or father have boxes there or even elsewhere?"

"Yes—why?"

"Have you checked them for Geitha's Tears?"

The Tears being the goddess-gifted necklace that had apparently disappeared on his mother's death.

Something flickered across his expression. Not surprise, not exactly. More... wariness. But why? He surely knew Treasa had asked me to find it—I doubted she would have lied about that.

"My father's security box did not hold the necklace."

"And your mother's?"

"Was closed long ago by my father. If the Tears were in there, he made no further note of where he'd moved it to."

"Damn."

"Indeed."

My gaze locked with his again, and for several seconds, I allowed myself to get lost in the warmth so visible in those gloriously smoky depths. Heat stirred through them, heat and something else. Something undefinable and rare. Something that made my heart leap and my head mock its foolishness.

"Bethany," he whispered, reaching out to me with one hand.

I stepped back, even though every inch of me wanted to do the opposite. His hand dropped, but his fingers were once again clenched.

"I need to know what the end game is here, Cynwrig, because I'm—" *in serious danger of losing my heart, and I'm not sure I could stand the devastation that will inevitably happen when you have to choose a wife.*

He didn't immediately reply, and I had the oddest feeling he knew exactly what I was thinking. Perhaps he did; perhaps the bond that seemed to be forming between us—the bond that had allowed him to hear my "resonance" on the earth—also gave him deeper insights into my heart and my mind.

"Do you trust me?" he asked eventually.

"With my life. But this is not a matter of trust; it's about expectations, and dreams, and I—" I took a deep breath and plowed on. "I don't think I'm strong enough *emotionally* to continue this relationship. I want to, you have to know that, but in three months' time, when you are forced to choose a wife... it will likely break me."

"I will *never* do anything to break you, that I promise."

"You can't *possibly* make such a promise, Cynwrig, because you have no control over my heart, and *it* has proven time and again to be extremely foolish."

"Sometimes foolishness is required if you intend to claim the greatest prize."

"And sometimes, no matter how hard you try, no matter how much you might wish otherwise, some things will always remain out of reach."

He studied me for a few seconds, his face impassive. But his hands remained clenched and there was anger in his eyes. Whether it was aimed at me or the situation, I couldn't say. Despite our connection, he was still better at reading me than I was him.

"The king," he said eventually, "is not forced to choose a wife at the crowning ceremony."

"No, because Geitha's Tears chooses one for you."

"Traditionally, yes, but no matter who the Tears or the goddess herself chooses, I am not duty bound to marry them."

I couldn't help the somewhat bitter laugh that escaped. "You would go against the wishes of your goddess to continue a relationship with a commoner like me?"

The anger flared brighter and echoed through the darkness around us. I had the strangest feeling its cause was my choice of words. "I never said that."

"Then what *are* you saying?"

"I am doing nothing more than stating a fact—there will be no betrothal or indeed marriage unless I love the woman, and she loves me."

"So, while you and the goddess's chosen one set about discovering your emotional compatibility, you and I just maintain our sexual relationship?"

"What we have is far more than merely sexual."

"And what does it matter if it *is*?" I cried. "It can never go anywhere, Cynwrig, because of who you are. You have to know that."

His face became set. "What is common knowledge and what *I* accept are two different things."

So his sister had said. I scrubbed a hand through my hair, not sure what to say, or do, next. I hadn't intended to get into a fight with him. Far from it. But seeing him, being so close to him, not only had all the doubts that had crowded my mind before putting on the bracelet clawing their way back in, but emphasized the danger I was in.

Because if I stayed with him, if I continued a relationship with him, what was little more than a promising whisper right now would bloom into full-blown love.

And he *would* break my heart—break *me*—sooner or later.

Did I dare risk that?

Dare I not?

For all I knew, the gods had set a very short time frame for their game, and I might not have any more than a few months left anyway. Shouldn't I accept the inevitable heartbreak and make the most of the time left to me while I still had it?

A wise woman probably would.

Trouble was, no one had ever accused me of being particularly wise.

"Bethany—"

I took another hasty step back, though I had no idea if he intended to reach for me or not. "If I do continue a relationship with you, I want it to be real. I don't want it to be nothing more than a dream, and if that means waiting three—"

"This *is* real," he cut in. "We are not dreaming. We are not walking the dreaming plane. We are here physically, not just spiritually."

I stared at him for a second then looked around. "If this place is real, then why does it feel otherwise?"

"Because we have yet to fashion it to our wills. Think of it as a canvas waiting for the paint."

I frowned. "Poetic as that sounds, it doesn't really explain what this place is, or how we can use it without the risk of you being seen breaking the rules of mourning."

"This is what we call a liminal space—a place that exists between time and space, a pocket of reality that can only be created and accessed by a certain kind of magic. The paired Bruadar bracelets contain that magic and each allows entry *only* to its mate."

"Then it works on the same lines as an Annwfyn bridge?"

"Similar, but a liminal space is anchored in this world rather than being the connection between two worlds." He waved a hand. "Did you never wonder why we royal dark elves were the only people who could open and close the gateways?"

"Not really, though I did think it unfair that it was only your people who held the task of guarding them."

He half laughed, a warm sound that was nevertheless edged with just a trace of bitterness. "There are few enough who thought even *that*. We have been patrolling and repairing the gateways for as long as they have existed, thanks to a godly game that anointed our ancestors the only ones capable of doing so."

"But you've discovered other uses for it, obviously."

"We do have a rather well-deserved reputation for lascivious behavior." His voice was dry and yet there was an edge to it that spoke of barely contained emotions. "Our ability to invite those we wish to seduce into a liminal space to ensure complete anonymity while the seduction occurs is certainly a key ingredient to that reputation."

"I thought the bracelets were rare, and only gifted to a favorite lover or to wives?"

"They mostly are."

"'Mostly' being defined as whoever you fancied at the time?"

He laughed, a rich, warm sound that ran over my skin as sweetly as any caress, fanning the fires of wanting to greater life. "There are always those who take advantage of a situation or a gift, but remember, we, unlike the Ljósálfar, are monogamous once married. Until then? Life is to be enjoyed."

"That sounds like you think marriage cannot be."

"What I think is it depends entirely on who you marry and why. A marriage of the heart is a very different matter to one of State and necessity."

Which was why he was determined to seek the former rather than the latter, even if it broke with royal tradition. "What type of marriage did your parents have?"

"The latter, of course, because the choosing is usually part of the crowning ceremony and neither had lost their hearts to others. But they did grow fond of each other, and my father deeply grieved her death." He paused, once again seeming on the verge of saying something before changing his mind. "I want more than fondness out of my marriage, Bethany. I have grown up in that environment, and as much as I loved my parents, I will not inflict it on any children I might be blessed enough to have."

"And yet you are the crown prince, and you have a duty to your people."

"I would rather walk away from both than be trapped in a loveless marriage." He thrust a hand through his dark hair. "But all this is nothing more than conjecture until the Tears are found."

"The possibility of you breaking my heart is not conjecture, Cynwrig. It is fact."

His hand flexed, and just for a second, his turmoil echoed through me, sharp and fierce. Nothing showed in his face however, which remained impassive.

"If you do not wish to continue the sexual nature of our relationship, I will understand. I won't like it, but I will understand. If that *is* your choice, however, I will ask that you keep the Bruadar on your wrist, as it will give you an escape 'room' if you ever need it."

"Will keeping it on affect the way it works?"

"No. In fact, until this relationship is ended, you will not be able to take it off. The magic will not allow it."

"Well, that's just fine and dandy," I growled. "What if I want to do something personal? What if I want to be with Eljin at some point?"

His eyebrows rose. "At some point? Does that mean your relationship with him has cooled?"

"It does not."

"Shame."

I scowled at him. *He* looked totally unperturbed.

"To answer your question," he continued, after a beat, "you can do as you wish. The Bruadar is not a tracer, and it will not spy on your activities. It was developed to do nothing more than bring you to this liminal space."

I glanced down at it for a moment. "How does it work if you're trying to contact me?"

"The stars will spin. If you wish to accept the call, simply say so, and we will meet here."

"And if I want to refuse the call?"

"You simply say 'reject call.'"

I hesitated. "And this place? Are there any restrictions on how long we can stay here?"

"Aside from the fact that there is neither food nor water here aside from what we might bring in, no."

"There's no bed, either, from what I can see."

His soft chuckle held the faintest edge, but it nevertheless had delight skittering down my spine, warming me in all the right places. "As I have said, we have not yet fashioned it to our wills. I suspect you are not quite ready to do that yet."

I wanted to. I wanted *him*. But the fear remained. While I had no doubt our sexual relationship would continue sooner rather than later, if for no other reason than the fact I was an absolute idiot, I just... wanted to delay the inevitable heartbreak just a fraction longer. I doubted I'd ever be able to harden my heart to it, though. Or to him.

When I didn't answer, he added, "I shall begin investigations into those who attended and work up a list of suspects. It may take me a day or so, but once a day, we shall meet here, if you wish, and discuss the matter."

I couldn't help arching an eyebrow. "Just discuss?"

"That, my dearest Bethany, is entirely up to you."

"I have dinner with Lugh and Darby tomorrow night, so if it is done by then, don't call early."

He bowed in formal acknowledgement of the request then stepped back and said, "Leave."

And with little fanfare, he did so, leaving me alone in the darkness and cursing the fucking fear that had stopped me taking what I so desperately wanted.

I drew in a deep, shuddering breath, then, like him, said, "Leave."

And found myself back in the bedroom, alone and aching.

Serves me right, I thought.

I stripped off, climbed back into bed, then tried to sleep.

It took a long, *long* time to find me.

But when it did, it came with dreams. Or maybe they were nightmares, because they were filled with the bitter taste of deception and death. Nothing was really clear, nothing beyond two things. A knife, flashing down into the flesh of a red-haired woman—a woman who now had a face. Mine.

But that wasn't the worst of it, because this time the dream included a calendar clock, ticking down.

If it were to be believed, death would find me in a little under nine months.

CHAPTER
FIVE

It was close to ten by the time I woke up. The building's cheery song told me Ingrid and the crew were already downstairs, setting up for the day, and my mind was helpfully providing a rundown of the things I had to do over the next couple of hours. I definitely needed to get up and get going, but for the longest of time, I couldn't. I just snuggled deeper under the comforter's warmth and did my best to ignore the mental list. Partially because I was still damnably tired, and partially because I was still mad at myself for not accepting the situation with Cynwrig, especially if those dreams were a precognitive warning rather than a natural result of the fear that had haunted me since my father's proclamation.

Besides, it wasn't as if *not* fucking him would, in any way, ease the anguish when he took a wife. I might not have known him all that long, we might still be strangers in every way beyond the bedroom, but I was already too far down the rabbit hole of caring not to fall apart when he married.

I rolled onto my back and stared up at the ceiling.

Maybe I needed to talk to Darby about Cynwrig *and* that ticking clock. I couldn't discuss it with Lugh, because it wouldn't be fair to burden him with that until I was absolutely certain there was no way I could win this game and stay alive. It probably wasn't entirely fair to burden Darby with it, either, but she was a forester class light elf, which meant that while she was far more emotionally connected, she still had an elf's practicalities when it came to men, life, and love. She would give me a straight, no-nonsense answer, whether I wanted to hear it or not.

Although when it came to Cynwrig, I already knew what her advice would be. But given she was the one who always picked up the pieces after a love affair of mine had gone south—and there'd been plenty of them over the decades because I was absolute shit at choosing partners— the least I could do was give her time to stock up on the cake, chocolate, and alcohol that were a standard requirement for our "he sucks, you're awesome" pity parties.

As for the clock... well, she was a healer who specialized in poisons, with a secondary specialization in wound repairs. Maybe she could suggest a way around fate's declaration. After all, my fucking aunt had used death to get around the restrictions of the red knife, so surely there was some way I could do the same.

The phone rang sharply into the silence and made me jump. I was tempted to ignore it, but the tone told me it was Mathi, and he rarely rang without reason. I groped for it on the bedside table, then hit the answer button.

"Hey," I said. "What's up? Not another theft, I hope, because I'm really not in the mood today."

"If your face is sore, you should have gone to either Darby or your doctor to get it repaired."

"Yes, I should have, but I didn't, and now I'm grumpy, tired, and have absolutely no patience."

He chuckled softly. "State normal, then."

"You, Mathi Dhār-Val, can be a bastard sometimes."

"Indeed, I can. It's part of my charm."

I rolled my eyes. "Why are you ringing?"

"Got the name of the person who owned that box our thief took the contents from. Thought we might do a little illicit searching of her property."

"It's not the cottage he hit yesterday, then?"

"No. Different."

I frowned. "So why not just go talk to her? Better yet, given your father or his team probably already have, why not just read the report?"

"Because they haven't found her yet, let alone talked to her. Apparently she hasn't lived at that address for quite a few years."

"But she still owns it?"

"Yes, and according to the neighbors, she randomly appears, stays for a couple of hours, and then leaves again."

"She doesn't rent it out?"

"No. She has gardeners and cleaners coming in once a month, though."

"Your father hasn't ordered an internal search to be done?"

"He has no cause—she is a victim, not a suspect."

"Having no cause hasn't stopped him in the past."

"No, but there are, believe it or not, some lines even my father won't cross."

"Are there lines the son won't?" I asked, amused.

"Depends entirely on the line. There is one problem, however."

"Of course there is, because when has any relic search gone smoothly?"

He chuckled. "My father has tasked the regular police with watching the building, and has also ordered me not to go near it. He doesn't want to risk spooking the owner on the off chance this was something other than a mere robbery."

"Like what?"

"Like a means to blackmail his target. It would certainly explain him only taking the contents of one box."

"Isn't it also possible that, given both lines of elves do like keeping little incriminating bits and pieces for possible use later, he was simply trying to retrieve the contents of that box, thereby stopping either a scandal or future problems for his family?"

If that were the case though, why go on and raid the cottage the next day?

"Indeed," Mathi was saying, "but until we can find the owner and talk to her, we won't know."

"Hence the illicit comment. But why? Your father's request isn't unreasonable, even though it does suggest he is unaware of the true extent of your breaking and entering skills."

"Not even my skills could get us past a twenty-four-hour ground watch. I might, however, have found another means of skirting them."

"Why are you so gung-ho about circumventing your father's orders?" I asked curiously.

"The mere fact he issued them."

"Given your grand age," I replied dryly, "I would have thought you beyond your teenage rebellion years."

"I," he responded, in much the same tone, "am barely

on the cusp of breeding age for an elf, so the rebellion is not out of place."

I laughed. "And the real reason?"

"He denied the council request you be sent in to investigate."

My eyebrows shot upward. "Why would they request that?"

"I tried to access the file this morning and couldn't. I subsequently told the council it was necessary we get into the house when I made my report this morning."

"Why couldn't you get into the file?"

"My access has been revoked."

Surprise rippled through me. "It has? By whom? Sgott?"

He didn't, after all, like Mathi's deep access into the system and had threatened a complete lockout more than once.

"No, by my father. In the interest of protecting the victims, apparently, who do not wish their names known or released."

Another reasonable point, given the suspected informational leaks throughout the IIT. "So, if this building is under twenty-four-hour watch, how are we going to get in without your father being informed?"

"I have enquiries open with a mage and a dwarf."

"I daresay you're hoping it's the former with the best breaking and entering option, given you and underground spaces are not compatible."

"As has been established recently, my dislike does not hamper my actions. The question is, can you control your loathing of rats if a tunnel turns out to be the better choice?"

Said loathing had been born out of having them

running over my face when I was a kid. "I've traversed them before; I can do so again."

Even if my brain was saying, *No, no you can't.*

He laughed. "Will a bacon butty sweeten the deal?"

"Add some chips, and yes it will."

"In what world are chips ever considered breakfast material?"

His horror was evident, and I couldn't help smiling. "It's closer to lunchtime than breakfast, so it's totally appropriate. How long have I got before you arrive?"

"Traffic is terrible, so we'll say twenty minutes, end of lane. I should have received calls from both by then."

"And if you haven't?"

"We will be forced to delay our adventure until another day."

"Given the adventure might well involve rats, I can't say I'd be sad about that."

He chuckled again and hung up. I tossed the comforter off and padded, shivering all the way, into the bathroom for a quick shower. Once I was dressed, I tucked my phone into my jeans pocket then ran up the loft ladder to get the knives. I might be able to call them to me, but they tended to come sans sheaths, and it wasn't exactly legal to carry bare blades about. Of course, it wasn't exactly legal to carry them sheathed either, even if, like Mom, I now had some leeway in that I worked for the council and the knives were an essential part of my relic hunting. I reached around the back of the flue to get them, but the minute I touched the hilts, the Eye came to life.

There were visions to be had.

I cursed softly, sent a text to Mathi, then walked over to the sofa. Once I'd made myself comfortable, I placed one hand on the blades and wrapped the other around the Eye.

The connection between me and the triune was strong enough now that my mind's eye was swept away so damn fast it was briefly disorientating.

I found myself surrounded by darkness and stone that sped by at alarming speed, reminding me somewhat of a roller coaster in which all forms of lighting had been cut and there was only the rush of wind past face and hair. Gradually, though, a soft luminescence appeared, lending a cold glimmer to the stone walls. A few seconds later, I was swept over a lake that looked foul and whose surface moved unnaturally in the stillness, and then came to an island on which the altar I'd seen in the Codex library stood. Beside it was a harp, and though the strings seemed to be moving, the vision wasn't allowing me to hear the music it made.

Was the harp the source of the distant, jarring music I'd heard in the wind yesterday? Aasym had said that if I found the altar, I would find the means of tracing the pectoral.

The vision pulled back, giving me a brief glimpse of two rivers and a stepping stone path that crossed one and led to the ruined castle I'd also seen in the library, then darkness swept in again and spun me into another location entirely. One that provided no images, only sound, meaning I was about to "see" Carla and whoever her damn boss was.

It was a damnably frustrating situation, but until I found some way of getting past whatever shield they were using and could force these visions into both sound *and* sight mode, there wasn't much I could do.

Why have you called me here at this hour? Carla's voice was sharp and annoyed. *It is dangerous, given the council still meet. I cannot be absent for too long. You know this.*

A statement that suggested Carla was not only the lover of one—or more—of the councilors but also worked there.

Elves of either variety were generally not adverse to engaging in an office romance or two, and many of the shifters had high sex drives as well. Given Carla's ability to basically take on any form she wished, it wouldn't be hard for her to uncover a councilor's preferences and subtly play to them.

You've heard of the robbery at Tylwyth Teg?

The man's tinny tone was curt. Aside from the fact he was still using the voice modulator—though why he was bothering when he and Carla were lovers and she obviously knew his identity, I had no idea—he was obviously very annoyed at her. Which was interesting. What the hell had she done?

It was the talk of the council meeting for the first hour or so, she replied dryly. *Why?*

You kept a box there, did you not?

There was a long pause. *Yes. How did you know? It was not under the name of my usual identities.*

I have known you for a very long time, remember, and my memory is keen. That identity's box was the target. He took everything within it, and nothing else.

If he had that information, it meant this man was either working for the bank or was a part of the IIT investigative team. Ruadhán was obviously right to lock the file down when he had, but maybe he needed to take a closer look at the people on this investigation.

What did you have in there? he added in a low growl.

Security, she replied. Though her voice was even, I had a vague sense that panic bubbled underneath that calmness.

What sort of security? Not names, I hope, because I will bury you so damn deep—

A comment that was *very* interesting, given that was a method favored by dark elves wanting to get rid of their foes. Up until this point, we'd suspected that those behind the theft of the hoard had come mainly from the light elf camp, as they were the ones responsible for protecting it. But perhaps we needed to look for suspects in the Myrkálfar camp, too.

And lose not only the best fuck you've had in decades, but also your best spy? Carla's laugh was harsh. *Come now, we both know that will not happen.*

Do not ever overestimate your value to me. The cause is worth far more to me than you ever will be.

And your cause would have stalled multiple times if not for me, she snapped back. *Who was it that gave you the information about the pixie witch? Without that, she might have succeeded in stopping the hoard's theft.*

Carla was the one who'd passed on the information about Mom? If that were true, then she was dead. *So* dead. There would be no justice for her, no court appearance. In darkness and in lightning she would die, as Mom had died, in agony....

I shivered and tried to rein in the furious darkness that roiled through me. The vision hadn't faded. There was more to be learned.

Her death landed us with an even bigger problem.

Which is not my fault. Who knew the bitch's offspring would turn out to have stronger gifts than her fucking mother? Carla sniffed. *What is being done to retrieve the box's contents?*

The usual, came the angry reply. *Now answer the question —what was in there, Brídín?*

Brídín? If that was the name she'd been born with, then we might have gotten our first useful clue.

No fucking names, remember? The witch may be listening in.

She is with Mathi. They are researching options to get past the guards stationed at the address registered with the bank.

How the fuck would he know that? Was Mathi's car or home bugged?

You've taken measures to stop that, I gather.

I can only do so much without risking my cover. Now answer the question—what was in the box?

Birth records, passports, property documents, stuff like that.

Nothing incriminating in regard to me or our plans, then?

There was just the tiniest hesitation before she said, *No.*

Liar, instinct whispered, and that only made it more important than ever we got the thief before the IIT did. Because once they had him, Carla would no doubt erase him, as she had erased other IIT prisoners. Even if the IIT locked him down, it was hard to protect him from someone who could assume the identity of almost any woman she touched.

Which meant, of course, they simply had to make sure everyone who dealt with or protected him was male.

And the address listed with the bank? Anything there we should be worried about?

I wouldn't have thought so, came Carla's reply. *I haven't lived there for quite a while.*

The witchling has second sight, remember. It might not take much to set it off.

The safe is empty, and there's nothing in the office.

Personal items?

Nothing that would now hold any resonance or memory.

The man grunted. It remained an unhappy sound. *If you lie—*

I have no reason to lie, and every reason to avoid capture, given it would ultimately mean my death. Trust that, even if you don't trust me.

Another grunt. *I will update once I have any news. I trust you will do the same.*

Your every wish is my command, Carla said, a weird mix of amusement and bitterness in her voice. It was almost as if she herself had no choice but to obey. Had she been pixied? Possibly, though not even a pixie's will could last the centuries that Carla had apparently been alive. Hell, I had no idea if it would even hold if she took on a completely different form. Technically, it should, but who really knew when it came to one form of magic against another?

The vision fell away, and the building's song rose around me again, informing me that Mathi was downstairs in my living area. I took a deep breath to calm my still-racing pulse but didn't immediately leave the loft, instead calling Sgott. He didn't answer, so I left a message telling him our face shifter's real name, and that one of her aliases owned the box that our thief had taken. Then I pushed to my feet and headed back down the ladder.

Mathi was in the process of making a pot of tea, but it was the heavenly scent of bacon that led my nose over to the living area and the brown paper bag that sat on the coffee table. There was also a takeout cup of coffee but that obviously wasn't meant for me, given he was making tea and he generally avoided it.

"Since when did you become so domesticated?" I picked up the bag and discovered two bacon butties along with the hot chips. "You're spoiling me here."

"It's more self-preservation," he drawled. "I have previous experience when it comes to you and a food-and-tea-deprived state, remember."

I laughed, sat down on the sofa, and pulled out the food, munching on some chips while I unwrapped the butties. He placed a mug and the cozy-covered teapot beside my chips, then moved over to the other sofa and picked up his coffee.

"What did you see?"

I gave him a detailed description of both visions, then added, "Wherever you were when you made that call, it sounds like it is bugged. There's no other way he could have known what we were up to, because Sgott still regularly sweeps for them up here."

Instead of answering, he retrieved his phone and made a call, placing it on speaker so that I could hear.

"Yes, sir?" Henrick said.

"Code one search. Immediately."

"Bagged or destroyed?" Henrick asked implacably. Obviously, code one searches were not new to him.

"Bagged. I want a trace-back done."

"Immediately, sir."

He hung up. Mathi placed his phone on the table and took a drink of his coffee. "There are few places the public has access to my car. It should be easy enough to get the security footage and uncover who did this."

"Why would they bother bugging you now and not before, though?"

He shrugged. "Until we find those responsible for the bugs, if indeed we find any, that is not a question I can answer. Have you googled the rivers you saw in the vision?"

"No, because I called Sgott first, then smelled the bacon and came straight down."

He half laughed, picked up his phone, and searched for various options while I ate my food and drank my tea.

"Well," he said, after a good ten minutes. "Let me assure you that there are plenty of ruined castles sitting on riverbanks within the UK."

"That's because rivers used to be strategically important back in those days. The question is, how many of them are near the convergence of two rivers?"

He gave me a somewhat pained look. "Far too many. It would help if your visions or the Codex itself were a little more detailed."

On that we both agreed. I wrinkled my nose. "I'll try to get something a little more detailed once we've checked out that cottage... but save the list so we can work out a plan of attack once we get more time."

"Done," he said, after a moment.

"Did you did get an answer to either of your calls?"

"I did, but thankfully, it was as I was walking down the lane. Option two is the best, I'm afraid."

"Surprised, I am not." I finished the final butty and licked the grease from my fingers. "What are the chances of your phone being bugged?"

"The police and the IIT could certainly be using IMSI catchers, but they'd need a court order to do so, and my father would have warned me."

"What the hell is an IMSI catcher?"

"An IMSI is your SIM's unique number. Once your phone connects with a catcher, it reveals this number. The catcher can then reveal your phone's location by measuring the strength of the signal from the phone."

My eyebrows rose. "That all sounds very convoluted. Whatever happened to good old-fashioned call scanners?"

"The use of scanners for that sort of thing is illegal in this country."

I grinned. "When has being illegal stopped anyone? When has it ever stopped you?"

"I will have you know that ninety-five per cent of the time, my actions are beyond legal reproach."

"It's the five per cent most people need to worry about."

He smiled and didn't deny it. "We should leave. I'll call an Uber on the way down."

"Why not call the emergency chauffeur and car?"

"Because if one car is bugged, the other might be. It will take time for Henrick to do a thorough check."

"Suggesting he's been trained for that sort of thing."

"Indeed. He's former military intelligence."

The things you learn…. I finished my tea, then picked up my purse, coat, and knives, and headed for the stairs. "Have bugs been a problem in the past?"

"Corporate espionage is a problem for any successful business. We Dhār-Vals are the top at what we do."

And what they did was run one of the largest forestry growth businesses in the UK. Basically, they tripled the growth rate of plantation forests in order to protect the remaining old growth forests from harvesting. Though Mathi was the son of a second son, his uncle had retired some eight years ago without male issue. Ruadhán normally would have taken over, but had been deemed ineligible because his ability to manipulate the energy of living flora was considered below acceptable limits. I personally doubted he'd have accepted the position anyway. He had his own little fiefdom in the form of the daytime IIT division, and he definitely enjoyed the power it gave him over all races.

"I never really thought about that." I glanced over my shoulder at him. "Do you bug competitors?"

"Of course. I would be a fool not to."

"You know, there are so many aspects of your personality and your life I've not seen until recently."

"Because until recently, neither of us realized the importance of the other in our lives."

"That is definitely true." I'd been comfortable with

Mathi, had enjoyed our sex life and being with him in general, but that was it, really. I'd always known he was not my forever man and had been happy to keep our relationship light and uncomplicated, without realizing the true worth of it.

Of course, I was also well aware that Cynwrig was not my forever man, but our relationship, despite it only being a few weeks old, was as complicated as it could get, thanks to my stupid heart.

But then, I did have a history of falling far too quickly for totally unsuitable men.

Mathi opened the tavern's front door for me, then rang for an Uber. I tucked my knives away, shoved on my coat, then slung my purse over my shoulder. The day was gray and rather bleak, but for the moment, there was no rain on the horizon. The wind danced lightly around me, filled with the promise of the frost that would blanket the night later, but she was thankfully clear of the scratchy noise I'd heard yesterday. Hopefully, that meant our thief wasn't currently active. Maybe he'd found what he'd wanted in the cottage —though if that were the case, why had he been hanging around in the park?—and maybe he was simply lying low until he decided on his next target.

Instinct suggested it was the latter. It didn't tell me why, of course. Instinct could be annoyingly obtuse sometimes.

Mathi tucked his phone away and then motioned me to the right. "He'll meet us near the Cross."

The Cross actually wasn't a cross, but rather a red sandstone shaft topped by a crown, a finial, and a ball. The wide, three-stepped plinth was used as seating by tourists and pigeons alike. "Where are we meeting our dwarf guide?"

"At the community pavilion in the Water Tower Gardens."

I glanced at him curiously. "Why there? Is it close to the woman's house?"

"Not particularly, but there is an old access grate into the even older sewer tunnel system located there that runs under our target. Locryn assures me it won't be much hassle to get us in."

"Knowing Locryn," I said wryly, "he undoubtedly demanded a very high fee for such an assurance."

Mathi glanced at me in surprise. "You've met him before?"

I nodded. "He helped Lugh break into Nialle's place a while ago. For an exorbitant fee, of course."

"Well, he is the best at what he does, so the price reflects that."

And what he—and Brega, his wife and partner in crime —did was tunnel, whether working as private contractors for the National Fae Museum or as freelancers willing to work with all comers. From what I'd seen, they didn't really care about the legalities of what they were employed to do, as long as the price was right.

"Has the cottage got any sort of security system we need to worry about?" I asked as we made our way down Eastgate Street.

"Nothing that will affect us."

"Meaning it has got something?"

"Ring doorbell devices on both front and back doors, and alarmed windows. No movement sensors inside or anything like that."

"And you know this how?"

"A rat shifter was sent inside to scout, and I read that part of the report before it was locked down."

"Lucky."

"Indeed."

The Uber arrived the same time as we did and quickly whisked us over to the Water Tower Gardens. I climbed out, zipped up my coat, then shoved my hands into my pockets and scanned the area while I waited for Mathi to join me. I couldn't see the pavilion from where I stood, thanks to all the trees on the right side of the gate, but the park looked quite lovely. The old stone water tower stood at the back of the gardens to the right of the gate and was surrounded on either side by trees, while somewhere to the left there was a play area for little kids. Their screams of delight and laughter drifted joyously on the air and made me smile.

Mathi joined me as the Uber sped off, and pressed a hand against my back, guiding me toward a lichen-covered wrought-iron gate that didn't appear to have been moved for decades. A concrete path led into the heart of the garden, then split into three; the right one went to the water tower and a nearby wooden jungle gym thing that looked recent while the left one angled toward the little kids' playground and some tennis courts. We took the third option, which led to the pavilion directly ahead. It was wooden, painted dark green, with a red shingle roof, and rather oddly reminded me of an old eighteenth century stable block, complete with clock tower.

Brega waited for us at the angled doubled doors that led into the building. Like all dwarves, she was short and thick-set, but her pale features were heavily wrinkled, her eyes a dark brown, and her silver hair long enough that, even though it had been plaited, it still ran down her back to her butt.

"Right on time, Mr. Dhār-Val. Thank you for the consideration." Her sharp gaze flicked to me. "I am surprised to find you on this adventure, young Bethany, given your distaste for tunnel inhabitants."

I smiled. "Given any choice at all, I'd certainly rather be walking through a front or back door."

She laughed, the sound ringing harshly against the distant noise of happiness. "These tunnels aren't as bad as the ones we took you and Lugh through."

"I do believe you said those ones weren't all that bad either."

My voice was dry, and she laughed again. "Could be right there. Come along, before someone starts getting too nosy."

She turned and, with a thick grunt, wrenched the door open then ushered us through. Locryn waited near a yet-to-be-opened grate in the middle of the pavilion. Not only was he older and a little more gnarled than his wife, but he was also very bald—a rare thing, given dwarves' reputation for hairiness.

"Bethany Aodhán, this is a surprise," he said, warmth touching his expression. "How is your brother doing? We've not heard from him since we broke into that basement."

"They've been concentrating on above ground pursuits rather than beneath."

"Shame. They're a good employer." He reached down and grabbed the two bags at his feet, then tossed them to Mathi and me. "You'll be needing to put these on so you don't ruin your nice clothing."

"These" turned out to be coveralls. I cast Brega a wry look. "So, no rats, but not exactly a pristine environment then."

"It's a sewer—what are you expecting?"

I snorted and climbed into the coverall, which not only covered my shoes but was large enough that I could keep my purse under it and still maintain complete maneuverability.

Once we were suited up, Locryn handed us each a pair of heavy synthetic gloves—the type they seemed to use in labs that dealt with chemicals, which was not a great sign in my opinion—then opened the grate. It made no noise, despite looking rusted over.

"This first bit is more a water drain than a tunnel and can get pretty nasty. It'll require you both to crawl, but it does open up into the main system after about ten minutes. Follow me."

He jumped into the hole and disappeared, though the sound of his boots hitting solid ground echoed a few seconds later.

Mathi glanced at me. "You want me to go next and scare away the rats?"

I gave him a very unamused look. He laughed. "I'll take that as a yes."

He sat on the edge, then lowered himself down. A few seconds later, he said, "Okay, Beth, your turn."

I wrinkled my nose. "How bad is it?"

"It's an old red-brick drain that's obviously still connected to the system somewhere. Wet and nasty just about sums it up."

"Oh joy," I muttered, then followed his lead, sitting down on the edge of the grate hole and slowly lowering myself down. I didn't have the upper arm strength that he did, so I dropped more than lowered, but managed to avoid doing myself any damage.

Mathi had definitely understated things when it said it was nasty, though. The smell... Nausea stirred briefly. A lot more than mere water flowed down this thing, if that smell was anything to go by. Thank gods for the coverall and the gloves. I bent and peered into the tunnel. Mathi and Locryn waited a few yards ahead, the latter holding a flashlight that lent the old red bricks an almost golden glow.

"Come along, lass, nothing here to bite."

"Yet," I muttered, then got down on hands and knees and scrambled after them. Behind me, there was a soft clang as the grate was moved back in place. Surprise flicked through me. "Brega's not coming?"

"No. We're familiar with the target area, and it won't take two of us to get into the cellar. She'll deter anyone wanting to use the pavilion and ensure we can get out easily enough."

I kept my eyes on Mathi's butt—never a bad sight, despite the loose coveralls—and studiously followed. As Locryn had promised, the drain tunnel soon opened into a larger, older one, giving us room to actually stand.

"This way," he said, and marched away at a good clip, his boots sending sprays of too-thick water flying.

Mathi glanced my way, eyebrow raised in silent question. I hurried after Locryn, letting him bring up the rear. It had occurred to me in the brick tunnel that if there were indeed rats here, then the middle position was likely to be safest.

Locryn's light played unevenly across the walls, and our footsteps echoed. The air was musty and odorous, and water ran steadily through the grasslands of slime and lichen that covered the ceilings and walls. Though the air remained foul, it was at least moving, suggesting there was an opening somewhere up ahead. That wasn't really surprising, given many of these tunnels had once provided safe passage to and from the various underground military installations during the Second World War. There were few —aside from the dwarves, I'd wager—alive these days who knew the full extent of them. Most of the maps had disappeared, though whether that was deliberate or merely a consequence of time and their perceived unimportance once the war had ended, no one could say.

We continued on at a good pace; the air got colder, fouler, while the moss now covered the stone underfoot and made each step that much more treacherous. I kept my gaze on the ground, watching every step, not wanting to fall in this rank place even if I was almost completely covered.

I had no idea how long we traversed this underground hell, but eventually, after turning into a smaller, narrower, and oddly squarish tunnel, Locryn stopped and pointed his flashlight up at the ceiling, highlighting not stone but rather wood.

"A trapdoor?" I said in disbelief. "The cottage has a fucking trapdoor in its basement?"

"Many of them around this area do. Before it became upmarket, it was something of a haven for black marketeers, thanks to its closeness to the river and all. This one was jammed, but with a little encouragement, we did get it open."

"Hence the comment that it wasn't much of a hassle to get in," Mathi said, voice dry.

"Indeed, lad, indeed. Now, there's an old metal ladder attached to that wall there." He motioned to the left but didn't move the light, which remained trained on the trapdoor. I squinted, and after a moment, saw the rusted remnants. "But I'd advise against using it. We've made some hand-and-foot holds in this here wall for you both."

"You'll wait here for us?" Mathi said.

Locryn's cheeks dimpled. "Lad, you're paying us by the hour, so yes. And please, feel free to take your time."

"The timing is up to Bethany, not me, I'm afraid."

He reached for the first handhold and climbed. Once close enough, he placed a hand on the trapdoor and pushed it upward with some force. It didn't, as I'd half expected, crash backward and make an ungodly noise.

Locryn obviously saw my surprise, because he said, "Rigged up a harness to stop it flipping completely open. I'll return the door to its normal state once we see you back to the pavilion."

Mathi clambered into the basement and briefly disappeared. I waited and, after a moment, he reappeared above me. "It's safe. Your turn."

I drew in a deeper breath, regretted it the moment the foul stench of the place coated my throat and made me cough, then gripped the first handhold. Locryn had spaced them perfectly apart, and I climbed without much problem. Mathi helped me over the edge, steadied me as I rose, then turned on his phone, which he'd obviously retrieved from under his coverall, and flicked on the flashlight. The shadows were banished, revealing a small room that had wine racks lining one side and different-sized plastic boxes on the other.

He stripped off the coveralls, then walked over to the racks, randomly pulled out a bottle, and blew off the dust. "A Vosne-Romanée Cros Parantoux 1999. Nice."

"And expensive." I tucked my coveralls next to his. "Christie's sold a bottle for over one hundred pounds a few years ago. I imagine it's gone up in value since then. You want to bring that light over here so I can check the boxes?"

He placed the bottle back in its rack and walked over, shining the light on the boxes while I opened them one by one to check the contents. Nothing stirred my second sight, and the Eye remained mute.

"I guess it was never going to be that easy," I said, replacing the last lid.

"No." Mathi turned and walked toward the stairs, taking them two at a time. He flicked off the light, then cautiously opened the basement door and looked out. "Clear."

"I know you said there wasn't internal security, but what happens if the cops outside are using motion sensors or infrared?"

"I doubt they are—it would be overkill for what is basically a watch and intercept operation. Besides, it's doubtful they know of the trapdoor's existence." He glanced back at me. "It would be advisable to keep away from the windows as much as possible, though, just in case."

He pushed the door all the way open and stepped out into a small kitchen. Thankfully, the window almost directly opposite had the blinds pulled all the way down. I followed, then cocked my head to one side and listened to the building's very distant wood song. It was a forlorn sound that spoke of abandonment and abuse, suggesting this house had gone through multiple changes over the years without the aid of a pixie, thereby all but severing the golden rivers of its life. That, unfortunately, was not uncommon in these redeveloped old cottages, as many saw the hiring of a pixie to reinstate and repair the rivers—and thereby the health of the entire house—a waste of time and money. It was also why so many newer houses had problems, be it mold or movement.

I did a quick search of the cupboards and drawers, but neither the Eye nor my second sight found anything. We moved on. There was no furniture in the small living room at the front of the cottage, though the carpet still bore the dents of several chairs and a coffee table. The blinds here were also drawn, so hopefully luck was with us and the rest of them would be, too.

After checking the understairs storage area—empty aside from a vacuum, a mop, and a bucket—we headed upstairs, discovering a bedroom on either side of the landing and a small bathroom directly opposite.

There was nothing in either bedroom—the smaller one had been set up as an office, but the wall safe was indeed empty and the desk held only dust bunnies—but the minute I stepped into the bathroom, the Eye flared to life, spearing red lightning through the semi-shadowed room.

"To state the obvious, it looks like there's something here," Mathi said.

I grunted in agreement and gripped the Eye's case. There was nothing in the bath or on the basin, so I continued on and opened the mirrored shaving cabinet. There were a few old medicine boxes stacked inside, along with a half-used box of earbuds and a rather dusty-looking bottle of micellar makeup remover. I picked up the closest box—antibiotics, prescribed to one Hattie Jones. I checked the rest, and discovered the same name, but none of them increased the intensity of the Eye's response. I handed one of the boxes over to Mathi, then rose onto my toes and swept my hand across the top shelf. Nothing but dust.

I stepped back, opened the under-sink cabinet, and then knelt to examine it. There was nothing inside—nothing but more dust bunnies, anyway—and yet the Eye flared brighter, casting a ruddy glow throughout the room. Whatever it was sensing, it was damnably close.

I pressed my fingers against the rear wall. It gave, suggesting it might be a false wall. I felt around, found a corner with a small angular cut, then slipped a finger through and gave it a gentle tug. The whole back wall came away, revealing the building's frame. Almost immediately, the building's pain sharpened. I frowned and deepened the contact, flowing into the fragmented rivers, seeing so many breaches across the entirety of the building that tears stung my eyes. But this pulse, *this* pain, was centered on a spot of burning agony that lay against the outer wall; a large hole had been punched through both the frame and the external cladding and, into that breach, a cold iron box had been inserted.

I swore, softly but venomously. Cold iron had long been used by humans and shifters to repel, contain, or harm ghosts, fairies, witches, and other so-called "malevolent" supernatural creatures. A side effect of this meant it also repelled those magics used by them, which in this case was the lifeblood of the building. Maybe the renovations weren't the reason for its dying song; maybe this fucking thing was slowly tearing it apart.

"Problem?" Mathi said from behind me.

"Cold iron box inserted into the wall."

"Haven't heard of someone doing that for centuries. Anything in it?"

"Don't know—about to check."

I leaned in a little more and felt around until I found the latch. Surprisingly, it wasn't any sort of modern lock but rather a simple latch slide. Perhaps, given the false wall and the unlikeliness of anyone looking past it, the owner simply hadn't bothered.

The door swung open; inside were several yellowed scrolls, each one sealed with red wax. I drew a knife and touched the tip of it onto each one; light flickered brightly down the fuller and there was a soft puff of smoke that suggested a spell had been killed. I placed the knife to one side, tugged the scrolls out and handed them to Mathi, then swept my hand through the box's innards again. At the very back I found a small leather book. I repeated the process with the knife, then dragged out the book, checked there was nothing else, then closed the door and slid the latch back into place. After a slight hesitation, I deepened the contact with the old building again and carefully rerouted the rivers, leaving the areas that touched the iron dead and unconnected, but allowing the rest to flow unimpeded. I couldn't repair all the breaches—I simply didn't have the time—but this would at least stop the continuing agony and perhaps allow a little bit of healing over time. After replacing the false back wall, I pushed to my feet.

"Anything interesting in that book at first glance?"

"Can't say, because it's not written in any language I know, and I do know a few."

I stopped in front of him and peered at the upside down pages. "That looks like gibberish."

"Might be code. Maybe the key is in the scrolls you found. We should leave."

I nodded and motioned him to lead the way. We'd just reached the bottom of the stairs when the soft scrape of a key in the lock echoed. Mathi glanced briefly at me, then immediately broke into a run; his steps were light, almost inaudible, mine not so much. There was a curse from the other side of the door, and it was flung open just as we reached the cellar. Mathi motioned me in first, but I shook my head and pointed to the frame. He nodded in under-standing and went down the stairs fast. I closed the door then quickly connected to the building again, weaving the fading song of the door into the slightly stronger frame. It probably wouldn't hold them for all that long, but we didn't need long.

I went down the stairs slowly in an effort to contain the

noise of my steps, then hurried over to Mathi. Locryn had just finished dismantling his harness and leapt back down. Mathi threw my coveralls at me and, once I had tugged them back on, motioned me to precede him. He followed, closing the trapdoor behind him. A heartbeat later, there was a loud crash; the basement door had just been forced open. I clambered back up the stone ladder once Mathi was clear and hastily fused the trapdoor to the surrounding frame, then jumped down and scurried after Locryn.

The thumping of something heavy against the trapdoor chased us into the deeper tunnels. We didn't speak; didn't say anything until we were back at the pavilion and safe.

As the grate was wedged back into place, Brega said, "I take it there was some excitement down there? I've never seen Locryn so flushed before."

"He definitely earned his fee today," Mathi said. "I'll throw in a bonus for the hasty footwork in the cellar too."

"Ah, that is mighty generous of you," Locryn said. "Now strip off the coveralls and gloves, and let's all get the fuck out of here, just in case they've got some hounds or rats out trying to track us."

"Hounds can't trace through water, can they?" We'd certainly run through enough of that muck to counter the possibility.

"No, but a rat could. Their sense of smell is extremely sensitive, and it's usually unfazed by water."

"It's unlikely they had one on watch," Mathi said, handing Brega his coverall and gloves. "But it's also better to be safe than sorry."

"Indeed," Brega said. "Now go, both of you, while we clean up the area to erase any possible evidence we were here and lock down the grate."

Mathi called the Uber, then thanked them and opened

the door, ushering me through. We'd obviously been underground for longer than it had seemed, because the faint blush of evening had spread across the sky and the earlier promise of frost was stronger in the air.

"How do you think they saw us?" I said, crossing my arms against the cold.

"Probably the Eye's light. The bathroom blind wasn't pulled all the way down."

I frowned. "There would have been a half inch gap, if that."

"Which is enough for light to shine through. Obviously, whoever was watching that side of the building was, unfortunately for us, paying attention."

I grunted. "Will today's excursion bring your father's wrath down?"

He shrugged. "There's no proof it was us—we weren't seen—and there will be no prints to find aside from those left on the false back wall and the iron box's door. It's unlikely the cops or my father know about either of those."

"I hope you're right." I paused and scooted through the gate ahead of Mathi. The Uber was waiting a little farther up the road. "I've dinner with Lugh and Darby tonight—why don't you come along? He might have more luck deciphering that book than either of us, given his familiarity with hieroglyphics and whatnot."

"I'm not sure either of us are in a fit state to attend a dinner—the scent of the sewer lingers, despite the coveralls."

"It wouldn't be the first time we've showered and changed there—and no, there will be no joint shower."

He laughed. "I'm getting predictable, and that is truly sad. You'd better call him, just to be sure it's okay."

"It will be—Darby always over caters."

I did nevertheless send a text warning her she had an extra guest for dinner, then climbed into the Uber and gave the driver Lugh's address. Night had well and truly fallen by the time we arrived at his place—a decommissioned power substation that was a bit of an eyesore compared to the rest of the lovely old Victorian houses in the street. Decades of grime had darkened the brown brick to black, and the wooden door—situated in the middle of the long, single-story building—still had the rusty old electrical warning signs screwed into it. It did, however, have the one thing vital to a man of Lugh's size that none of the lovely old Victorians did—tons of head height and, more importantly, tons of storage space.

I punched in the code, then opened the door and yelled, "We're here."

"Feel free to come in," came the amused response.

We stepped inside the building's large, airy foyer and hung up our coats on the spare hooks on the wall behind the front door. There were two other doors here—the one on the left went into the main living area and the two bedrooms, the one on the right into his office and the storage area.

Darby was in the process of pulling a roast out of the oven—which was new, I noted, meaning she'd finally done something about the decades-old stove that had been secondhand when Lugh had installed it, and which had never worked reliably—but glanced around as we entered, her grin wide. She was a typical light elf in looks—tall and slender, with long pale gold hair plaited into a thick rope that ran down her spine, eyes the color of summer skies, and features sharp but ethereally beautiful.

"Now that is what I call perfect timing."

"Not really," I said. "We've been doing a sewer run and are little odious right now."

"I did wonder what that smell was," Lugh said as he came into the room behind us. At six foot five inches—a good nine inches taller than me—he broke every expectation when it came to pixies, even amongst those familiar with the fact that both the Talien and Aodhán pixies were human sized. "I hope you're planning to shower before we eat, because it really is enough to put us off dinner."

"The most odious smell on this Earth would never put *you* off your food," I noted dryly. "Not ever."

"True, but I was more worried about Darby's sensibilities, not mine."

"I'm a healer *and* a Ljósálfar elf. My sensibilities are capable of handling just about anything." Her gaze came back to mine. "What happened to your face, and why didn't you get it fixed?"

I wrinkled my nose. "Collided with a rock wall and didn't have time."

She tsked. "Get thee to a shower, and I'll come in and fix it before we eat."

"We'll need to borrow some clothes," Mathi said. "It is pointless cleaning up if we just put the same clothes back on."

"Beth has her emergency clothing here, but I'll grab you some sweats," Lugh said.

Darby laughed. "He'll swim in yours. Mine would be a better fit."

"As long as they're not pink, fine." There was just a hint of resignation in Mathi's voice. He knew, like I knew, the sweats were never going to be a "normal" color, given Darby did like pastels.

"Baby blue it is then," she replied with a laugh. "At least it'll match your lovely eyes."

He rolled said eyes and headed into the guest room to use the shower there. I grabbed jeans, a sweater, and fresh knickers out of my spares drawer, caught the sweats Darby tossed me and left them on the bed for Mathi, then closed the door and headed for the shower in Lugh's bedroom.

I was in the process of toweling off when there was a knock at the door. "Okay to come in?"

"Yep."

Darby slipped inside and closed the door again. "Okay, I'll—" She stopped abruptly, her gaze dropping to my wrist. "You're wearing the bracelet."

"I am."

Her gaze widened. "Does that mean...?"

"It means I went onto the plane—which apparently is a real place and not a dreaming realm, as such—and talked to him."

"Just talked? Are you insane?" She stopped in front of me and raised the back of her hand to my forehead. "No temperature..."

I laughed and knocked her hand away. "You know well enough why I only talked to the man."

"Because you're afraid," she said with a nod. "Thing is, you and I both know the time to be worrying about heartache has long passed. The term 'falling hard and fast' is rather apt when it comes to your relationship with Cynwrig. Sadly, that does leave poor Eljin out in the cold emotionally, at least for the time being, anyway."

"That's presuming poor Eljin isn't playing some game of his own," I said darkly.

Her eyebrows rose. "Really? Do tell."

I waved the comment away. "Later, if there is something to tell. It might be nothing more than my hormones determinedly fixating on the totally unsuitable man in my life rather than the logically better option."

"Love is never logical."

"It can't be love. I barely even know the man."

"Time has very little to do with emotions, and besides, sometimes you just got to take a leap of faith."

"You're saying that to someone who has a very bad record when it comes to picking suitable lovers."

My voice was dry, and she laughed. "Well, yes, but let's be honest here—aside from the whole royalty never marrying commoners issue, Cynwrig is the most suitable man you've ever had a relationship with, and you two are very obviously in sync both physically and spiritually."

"Because his presence was thrown into the game by the opposing force to distract me."

"That doesn't alter anything I've said about you and him." She pressed her fingers against my temples, and her magic rose, a warm caress of energy that swept my length, checking for any other injuries, before returning to buzz around my scraped cheek. "But go on, what did you talk to him about?"

"I asked the man what his plans were and where he saw the relationship going."

"I bet the one thing he didn't do was answer *that* question."

"Got it in one." I paused. "He did say he'd never intentionally break my heart and that he would never marry anyone unless he was in love. He also said he'd rather walk away from the throne than be told who he could take as a wife."

Her eyebrows rose sharply. "Now *that* is an interesting comment."

The heat of her magic increased, its warmth centering around the wounds, making my skin tingle and twitch uncomfortably as she worked.

"And *you* had best explain the emphasis you placed on 'that.'"

"Beth, I saw his face when he brought you to the hospital after he and Mathi rescued you. The man cares, and deeply."

"Caring isn't love. Caring doesn't mean he will ever marry me. He can't. His people will never accept it."

"Perhaps he never plans to marry and simply wants to play around with you for the rest of his life."

"That is hardly fair to me. Besides, he has a duty to produce heirs."

She released me, stepped back, and shoved her hands on her hips. "Well, whatever that man intends, it's pretty clear you have two options—and you're already well aware of both."

I gave her a twisted smile. "Yeah, which is why I'm giving you advance warning to stock the pantry with all the usual items required for the breakup wake."

She laughed. "Anything else? Because I've got the decidedly big impression that there is something else worrying you."

I hesitated. "You can't tell anyone what I'm about to reveal—especially not Lugh."

Alarm flitted through her expression, and she touched my arm, her grip tight. "What the fuck has happened? What's wrong?"

I took a deeper breath and said, "I had that dream again."

I'm not sure why I said that rather than tell her about my father's proclamation, but it wasn't really a lie given I *had* dreamed of that knife last night. Only difference now was, I knew the truth of who it was.

She frowned. "Which dream? You have enough of them."

"The one about a red-haired woman on a sacrifice table and a knife flashing down. It wasn't a stranger. It was me, Darby. I saw my death."

Her grip on my arm tightened. "Prophetic dreams are visions of a future not yet set in stone. What you saw may not come to pass."

"That's not the worst of it."

"How the fuck can death not be the worst of it?"

"There's a countdown. Nine months."

"Well, we'll just make damn sure you get to ten months, and kick that fucking dream back to the hell it came from."

The determined outrage in her voice made me smile. "I like this plan. But, on the off chance it does come true, is it possible to revive someone who has been stabbed through the heart?"

"Anything is possible. It just depends on the time between death and healing. A heart is easy enough, but not even the best healer on this planet can revive a brain deprived of oxygen for too long. Not without dire consequences."

"But there are drugs that can help extend brain survival, aren't there?"

"Yes but—"

"Can you research it? It needs to be something I can use if I'm restrained. Something that is fast acting."

She hesitated. "I think we need to talk to Lugh and Mathi about—"

"I will," I cut in. "Once we've explored all the options.

As you said, it's a dream, not a certainty, and I don't want to worry them just yet."

"You should at least tell them about the game being over in nine months, even if you don't go into the whole death thing."

"That I can do." And it did make sense not to keep them completely in the dark.

"Tonight?"

I rolled my eyes. "Fine. Tonight."

"Then, on the proviso we tell them the full truth once we have the answer, I shall start researching. In the meantime, you need to start using a tracer. Extending the timeframe of life between body and brain death will be useless if we have no means of finding you quickly."

"Tracers have range limits."

"Magical tracers don't; given this latest dream, I think it's way past time you got one. Promise me you will, or I'll ask Mathi to get you one."

Another eye roll. "Please don't. Cynwrig's already demanded he protect me; I don't need you adding more weight onto his shoulders."

"Cynwrig did that, huh?"

"Yes, but I'm not reading all that much into it, and neither should you."

"Way too late for that, my friend." She paused. "Even if you don't want to mention this dream to your brother or Mathi, you need to tell Cynwrig about it. He was the one who found and rescued you from your aunt. He's the likeliest to find you with or without aid of a tracer."

I wrinkled my nose. "What if he decides to end our relationship there and then? It might ultimately be the sensible thing for us both, but I'm not sure my hormones would be pleased."

Her eyebrows rose. "These would be the same hormones that didn't jump that man's bones when they had the chance?"

"The hormones wanted to," I replied glumly. "But fear and common sense held them hostage."

She laughed. "Dark elves are renowned for hanging on to relationships until they're good and ready to leave, and that man is far from finished with you yet. However, knowing about the dream might mean he'll keep a more vigilant eye on you."

"He can't."

"Physically, no. But he used the song of your weight on the earth to find you, meaning he's more than capable of keeping track of your movements if he wishes."

Which was both an unsettling yet somehow deliciously erotic thought.

My hormones really *did* need to be bitch-slapped. Or maybe it was fear and sense that did.

"You two all right in there?" came Lugh's question. "The food is getting cold out here."

"Coming right out," Darby shouted back, then opened the door and waved me through ahead of her.

Lugh scanned my face and smiled. "Now that looks much better."

"But not as good as Mathi does in powder blue," Darby said behind me. "It really does match his lovely eyes."

He rolled said eyes once again. "Ladies, can we focus here? The table has been set and the food is going to waste."

I laughed. "With Lugh around, there is no such thing as food wastage."

"That is certainly true." Darby's grin was wide as she walked to the far side of the table and sat down beside my brother. "The man has the appetite of a bear, be it—"

"There will be no discussion about any other kind of appetite," he cut in dryly. "Not at the table while we're eating."

She chuckled but didn't finish her sentence. Mathi pulled out my chair, then sat beside me, and conversation rolled easily over dinner. Once we'd finished and the dishes had been stacked in the dishwasher, I made tea and coffee while Darby served up dessert—a simple chocolate cake I knew from past eating experience was absolutely divine.

As we sat back down, Lugh said, "I managed to get hold of Frank today."

"And who might Frank be?" Mathi asked.

"One of the archeologists pictured in that article Treasa gave me about the dig in Portugal," I replied, and returned my gaze to my brother. "What did he say?"

"That it was a bitch of a dig, and he wished he'd never gone."

I grinned. "Meaning he thinks it was cursed, as the article suggested?"

"Not cursed so much as just badly run." Lugh shrugged. "The authorities were also less than helpful when thieves hit the dig."

"Did they take much?"

"Yes, but he didn't go into detail. He did, however, remember the names of those involved."

There was something in the way he said that that had the small hairs on the back of my neck rising. "And?"

He retrieved a folded piece of paper from his pocket and spread it out on the table. It was the article I'd sent him, newly printed.

"This man here," he said, tapping the grainy image of a tall, middle-aged man with darkish hair and a rakish smile, "is none other than Eljin Lavigne."

CHAPTER

SIX

"**B**ut not our Eljin," I said automatically. "They look nothing alike."

"It could be his father or even grandfather, although you'd think there'd be *some* genetic resemblance," Lugh said. "You could ask the man."

"I'd rather not at the moment."

Lugh raised an eyebrow. "Why not? Problems in paradise?"

"Just a vague notion he's not being completely honest with me."

His eyes narrowed dangerously; big brother mode had just been engaged. "In what way?"

I hesitated, not wanting to destroy his relationship with Eljin without any justifiable cause. "It's just a vague feeling, and if I'm being honest, it might be based more on Cynwrig's absence than Eljin himself."

"Hmm," was all he said. He did relax a little, though I suspected he'd be keeping a closer eye on Eljin from now on.

"What about doing a search of his place while he's in

London?" Mathi said. "You've a key and the code, haven't you?"

"Yes, but if I disengage the alarm, he'll be sent a notification."

"So?" Darby said. "Send him a text beforehand, saying you left something there and ask if it's okay if you go in and get it. Worked for me with past lovers when I wanted to suss out if they had any dark secrets."

"I am shocked and appalled you would do such a thing," Lugh said, even as amusement twitched his lips. "Luckily for me, I have no dark secrets."

She patted his knee. "Even if you did, Beth would have told me them a long time ago."

"That is totally true," I agreed. "There are no secrets between us."

"Apparently even when it comes to sex." He glanced at Mathi. "Don't be surprised if you were the topic of many conversations over the years."

"I have no fear when it comes to sex and my performance." His voice was pure royal elf arrogance, but amusement danced in his eyes. "We are renowned for end game satisfaction, and I more so than many."

"Nothing like tooting your own horn." Lugh tapped the printout. "Any chance you can use your IIT access to run a search on *this* Eljin? I can grab his full details for you, as the museum should have them on file somewhere."

I frowned. "Why would they be on file there?"

"He worked for our museum for a couple of years, and they keep passport information of all active antiquarians on file to make it easier when they're booking flights for hunts or digs."

"He's not active though," Darby pointed out.

"No, but it should still be in the archived records."

"Legally, they should destroy all personal information when the antiquarian retires," Mathi pointed out. "But to answer your question, it might be better if Sgott does the search. It would appear we have a serious leak in the day division."

"Him searching might still raise the wrong eyebrows if this Eljin is somehow linked to ours and both are up to no good," I said.

"Yes, but he has off-site access. I do not."

My eyebrows rose. "Since when?"

"Since my father revoked my access."

"I thought *that* was just to this case."

"No. It was all access."

"Well, that's inconvenient."

"Indeed. I will be discussing the matter with him."

"Eljin told me he was getting back in tomorrow evening," Lugh said. "So that gives you more than enough time to do a thorough check of his apartment."

"Unless our thief jumps into action again," I said.

"Thief?" Darby asked. "That got anything to do with the Tylwyth Teg break-in?"

"Yep. He used a hoard artifact to get in."

"Much stolen? I have an account and locked box there, but the bank hasn't contacted me as yet—"

"Which means," Mathi said, "that yours is safe. They've already contacted the owners of the twenty involved."

"Only twenty? That sounds targeted," Lugh noted.

"It was. Thankfully, we do have a means of finding him—"

"One that involves finding a convergence of two rivers, a ruined castle accessed by stepping stones over one of those rivers, and a dark tunnel whose entrance is hidden in a stone wall." Mathi's voice was dry. "Simple, really."

Lugh laughed. "Have you googled it? It's usually pretty good at pinning down that sort of thing."

"We have," I said. "There's a short list."

"Of twenty," Mathi added. "We haven't the time to physically search each and every one."

"Then don't," Darby said. "Use Google Earth."

I blinked. "I never thought about using that."

"I'm not just here for my good looks and healing ability, you know. Hang on while I get my laptop."

While she rose and headed into the bedroom, Mathi dragged out his phone and brought up the search list he'd saved.

"Right," she said, sitting back down beside Lugh. "Hit me with the first address."

Mathi did so, and after a few minutes she turned the computer around so I could see the castle. I shook my head, and she said, "Next."

That continued on for the next twenty minutes. It wasn't until we'd hit the nineteenth option that I recognized the castle I'd seen in my dream. "That's it. That's the one."

"And naturally it's one of the farthest away," Mathi noted. "Given we'll be heading underground, I'll contact Cynwrig and ask him to recommend a guide."

"Wise, given we have no idea what condition those tunnels will be in." I studiously avoided Darby's gaze when I said that and was totally surprised she resisted the urge to mention the fact I could ask him myself. "We'll also need a blow-up boat of some kind. The lake that surrounds the altar seems to have life in it."

"Which is never a good thing when it comes to godly artifacts," Lugh said. "I'll come with you and bring Jack and Jill with me, just in case."

Jack—made of cold iron—and Jill—silver with an iron core—were the rather incongruous names he'd given the hefty, foot-long metal stakes he'd had made to deal with the wide range of hellish ghouls that often hung around ancient relic sites.

"Good idea," Darby said. "I'll stay above ground and provide the medical assistance that will invariably be needed, given said nasties in the water."

Lugh glanced at her. "That isn't necess—"

"It is, and I will be taking no protective nonsense from you, Lugh Aodhán. I have the next two days off, and I've not been to that part of Wales."

"You could be sitting in the car for ages," he tried again. "I really don't think—"

"There will be no car sitting, either, because that would be far too obvious to anyone who might be keeping an eye on the place. I'll check out the ruin and then wander over to the cake and coffee shop that's not even five minutes away."

He grumbled something I couldn't quite catch, but Darby smiled and patted his leg. "Yes, you are indeed lucky to have two stubborn women in your life, and no, we will not be discussing it later."

"That being settled," Mathi said, a smile twitching his lips, "shall we aim for Monday? It gives us time to procure everything we need."

Lugh nodded. "I'll drive, given I've all the necessary caving gear in—"

"It'll be quicker and easier if I arrange the use of a private plane—"

"Which will be the Dhār-Val private company jet, because he can charge the costs back to the council for a wee profit," I cut in.

"There is no 'wee' about it," he said. "It's not like they're offering me a retainer for my services, so inflated expenditure claims are to be expected."

"Meaning you'll also hire the car?" Darby asked, amused.

"Indeed. Shall we say a 7:00 am start?"

"Only if we must," I said, with a slight groan.

"You'll just have to get yourself to bed early, won't you?" Darby said, a twinkle in her eyes.

"Yeah," I replied dryly. "I guess I will."

Lugh's gaze shot between us. "I have a vague feeling there's something Mathi and I are missing right now."

"I find it best not to ask when women are being deliberately vague," Mathi commented. "It generally only gets you in trouble."

"It does depend on the reason for the vagueness. There is one other thing." I rose and retrieved the scrolls and the little black book from my purse. "We found these in a house the thief was targeting, and we're wondering if they make any sort of sense to you."

"In other words," Lugh said, "can you please transcribe them."

"Yes," Mathi said. "Though I would suggest it be done here rather than at the museum, given we are unclear as to where Eljin's loyalties lie."

Lugh rose, washed his hands, then carefully unrolled the first scroll, keeping his fingers to the edges to lessen the risk of contaminating the old vellum with skin oil. He studied it for several minutes, gaze narrowed and expression thoughtful.

"It appears to be based on hieroglyphs, with a few other random ancient languages thrown in." He let the scroll roll back up and opened up the black book. "And this contains the means of deciphering them. Handy."

"How long will it take you?" I asked.

"A couple of days, most likely. Glyphs can be tricky even at the best of times." He glanced up. "And if I'm honest, tracking down the truth about both the article Eljin and ours is more of a priority right now."

On that we both agreed. I glanced at the clock and saw it was close to ten. "I should go. I promised Ingrid I'd help her close again tonight."

Darby cleared her throat and gave me a pointed stare. "Aren't you forgetting something?"

"Oh, yeah." I waved a hand. "I had another dream. Apparently we're on the clock and this godly game will be over in nine months."

"Well, it's always good to have a timeframe to work with," Lugh said. "But I'm thinking the result is not currently guaranteed to go our way."

"No, but we now have Beira *and* my father on our side, so that's got to swing things a little in our favor."

"When it comes to gods, nothing is ever guaranteed." Mathi's phone pinged. He glanced at it, then pushed to his feet. "We can share an Uber. I need to get back to the office."

"Neither of your drivers working tonight?" Lugh asked, expression surprised.

"Henrick's vehicle was bugged. We found one tracer, but until both vehicles have been fully swept and cleared, they cannot be used."

"Competitors? Or something else?"

"Unknown at this stage, but I intend to find out."

"And woe betide those responsible," Darby said.

Mathi glanced at her. "Indeed."

We grabbed our smelly clothes and our coats, and headed out. Mathi called the Uber, and we walked up to the end of the street to wait. It arrived a few minutes later and quickly scooted us across to the tavern.

"Ring if you want company to Eljin's tomorrow," he said as I climbed out.

I shook my head. "If he is up to something, then he might well have set up a camera or two. When will you get the report back from your friend? Or is that the reason you suddenly have to go into the office?"

He smiled. "Indeed. According to Dawson, he's almost finished compiling his initial report and will send it to my computer later this evening. He's going to run a background on the woman, just to be certain as to her identity, but that probably won't be available for a day or so, given you said she was from France."

I nodded. "You'll let me know tomorrow if there's anything untoward in the initial report, though?"

"You know I will."

I blew him a kiss, then jogged down the lane to the rear door and let myself in. We had another good crowd in, although it wasn't as busy at this hour as it had been last night. I found Ingrid and checked that everything was okay, then headed upstairs, dumping my clothes into the washing machine before heading into the kitchenette to put the kettle on. Once my tea was made, I settled on the sofa, dragged out my phone, and found Eljin's number.

Hey, I sent. *I'm really sorry to text on your weekend away, but I was looking for a brooch Mom gave me, and I think it might have fallen off at your place. You mind if I go over tomorrow morning and search for it?*

I didn't expect an immediate reply, and I didn't get one. He was likely out with his sister having dinner somewhere, so I grabbed my iPad, drank my tea while I doom-scrolled my favorite social media sites, and watched a few YouTube videos. It was a good hour before my phone pinged.

Brooch? came his reply. *Can't remember seeing you wear anything other than the pendant that hates me.*

It was no doubt meant as a joke, but it was a strong reminder that if the Eye had reservations about this man, I really needed to start listening.

It was pinned on the coat I was wearing last time I was there. I only just noticed it was missing and did a search here, to no avail.

Would it have fallen off anywhere else? In the street perhaps?

Possibly, but I thought I'd check your place first before I put in a police report, because it's fair to say we were in a heated haze last time I went there, and it could have fallen off in the hasty stripping off.

Heated haze is something of an understatement, he replied, and followed it up with a LOL emoji. *What time you going over? I'll turn off notifications for that period. You remember the security code?*

About midday and, yes, I do. A little bit of the inner tension untwined. Surely if he'd had anything incriminating hidden in his house, he would not have been so easygoing about me going in. *How's your sister?*

The three little dots indicating he was replying appeared. *She's good. Missing her kids something fierce, though, which is crazy to me. You'd think she'd enjoy the break.*

If they're only young, it's understandable.

I suppose. What are you up to? Why are you searching for the brooch?

I hesitated, then sent, *Got a date, and I just noticed it was missing when I put the coat on. As I said, a quick search didn't uncover it.*

I thought the competition was unavailable for the next few months.

He is.

Darby, then?

No.

There was a long moment of text silence before he sent back, *Ask no questions, be told no lies?*

I sent several smiley emojis. *We're not exclusive and I was bored.*

Then I shall have to up my game and ensure boredom is not a problem. He added a number of sexual emojis.

He did not, I couldn't help but notice, even jest about going exclusive, which was interesting given my statement was the perfect opening for it. *Don't make promises you can't keep.*

Challenge accepted, my dear. I shall see you when I get home.

You will.

And if I *did* find something untoward in his apartment tomorrow, at least I had Monday to think about my next step with him. Because as much as I'd want to confront him straight away, that might not be the best option. I could always attempt to use my magic on him—male pixies were not immune to it, even if elves were—but if he'd been deliberately placed in my path to keep an eye on me, it was more than possible he'd be immune to being pixied, whether that be via magic or some sort of telepathic overrule to prevent him from saying too much.

I finished my tea then went downstairs to help Ingrid, as I'd promised, so it was close to midnight by the time I got back upstairs.

The Bruadar remained stubbornly silent, and the disappointment levels were high. I stripped off, climbed into bed, and slept. Dreams spun through the night, none powerful enough to wake me, but still filled with the warning of danger, of death.

To say I woke up feeling less than rested and particularly grumpy would be an understatement. I took my time eating breakfast, then went downstairs to Mom's office to finally go through the multiple boxes that were stored there. Most of them were old bills that she hadn't gotten around to filing, but the two at the very bottom of the stack held a number of leather-bound accounting and appointment books. A quick look at one revealed Mom's handwritten and rather meticulous accounting of expenses and profits—not for the tavern, but rather her relic hunting side business. My pulse skipped several beats. Maybe, just maybe, there'd be something here that would lead me to Geitha's Tears—presuming she *had* made an appointment to meet with Cynwrig's father to discuss finding the missing necklace.

I stacked the boxes on top of each other then made my way through the tavern and up the stairs—to find Beira sitting on the sofa, a bottle of whisky on the coffee table in front of her and a full glass, sans ice, held in one slightly clawed hand.

I stopped abruptly. "How the fuck did you get up here?"

"Walked up the stairs like any normal person."

"The door at the bottom of these stairs was locked."

She waved a hand. "That sort of lock is easy to get around."

"It's electronic, and key coded."

"And the right amount of lightning properly applied

can short it out just enough to open it without destroying it. You might want to look into that."

I put the boxes on the floor next to the coffee table, then stepped over them and walked across to the kitchenette, flicking on the kettle. While I did like the whisky The Lakes Distillery produced, it was a wee bit early for me to be drinking. Once I'd popped the leaves into the teapot, I turned and crossed my arms. "And to what do I owe this particular honor?"

"I heard the harp's discordant song on the wind and was wondering if you did."

I frowned. "I've been hearing something, but it's been too fleeting to trace. I'd actually attributed it to a relic our thief is using, given the noise generally happened at the same time he was active."

She wasn't facing me, but I could almost feel her eyes rolling. "If the blade had had a similar resonance to another relic, I would have mentioned it."

"Hate to be disrespectful and all, but you're a god involved in a current game—even if unofficially—so there is no real guarantee of help in any given situation."

She snorted and didn't deny the statement. "Have you tried asking the wind to trace it?"

"What? The blade or the relic?"

"The blade, of course."

"Not yet, but if you're feeling in a generous mood, you can always ask the wind to trace the relic for me. You're better at that sort of stuff."

"And you will not get any better if you do not *practice*. As to the blade, I am not, as you noted earlier, an active participant in the game."

"Then what are you doing here?"

"Trying to shove a poker up your ass to get it moving."

I couldn't help but laugh. "You certainly do have a unique turn of phrase."

She harrumphed. "What is the relic you have been tasked to find this time?"

I made my tea and then carried the pot, a mug, and a small jug of milk over to the sitting area. "Aamon's Pectoral."

Surprised flitted through her expression. "It's been released? That's the artifact your thief is using?"

"Apparently."

"Interesting."

"Why?"

"Because Aamon has rarely participated in the games. If his relic is now active, then it's because he wished it."

"Meaning it was never part of the hoard?"

"No."

I frowned and poured my tea. "I got the impression when I was talking to Aasym that he'd moved on from this world."

Her eyebrows shot up. "You know the librarian's name?"

"Well, it seemed rude not to."

She chuckled. "It must like you, Bethany, because it has not shared that information with anyone for eons."

"Because no one has gone there for eons."

"Humanity, no, but gods do still use it as a resource. Perhaps you should ask next time what godly figure has accessed the library recently."

"To what end?"

She shrugged. "Information never goes astray. But to answer your question, no, he has not moved on, and he closely guards his relics. If his pectoral has been tossed into the gaming ring, it will be as a countermeasure to some other development."

"Seems to be a bit random to me."

She took a long drink. "It isn't. As I said, Aamon rarely plays the game, so if he is involved then it will be with reason."

"Whose side is he on? Do you know?"

"He has never been fond of Ninkil, so in this case, it will be ours."

Suggesting our thief getting hold of it was no accident. Now we just had to figure out the *why* behind it. I sipped my tea. "I don't suppose you can ask him what the intent was, can you?"

"I don't suppose I can, and you know this."

"One has to try."

"One has to try a lot harder. Time is a-ticking, my dear."

I just about choked on my tea. "Really? You had to remind me?"

"Well, if the hot poker doesn't work, one has to try other methods of ass movement."

I rolled my eyes. "And the pectoral? Does he want it back, or shall I destroy it?"

"Return it to Liadon. She will ensure he receives it." She thrust to her feet, drained her glass, then exchanged said glass for the bottle. "I shall be taking this with me, of course."

"You only come here to replenish your whisky supply, don't you?"

"And who can blame me if that were true? You do keep a mighty fine stock." She skirted around the sofa I was sitting on and clomped down the stairs. But as she neared the door, she added, "Find the harp, find the thief, find the blade. The trail lies at your doorstep, Bethany."

"Yeah," I muttered. "Because it's that damn easy."

"If it were easy," came her retreating reply, "the game would be no fun."

"For the gods," I shouted after her. "We humans could do without such fun."

"You are neither human nor fae, my dear." Her reply floated around me on a soft breeze. "Never was, never will be."

And aside from the ability to read the wind and use storms as a weapon, what advantage had being a godling given me? Godlings could still die—the fact my father's very first daughter had found her death in these goddamn games proved that, not to mention the fact I'd barely escaped the death my aunt had planned for me—but what if the divine blood that ran through my veins provided me with an advantage I hadn't yet tested? What if it gave me a greater means of escaping death's grip? Perhaps I'd survived my aunt's poisoning for the very reason that I *wasn't* entirely fae. What if my godly blood had dramatically slowed the poison's progress through my body, thereby giving me that chance? What if it could also keep my brain active for longer, meaning Darby would have more time to reach and save me?

If that *were* true, then there was hope of life beyond my father's proclamation, and damned if I wasn't going to hold on tight to it. Which also meant, of course, that I needed to get a magical tracer sooner rather than later.

I glanced at the time, saw it was close to twelve, and swore. I hastily drained the rest of my cup and rose, quickly collecting my bag and coat before heading down the stairs after Beira. Despite the fact there was little more than a minute between her departure and mine, she was nowhere in sight. But then, she was goddess of winter and storms and really *could* move like the wind when she wanted to.

It was starting to drizzle by the time I got outside, so I zipped up my coat, tugged on the hood, and shoved my hands into my pockets. I didn't bother calling a cab. Eljin's wasn't all that far away, and I'd never really been averse to walking in rain anyway—an inclination no doubt due to who my father was.

I was at the end of Eastgate Street when my phone rang. I hit Answer and said, "Hey Mathi, what's up?"

"Got the report a little later than he'd said, but there's nothing in it that raises immediate alarms."

More of the inner tension unwound. I'd definitely been expecting the opposite. Of course, where he and I were concerned romantically, it didn't make a whole lot of difference. Eljin was a fun time, not a long time.

Of course, Cynwrig was supposed to fall under the same category too, but here we were....

"So, he did the touristy thing and spent time with his sister, nothing else?"

"Yep. Dawson even checked with the hotel to ensure they had separate rooms."

"I would hope so, given they're brother and sister, not lovers."

"According to Dawson, one of the most popular excuses given by cheating partners is that they have to meet a family member."

His voice was dry, and I smiled. "I'm surprised their lovers don't demand to meet said family members."

"Did you?"

"No, because he made it patently clear he wanted to spend time alone with his sister. Without actually saying that, of course." I paused, glancing left and right before crossing the street. "Besides, we're casual, nothing more. The only reason I wanted to check—"

"Was instinct saying something was off," Mathi finished for me. "So, we do the background on the woman, just to be safe. Right?"

"Yes, because we've got a shapeshifter capable of attaining other forms running around with a knife that can enforce her will on others. There's a chance he's a victim and has no control over what he is doing."

"You don't truly believe that, do you?"

"Right now, I'm not sure what to believe."

He sniffed. It was an unimpressed sound. "I shall see you tomorrow morning."

"You will." I hung up, tucked the phone away, and continued on. The wind stole around me as I stepped onto the curb, and a myriad of different images hit my mind, briefly making me stumble. I grabbed the nearby street light pole, holding on tightly as I came to grips with the giddying array of information. Basically, all the images confirmed what Mathi had just said—Eljin, in London, with a woman who had gorgeous mahogany hair that fell in waves to her butt. She was slender but beautiful, with pale skin that held an almost elvish luminosity.

"You alright, love?" someone off to my right said. "Do you need some help?"

I took a deeper breath, banished the wind's whispering, and looked up. A kindly looking old woman was studying me with concern. I smiled and nodded. "Just had a bit of a dizzy spell, that's all."

"You should get yourself to the doctors and have that checked," she said in a motherly tone. "Dizzy spells are never good at the best of times, let alone in someone so young."

"I will, thank you."

She hesitated. "Are you sure you're okay? You don't need me to call a cab or something?"

"I'm fine, really. I haven't far to go until I'm home, anyway."

"Perfect, then. Just make sure you take it easy," she said and continued on.

I watched her for several seconds, then pushed away from the light pole and continued, following Volunteer Street down to the end before turning into Albion.

Eljin lived in the penthouse apartment of a gorgeous old church whose conversion had been done so well that the song of the old beams was so clear and loud I could hear it from the street. I bounced up the steps, punched in the code, and opened the door. The scent of Eljin's aftershave—warm leather and exotic spices—hung lightly in the crisp, cold air, oddly fresher than it should have been given he'd been away for a couple of days. I swung off my purse, took off my coat, and hung it up on the nearby hooks to dry off. Then, after picking my purse back up, I walked into the main room. It was a large, double-height expanse, with the lovely old oak trusses painted white to give the room an even airier feeling. The wood song reverberated around me, rich and warm, and, on the street side of the building the light coming in from the two beautifully simple stained windows sent rainbows of color spinning through the room. At the far end of the room was a compact but well-equipped kitchen and beside it, a chrome and glass staircase that wound up to the loft bedroom.

I walked down to the end and put on the kettle, and at that precise moment realized I was not alone in the apartment.

Eljin wasn't in London.

He was here.

CHAPTER
SEVEN

I ignored the sudden leap of trepidation and glanced up, spotting his shadow more so than him. "That you hiding up there, Eljin? Or do I need to get my knives out?"

His laugh floated down from the loft, warm and unconcerned. "If you were going to get your knives out, you would have done so by now. I was just getting dressed after stepping out of the shower—would you like to come up here and play for a while?"

"Haven't got time to play, sadly."

"Another date?"

"No, a staff member down. I need to get back to the tavern to help out." The wood song told me he was standing next to the bed, placing something into the bedside table's top drawer. Something that was on the small side, made of wood, but also inlaid with some sort of silver. A gift? Or something else?

Instinct said the latter, meaning I probably needed to check it out when—if—I got the chance.

"Ah. Shame," he commented.

"In an even bigger shame, I have an early start tomorrow morning, so there can be no after work activities."

He appeared at the top of the stairs, wearing jeans but little else. "And now, I am bereft."

I smiled, enjoying the muscular goodness on show as he came down the stairs. Bad guy or not, he was very well built for a Talien pixie. They did tend to be on the leaner side than us Aodhán. I crossed my arms and leaned a hip on the kitchen bench. "How come you're home so early?"

He walked over, tugged me into his arms, and kissed me, long and soundly. There was a part of me that wanted to pull back, to ask him to stop, but I didn't. I had to play it carefully, because if he was a pawn in the other side's game, the last thing I wanted was to spook him into running before we could get any information out of him. And if he wasn't a pawn, well, the sex was good.

His eyes gleamed knowingly when he finally stepped back; that kiss had been deliberately intense and definitely *did* have the desired effect. My lips were tingling, my body trembling and achingly hot with desire.

But he didn't immediately take advantage of the situation, as I'd have expected. He simply walked around the bench and got two cups out of the cupboard. "If I said a sudden bout of jealously, would you believe me?"

"After that kiss? Maybe."

I lightly ran a finger across my lips, but the burning didn't immediately go away. I frowned, reached for one of the cups, then turned on the tap and drank some water. It helped. And yet, the stirring unease increased. Instinct— and the Eye—remained mute to any immediate danger, so the unease might be nothing more than the need not to be intimate with one man when I was so hung up on the other... but even as that thought crossed my mind, I smacked it away. This wasn't guilt. This was something else.

He laughed. "Remember I said my sister was missing her kids? Well, she decided to go back early. That left me with little to do in London, so I came back."

"Little to do in London? Are you insane?"

He shrugged. "I have been to London many times. It holds no particular appeal to me these days."

"Huh." I finished the water and pushed the cup back to him. "While you're making that, I might have a quick look around for the brooch."

"I doubt it's upstairs. I vacuumed before I left and would have found it."

"It was on my coat, so it wouldn't be up there anyway."

I turned and made a show of checking the sofas, thrusting a hand between each cushion, and then kneeling to look underneath. All the while aware of his gaze on me, of the heat rising within and the growing tide of need. I wanted him with an urgency that was almost surreal, but it wasn't as if I hadn't felt this level of overriding need before with him. It was just... troubling.

"Anything?" he said eventually.

I sighed and shook my head. "It must have come off somewhere else. I'll make a report, but it's likely gone."

"Was it a valuable piece?"

I walked back to the bench and sat down on one of the stools. "It was a gift from Mom, so to me, yes."

"Of course, sorry." He pushed my tea across the bench, then moved back around and sat beside me on the stool. His bare arm brushed against mine, and though I was wearing a sweater it felt like I was being touched by flame. My whole body went up, and it was all I could do to remain where I was and not climb into his lap and take what my body so desperately needed.

I needed to get out of there. *Now.* Before I did something I might—or might not—regret.

Perhaps the gods on my side of the game were listening, because at that precise moment, my phone pinged. I thrust to my feet, hurried over to my purse, and dragged it out. It was nothing more than an advert from a favorite dress shop, but I wasn't about to let it go to waste.

I grimaced and swung my purse over my shoulder. "Sorry, duty calls. I have to go."

"Now *that* is a damn shame." He followed me over and helped me into my coat, his fingers brushing my skin and causing utter havoc. Then he tugged me close, kissed me again, long and slow, before whispering, "Are you really sure you want to leave?"

No, gods no. I swallowed hard and stepped out of his arms. "I can't stay. Ingrid already does way too much."

"Tuesday then?"

"Tuesday," I agreed breathlessly, then turned and hurried out of the apartment.

He watched me all the way down to the street, a heat I could feel even after I was long gone from his sight. Even then, the wanting did not leave me. It was intensifying rather than easing.

I dug out my phone again and called Darby. "Hey, you busy right now?"

"Just coming home from seeing Rossita and Ruairí. Why?"

"Your home, or Lugh's?"

"Mine for now." A hint of concern now touched her tone. "To repeat, why?"

"It's possible I might have been drugged. I need you to check."

"Fuck, Beth, where are you? I'll come to you."

"I'm near the tavern but—"

"No buts—just get there and stop moving about."

"You'll find me in the shower. A very *cold* shower."

"What the fuck?"

"I'll explain when you get there."

"Oh, you certainly will, my friend."

She hung up and I continued on, doing my best to ignore the desire raging through my body. I made it to the tavern without giving in to the almost overwhelming urge to jump the nearest man's bones, and hurried upstairs, stripping off as I all but ran into the shower. In the end, ice water didn't do all that much, but masturbating did at least ease the all-consuming need. It remained in the background, though, a heated river that showed no inclination to cool.

The question was, if the raging desire was due to some sort of drug, how had he given it to me? I'd never gotten around to drinking the tea, and if he'd somehow done it via the kiss, surely it would have affected him as much as me. The why, however, was easy enough—to get information— but what type? Was he really working for the other side of this godly game, or was something else going on? Was he indeed under the control of Bia's Blade and its wielder?

Was I really that bad a judge of character?

Yes, that inner voice replied glumly. *Yes, you certainly are.*

The thunder of Darby's hurried steps echoed through the building long before she actually appeared.

"I'm okay," I called out, grabbing a robe and tying it on as I padded barefoot over to the fireplace. I hadn't lit it for well over a day, and the chill in the air was getting noticeable.

She appeared on the landing just as the fire caught, her face flushed with concern. "I thought I told you to sit down and not move."

"It's not that sort of drug. No death waiting in the wings."

"I think you'd best let me be the judge of that." She pointed imperiously at the sofa. "Sit. Now."

I sat. She squatted in front of me, pressed her fingertips against my temples, then closed her eyes. Her healing energy surged, bathing me in warmth, sweeping every inch of my body slowly and carefully.

"Well, fuck," she murmured. "You're right. It's definitely *not* that sort of drug."

"Do you know what caused it?"

"Yes, although it's a combination I've not seen before. Sit still while I chase it from your system."

"How did it get into said system?"

"Sitting still also means not moving your mouth."

I chuckled softly but obeyed, waiting patiently while she worked her magic. After a few seconds, the inner urge to get down and dirty with the nearest man eased; after a few seconds more, it fled altogether.

She sat back on her heels and sighed. "Right, you're now safe from the procreation urge."

"What the hell caused it?"

"A creative mix of Devil's Breath and Damiana."

I frowned, vaguely remembering Damiana being mentioned in one of the conversations I'd "overheard" between Carla and her boss. I'd presumed they'd been talking about drugging a council member, but what if it had been me?

Did that mean Eljin was indeed working with them? And if he was, was it willingly or unwillingly?

"I know Devil's Breath can make you feel so drowsy that you can't remember what was going on or what you were doing, but what does Damiana do?"

She picked up the teapot I'd left on the coffee table earlier, then rose and walked over to the kitchen. "It's a herb that dates back to the ancient Mayans, who used it to improve sexual interest and desire. It's quite powerful."

"Yeah, it is," I muttered. "But how does it get into the system?"

"Usually via food or drink, but it can be applied through transdermal administration."

"Would that include a kiss?"

"Yes, although using such a method would affect the kisser as much as the kissee." She made the tea and returned, placing a tray containing the refilled pot, two new cups, and an unopened packet of Chocolate Hob Nobs on the table. "Given where you were going today, I'm guessing Eljin is behind this whole misadventure?"

"I was perfectly fine until I got there and he kissed me, so yes." I paused and frowned. "Can it work that fast? I thought it took time for a transdermal application to take effect."

"There were some other smaller ingredients I couldn't quite pin down, so it's likely they used some sort of accelerant." She poured the tea, then broke open the biscuits, taking two before offering them to me. "Why was he even home? He wasn't due back until later tonight."

I helped myself to a couple of biscuits and nodded my thanks as she slid my mug over. "Apparently his sister left early this morning, and he decided to come home."

"On the face of it, that's not suspicious."

"Except for the fact that I did as you suggested and sent him a text last night saying I'd lost a brooch and was it okay if I went in and searched."

"Instant guilty verdict," she said darkly. "We should send Lugh and Mathi there, not only to knock some sense into him, but to get the name of whoever set him onto you."

"While I like this plan, we need to proceed carefully. Or, at the very least, we should wait until we have more information about the Eljin in that article."

"I see the sense in all that, but I still prefer my option."

I chuckled. "Who knew you had such a vicious streak in you."

"Bethany, I am Ljósálfar. We all have that streak—it's just less pronounced in the middle and lower classes." Her voice was dry, and her bright eyes danced. "But anyone with any common sense would not test us, especially when it comes to family and best friends."

I smiled, raised my mug, and clicked it lightly against hers. "To bloody-minded best friends."

"Indeed." She took a sip, then wrinkled her nose and added a bit of sugar. "Are we certain that the woman he was meeting in London is actually his sister?"

"No, which is why Mathi arranged for an investigative friend to follow the two of them around yesterday, and then do a trace on the woman herself."

"Mathi always had style."

"And he's as fierce as you when it comes to protecting his friends."

"Yes, I noticed that when you went missing. Under that cold uncaring exterior there beats a good heart."

"Don't tell him that," I drawled. "He'll be offended."

She laughed. "We should at least warn Lugh. He'll need to keep a closer eye on his movements at the museum."

"If I tell my brother Eljin drugged me, there will be an ugly confrontation. We can't afford that just yet." I munched on the biscuit for a bit. "Besides, given the information he got from Frank and the suspicions it raised, he'll already be on alert."

"I'm not happy about keeping so many secrets from him, Beth. Not when it comes to you."

I hesitated, but in truth, I could see her point. Their romantic relationship was still new, and given we had vowed long ago never to keep secrets from each other, it was natural she'd want to extend that to Lugh.

"Fine, tell him about Eljin but make him promise he'll take no action until we get that report back from Mathi's friend. And if he's reluctant to promise, tell him I'll pixie him."

"As long as he's included in any confrontation with the man, I'm sure he'll be perfectly fine with sitting back and waiting."

"Yeah, but only because it'll give him more time to plot Eljin's punishment."

My voice was dry, and she smiled in acknowledgement of *that* particular truth. "If Eljin is working for whoever stole the hoard, do you really think he'll live long enough to tell any tales once it's known we're onto him?"

"No, which is why we've got to step carefully." I finished my biscuit and chased it down with some tea. "In fact, it might be best if Sgott has nothing to do with chasing down the identity of older Eljin. It might be better if we get Mathi's friend to do it."

"Better yet, why not ask Treasa or even Cynwrig? They obviously know a lot more about him than they've said so far." She paused and wrinkled her nose again. "Though having said that, if Cynwrig had been aware that Eljin was playing for the other side in this battle, he would have reacted."

"Treasa did say she'd debated the wisdom of giving me that article, so maybe she also kept it from him."

"Maybe she didn't want you to think she was trying to sabotage your relationship with Eljin when you were also seeing Cynwrig."

"More likely she didn't want him reacting against Eljin until I'd had a chance to come to my senses."

"Well, they are twins. She knows him better than anyone." She glanced at her phone and rose. "I'd better get going. I promised I'd drive Mom to the hairdresser this afternoon."

Darby's mother—Ffion—along with her father, Dyfri, tended to spend a good portion of their time in Knolls Gardens, a specially designed retirement community for elderly but well-off Ljósálfar elves who wanted the convenience of being close to Deva without having to live in the hustle and bustle of the old city or its surrounds.

"Damn, sorry if I've made you late."

"Don't be daft, woman." She dropped a kiss on my cheek. "By the way, Lugh said he was going into the museum this morning to search the archives. He'll either call or send a text if he finds anything."

"I might get in first and tell him to cc Mathi in on anything he finds. Mathi's friend is already looking into the sister, so he might as well do a full background on the Eljin in that photo." I paused. "Did he happen to work on those scrolls last night, do you know?"

"He did indeed. Not sure when he came back to bed, because I was fast asleep." She touched my shoulder and then headed out.

I finished my second biscuit then grabbed my phone, first sending the text to my brother, and then calling Mathi.

"And to what do I owe this great honor?" he said, voice dry.

"Thought you might like to know that Eljin is definitely not on the side of the angels, though the jury is out as to whether he's a total black sheep."

"Why? What has he done?" His voice was flat, and yet so filled with threat that a shiver stole down my spine.

"We suspect—"

"We?" he cut in sharply.

"Me and Darby."

"To repeat, what has he done?"

"He didn't hurt me, Mathi, so stand down."

"Tell me," he growled.

"He was drugging me, probably to get information."

"How did you find out?"

I gave him a very brief version of events, then added, "Do you think Dawson will be able to run a check on the Eljin in that article? I just think it wise to keep Sgott totally out of any search right now in case our Eljin is connected to the spies at the IIT."

"Easily enough done. Get Lugh to cc me with anything he finds."

"Already sent him a text. Thanks."

He hesitated. "And you really are fine?"

"Yeah."

"Good." He paused. "But if you're still feeling heated, you know where I am. Always happy to help out a friend in need."

I rolled my eyes, even though he wasn't in the room to see. "Give it up, Mathi."

"Never."

I laughed. "No more news on our thief, then?"

"No. I've a meeting with my father in an hour, so I'll see what I can get."

"You'll let me know?"

"Of course," he replied, and hung up.

I finished my tea, poured myself another, then swiped through my contacts list until I found Treasa's number. I was tempted to call her, but in the end, chickened out and sent a text instead, asking her what she knew about the connection between the Eljin in that article and ours.

Then I rose, grabbed the first of the boxes, and placed it on the table, spending the next few hours going through each of the accounting books. If I learned one thing, it was the fact Mom not only worked for a good number of museums, but also for a lot of insurance companies, hunting down relics stolen from private collectors.

The first box didn't hold anything that mentioned either Gethen—Cynwrig's father—or Geitha's Tears. I shoved it under the coffee table, wearily rubbed the crick at my neck, then rose to stoke the fire, saying a soft prayer for the wood's sacrifice before tossing it in. Then I turned to warm my butt while listening to the rising tide of the wind outside the old building.

That wind held whispers of evil on the move. Beira, despite grumbling about me needing the practice, had obviously asked the wind to find the pectoral and its wielder.

I swore, ran over to grab my phone, and called Mathi as I swept up my coat and ran down the stairs.

"Two calls in one day," he said. "This can't be good."

"It's not. Our thief is active."

"Where are you?"

"Running down the tavern's stairs so I can go out and read the wind better."

"We'll meet you at the end of the lane in ten."

"Hurry."

He didn't answer. He'd already hung up.

I slid around the corner on the ground floor and belted toward the back door.

"Everything all right?" Ingrid called after me.

"Hope so," I shouted back. "Just late."

I thrust through the door then out into the lane. Evening was closing in, and what remained of the day was filled with a fog-like drizzle. I threw my coat over my head and hurried down the lane. The whispers suggested the thief was surprisingly close... if there was such a thing as close when it came to the wind and her definition of distance.

I continued on, and while most of my attention remained on the wind and its flow of information, I was nevertheless aware when Mathi's car pulled up and he climbed out.

"He still active?"

"According to the wind, yes."

It was absently said, and I felt more than saw his frown. "Any idea where?"

"East."

He snorted. "That really pins the area down somewhat."

"Listening to the wind is an art I haven't quite gotten a handle on yet, so just hold onto your britches for a second," I replied crossly.

He raised his eyebrows but otherwise didn't reply.

I wrapped my fingers around the Eye, closed my eyes, and focused on the wind. For several seconds all I saw was a veil of gray—a thick fog that had more to do with my inexperience when it came to focusing on what the wind was trying to show me than any true impediment. Then the Eye pulsed, and the fog lifted; images immediately flowed through my mind, as fast as the wind herself—a white-painted two-story house, fields of orderly green marked with flags, our thief walking through the front door. As he disappeared inside, the images shifted, revealing a silver SUV sitting almost opposite the house and two shadowy figures within, watching, waiting. Backup, perhaps? Had our thief been spooked enough by my appearance at the cottage to have brought help this time?

"Golf course," I said. "They're on a street that runs alongside it."

"The golf course up that way has streets on all four sides, but that at least is a good start."

He waved me inside the vehicle. I scrambled in, did up the seat belt, and then said, "This one has some sort of crossover point from one part of the golf course to the other."

"That would be Church Lane, sir," Henrick said. "I'm a member there and know the crossing well."

If Henrick could afford to be a member, then Mathi certainly was paying him *extremely* well. It was one of the finest—and most expensive—parkland golf courses in the entire region.

"Get us there at speed please, Henrick."

"At once, sir." The privacy screen slid up, and Henrick obeyed, the wheels spinning just a little on the wet road surface before gripping and sending us rocketing forward.

"Did you see anything else?" Mathi asked. "I take it he isn't alone, given you said 'they're.'"

"He's brought two people with him this time—they're

sitting in an SUV outside a two-story modern brick home a couple of doors up from the target house and the cross-over." I glanced at him. "I don't suppose your father gave you any insights about Carla and her many identities?"

"No, he was surprisingly uncooperative."

I raised my eyebrows at the deep annoyance in his expression. Mathi and Ruadhán had never been particularly close, even by light elf standards, but there had always been a mutual respect and understanding between the two. I'd never, in all the years I'd been in Mathi's life, known Ruadhán to knock back an information request from his son.

"Do you know why?"

"He quoted the delicacy of the situation and the need not to alarm the public."

"The public are well aware that the bank was raided, so that horse has already bolted." I grabbed the "oh shit" handle as Henrick expertly spun the car around a corner at speed, then flattened his foot again. "And he's not the type to bow to external pressure, be it the council or even Ljósálfar or Myrkálfar elders."

"I think it likely the bank's board are pressing for a quick result. They believe it will help restore faith in the bank."

"Why would one targeted theft in the how many hundreds of years they've been safekeeping other people's savings greatly affect their standing?"

"They pride themselves as being the only bank never to have fallen foul of robbery."

"Well, that's the problem right there," I replied, amused. "Put that sort of statement out in the world, and Fate will eventually take up the challenge. She can be a bitch like that."

He snorted and fell silent. I watched the world speed by, the Eye pulsing lightly on my chest, perhaps in time to the scratching in the wind I currently couldn't hear. We turned sharply left at a roundabout and entered Church Lane. Henrick slowed, moving past a large white van that was partially parked up on the curb but still taking a good portion of our side of the road, before continuing on, sweeping around a long curve to the right. Up ahead, a white SUV was parked up on the wrong side of the road, its darkened windows not allowing us to see if anyone remained inside.

"That's it," I said. "That's the vehicle."

Mathi pressed a button, and the privacy screen slid down. "Please slow, Henrick; the target car is that white SUV."

"The number plate has been recorded, sir."

"Excellent." Mathi glanced at me. "Any suggestions as to how we play this?"

"You and Henrick tackle the car while I—"

I stopped, frowning as the SUV lights briefly flashed. Perhaps the two men in the SUV had just gotten word from our thief and were preparing to leave. If that were the case, then maybe our best bet was to park up and follow them.

As it turned out, that wasn't the case.

Without anyone else getting into the vehicle, it moved. It didn't drive away, however.

It reversed.

Straight at the damn Mercedes.

Henrick immediately threw the Merc into reverse and hit the accelerator again. We shot backward at speed, and yet the SUV seemed to be gaining. Neither Henrick nor Mathi appeared to be fazed, however, so perhaps this wasn't the first time someone had tried to ram them.

Then, from the street behind us, came the sharp blast of a horn. My heart leapt, and I twisted around. Another car, though if the brief glimpse of the woman's horrified face was anything to go by, she wasn't connected to either the SUV or our thief.

"Please hold on to something," Henrick said, his tone cool and calm.

I barely had time to grab the "oh shit" handle again before he threw the car to the right, rocking it briefly onto two wheels as he neatly reversed into the nearest driveway, then slammed on the brakes.

We almost got out of the way.

Almost.

EIGHT

The rear of the SUV slammed into the front end of the Merc, throwing me sideways as the car was pushed into the nearby fence and sent bricks flying. There was a screech of tires as the woman tried to avoid the SUV, but her car slid on the wet road and spun, the rear end of her vehicle finishing off the bit of fence we'd left untouched.

The SUV peeled away from us and sped down the street.

"Oh, no you fucking don't," I growled, and scrambled out of the Merc. The wind whipped around me, sharp, cold, and eager to be used. I flung it after the retreating vehicle, slipped a thick knot of it under the SUV's tail end, and then flipped it up and over. The vehicle landed on its roof hard enough to buckle and slid down the road for several yards before coming to rest hard up against a light pole.

Mathi was already running toward it, Henrick two steps behind him.

I didn't chase after them; the wind continued her whispering, telling me our thief was on the run. I scrambled over the small brick fence separating the house behind us with the one next door, and headed for the crossover and the white house on the left side of it.

The front door was wide open, an invitation to enter if ever I saw one, and one I wasn't foolish enough to accept. Instead, I followed the asphalt path down the side of the house to the gate, pushing it open with a blast of wind and running on to the end of the double-story building. I paused briefly, scanning the backyard, looking for any hint of fog or vapor to suggest the thief was still here.

There was nothing to be seen, but a tremor now ran through the ground. The bastard was tunneling again.

I swore, gathered another whip of wind and flung it toward what seemed to be the epicenter of the trembling, then chased after it. I'd barely gone a few yards when the ground stopped moving. The wind trailed back to me, whispering of earth closing down on top of it, sheering it in half.

The bastard hadn't been opening a new tunnel, he'd been closing it down behind him.

I swore once again but nevertheless continued on. A thick hedge of common box divided the yard from the golf course beyond, but there was no gateway cut through it that would have provided access onto the course. That shouldn't have been a problem for our vaporous thief, of course, but for whatever reason, he'd obviously regained human form *beforehand,* then dived through the hedge, leaving behind a broken mess of branches, leaves, and a thick song of distress.

Why? It made absolutely no sense. Even if he *had* created his escape tunnel just beyond the hedge, why not simply keep to his vaporous form until he'd reached its safety? Why become flesh and blood and then inflict damage on himself by diving through such a thick hedge? And he obviously *had* suffered multiple cuts—even from here I could see the small bits of material and maybe even some hair fluttering in the shattered pathway he'd made. There'd also likely be some blood, though I couldn't immediately see the dark gleam of it.

The common box's song of distress sharpened as I stopped in front of it; perhaps the rivers of golden life that pulsed through the thick greenery sensed the closeness of someone who could ease their agony. I slipped deep into the flow, carefully chased down every broken end, and then looped the rivers away from each point. It would mean some die off in the plant overall, but with the still-healthy flow of energies intact further down the branches and limbs, the gap would eventually close over.

As I pulled out of the rivers, the wind stirred yet again, though this time it was filled with nothing more than the warning of impending rain and the wail of sirens. I dragged my phone out of my pocket to check the time; it was close to six, which hopefully meant it would be Sgott's crew in those cars rather than Ruadhán's. But if it *was* the latter, I only had a couple of minutes, if that, to take advantage of the back door being wide open.

I ran back up the yard. While neither the Eye nor my instincts were giving any indication that danger or a trap waited inside the back half of the house—as it had when I'd run past the front door—I nevertheless paused before entering and listened to the building's rich, warm song. There was nothing untoward within it. Nothing to suggest anyone was currently inside the home. I nevertheless connected to the rivers and quickly skimmed through them, looking for any "hot spots" that would indicate someone standing or sitting within.

Again, nothing.

Which didn't mean there wasn't any danger or trap

waiting within, especially given the wide-open front door. I called my knives from my purse, which was still sitting in the backseat of the Mercedes. Once they'd thudded into my hands, I tucked one blade into my belt under my coat, angling it so that I didn't stab my butt, then gripped the other tightly, feeling oddly reassured with its weight in my hand as I carefully stepped inside. Lightning flickered down the blade's fuller, a warning that echoed through the Eye. There was magic here, though it was much deeper inside the house and held no immediate threat.

I walked through the small laundry into a combined kitchen-dining-living space that ran the remaining width of the building. Glass sliding doors dominated the living area and would have provided great views over the golf course if the hedge wasn't there. Said hedge, no doubt, was there to prevent wayward golf balls smashing those same glass doors or the nearby windows.

I did a quick scout around the room, but nothing stirred my instincts. I continued on, into a hall from which there were entrances into several more rooms. A vague scent hung on the air, soft and definitely feminine. I frowned, drawing in a deeper breath; orange flowers, I thought after a moment, with just a hint of musk. Definitely not the scent of our thief, suggesting someone else had been here. Whether the scent wearer had been with him or had arrived beforehand was impossible to say.

At the far end of the hall was the open front door, and near it, to its right, were the stairs leading up to the first floor. Between it and me was some sort of weird haze.

I didn't need the faint flicker of lightning down the blade to tell me that haze was magic.

Outside, the sirens stopped and the sound of car doors

slamming rode the wind. The clock was definitely running down now....

I edged forward, my gaze on the haze. As I got closer, the lightning rolling down the knife's fuller intensified and the vague sense of danger increased.

I stopped again several feet away and sat on my heels, studying the haze through narrowed eyes. After a moment, I spotted the wire. It was hair fine, barely visible to the naked eye, and stretched the entire width of the hall, sitting only an inch or so off the oak flooring. It was attached to the skirting board on one side and a small round disk that was barely visible against the understairs storage doors on the other.

Footsteps approached and I glanced up. A big bear of a man with thick, wiry brown hair, brown skin, and a fierce, untamable beard strode up the path toward me.

Sgott, just as I'd hoped. And while he might be no happier than Ruadhán to find me inside this house, he was more likely to accept my reasons. His expression was certainly more resigned than annoyed.

"Lass, one of these days you're going to put yourself in deep trouble by trespassing like this."

The Scottish brogue was heavy in his voice, making it sound like it was coming from the vicinity of his boots.

"One of these days, I undoubtedly will, but hopefully it won't be today." I pointed toward the wire. "There's a trip wire here, attached to a disk and protected by a haze of magic."

He stopped on the threshold and squatted on his heels, brown eyes narrowing as his gaze swept the hall in front of me. "I'm not seeing anything."

"I think that's because of the magic. The only reason I saw it was because the knife gave me warning."

"Are you able to defuse the magic with your knife without tripping the wire? I can call someone in, but that'll take time we might not have."

I hesitated. "I should be able to, but it still might be wise if you step back."

"I'll step back when you step back, lass."

"That's not—"

"I said what I said, and I mean it."

I stared at him for a second, then rolled my eyes and gave in to the inevitable. "Fine. I'll task the wind with yanking me backward the minute I stab the haze."

"Good." He rose, glanced around at the sound of steps, and motioned to whoever it was to stop.

I silently reached for the wind, tied it around my waist, then returned my attention to Sgott. "Ready?"

He nodded, balancing lightly on the balls of his feet, ready to turn and run. I tightened the finger of air a fraction more, slashed the knife through the haze, and then ordered the wind to rip me back down the hall.

For a heartbeat, nothing happened. Then the haze ignited, and the disk exploded with enough force to shake the whole building. Dust and plaster began to chase me down the hall, and huge cracks appeared in the ceiling above. The building's gentle song switched to one of utter distress... it was coming down.

The whole fucking house was coming down.

Plaster, wood and even furniture now crashed all around me; wood, metal, and glass spun through the air, many deadly daggers that came close but never touched, thanks to the fierceness of the wind that remained wrapped around me. I was ripped through the living area, into the laundry, and then out through the back door. I was halfway down the backyard when I finally unleashed myself, and I hit the ground hard enough that a grunt escaped. I scrambled upright and watched in disbelief as the entire house—every brick, every tile, and everything else that lay within those four walls—disintegrated before my very eyes.

Our thief definitely hadn't set this trap. He might be Myrkálfar, but the complete and utter destructiveness of this spell wasn't in their skillset; not as far as I was aware, anyway. Their control lay over stone and precious metal, not timber or glass or any of the other manmade items that had lain within that house. While they *could* force stone to explode, it wouldn't have reduced the rest of the building's contents to splinters.

This had been done by someone else, possibly whoever that faint scent had belonged to. Whoever it was, she'd been very determined there would be absolutely nothing left to find.

My gaze met Sgott's over what little remained, the relief visible in his expression echoing through me. We'd both been lucky. *Very* damn lucky.

"You okay?" he asked, raising his voice to ensure he could be heard over the dying sounds of the building.

"Yeah." I brushed my fingers across my chin, smearing warmth. Obviously, I'd either cut it when I'd landed, or debris had gotten through my barrier, and I hadn't noticed. It didn't feel particularly bad and certainly wasn't bucketing blood, so all in all, I'd been pretty damn lucky. I grabbed an old tissue out of my coat pocket and dabbed the scrape lightly as I walked back to the still-open—and totally untouched—side gate.

Sgott met me at the front corner, his gaze briefly scanning me and coming up relieved. "I take it our thief wasn't inside, given you didn't mention him earlier."

"He wasn't, but I only just missed him. He dived

through the hedge at the back of the yard and went down a tunnel, and I wasn't fast enough to stop him. There's clothing threads and likely bits of flesh hanging off the broken branches, though, so we at least have DNA evidence now."

"I take it you did a search of the rear interior half of the house before you found the trap in the hallway?"

I nodded. "It was only cursory though, and I didn't find anything. But he didn't set the trap—someone else did."

"What makes you so sure? Aside from the fact Myrkálfar magic isn't capable of the utter destruction that spell entailed?"

"I smelled a scent—orange flower and musk. Feminine, not masculine."

"Could it have been one of those scent infusers?"

I hesitated. "Possibly?"

His eyebrows rose. "But you think not?"

"I do. No evidence beyond my gut to back it up though."

"Lass, instinct is good enough for me, given you are your mother's daughter."

"Instinct doesn't help us track the woman down though. What happened to the men in the SUV?"

"They're currently being examined by medics."

Frankie—a wolf shifter I'd met a few times now—came through the gate, her gaze on the destruction and her expression shocked. "Man, someone made damn sure there was no evidence to find in that house, didn't they?"

"Aye," Sgott replied. "Fetch forensics and get them to look over the hedge in the backyard. He's left evidence behind in the breakthrough."

She nodded. "The medics declared the two men fit to be questioned, though they would prefer it to be done *after* a full medical check has been completed at the hospital. I stressed the urgency and they're giving us a few minutes. Our suspects, however, are making like clamshells."

Sgott glanced at me. "I know this is a daft question, but care to make our clams a little more amenable?"

I grinned. "As you said, daft question."

I followed him out the gate and down the road. The SUV remained on its roof, but an ambulance was parked close by now, its back doors open. There were two men—aside from the medics—inside, one on the trolley and one on a seat. The swarthier of the two had his right arm in a sling, but that aside, it appeared they'd both come through the rollover with little more than a few cuts.

I couldn't see Henrick—he was likely back at the Merc, arranging for it to be towed—but Mathi leaned against one of the ambulance doors, his arms crossed and his expression less than pleased. I rather suspected its cause was the clams' refusal to answer his questions.

His gaze met mine, and relief stirred lightly through those blue depths. "Given you remain in one piece aside from that cut on your chin, I take it you weren't inside the house when it exploded?"

"Oh, she was," Sgott growled before I could answer. "And if I hadn't insisted she take precautions, she'd now be little more than another pile of splinters in that mess."

"Hey," I said lightly—and perhaps unwisely—"when death comes for me, it won't find me via a magical bomb, you can be sure of that."

Sgott frowned. "Suggesting you've seen your end. If that's—"

"I only meant that the knives would protect me from the effects of any spell, be it an explosion or something else." Which wasn't a lie and neatly avoided the whole death-ticking-clock thing I didn't want him to know about yet.

He studied me for a long second, suggesting he suspected there was far more to my explanation than that, but nevertheless motioned me to proceed. Mathi helped me up into the ambulance, then he and Sgott followed, making for rather cramped conditions. Both our suspects had been handcuffed, and were studying me curiously rather than with any sort of surliness or hostility, suggesting our thief hadn't warned them that I might be a problem. Perhaps he didn't think I would be.

I stepped past them, then turned around and pressed a couple of fingers against the exposed back of their necks, quickly saying, "You will offer no violence or react in any way. You will obey all orders given to you by the IIT and the ambulance officers, and answer all questions asked from this moment on."

Both men swore, but could do little else as my magic flowed through. I glanced up at Sgott and nodded.

"Right," he immediately said. "Tell me your names and why you are here."

"Raul Torrez," the swarthy man muttered. "SUV driver and backup muscle."

"Jason Gould," the blond said. "Muscle. We were both employed to watch and deflect by any means necessary."

"Deflect being code for ramming your vehicle into mine?" Mathi said mildly.

Raul glanced at him. "Yeah. We were given your license plate and car model and told to stop you getting into that house until we were told otherwise."

"We weren't warned you had skills," Jason added. "I mean, how the fuck did you flip the car like that?"

"I did not," Mathi replied, cool amusement touching his

lips. "Might I suggest that the next time you accept such an assignment, you thoroughly investigate just who and what you're going up against? Trust me when I say that an annoyed Ljósálfar elf is the least of your problems right now."

The two men shared a glance. Neither looked happy. "Look, man, we didn't know—"

"We're not interested in what you didn't know," Sgott cut in, "but rather what you *did*. Who employed you?"

"Don't know his name. Best not to with these sorts of jobs, you know?" Jason said.

"Then how did he get in contact with you?"

"He rang us."

"Then you've worked with him before?"

"No," Raul replied. "He got our number via a broker. We did check and they did recommend us. No contract or fee required."

"*That* is extremely unusual," I commented. "Brokers don't work for the love of it."

"No," Mathi agreed. "But some do sometimes give out contact details, either because they are related to the contractor or because they have a beef against the target."

"So which scenario applied here?" I asked.

Jason sniffed. "I got the impression it might have been both, but it's not like I could ask. I mean, she wasn't going to confirm it anyways, was she?"

She? While there was more than one female broker active within Deva, there was only one who might hold a grudge against me or Mathi—Kaitlyn Avery. And she'd certainly be familiar with the Merc's registration number given how many times he—and we—had visited her of late.

Except the last I'd heard she was still in hospital recovering from the frost burns she'd received in the ice attack that had destroyed her place of business. Surely even she wouldn't be running her business from her hospital bed.

"Does this someone have a name?" Sgott asked.

"Obviously, yes."

"And what is their name?"

Sgott had the patience of a saint. I was ready to clip the fellow over the head.

"Kaitlyn Avery."

So much for the thought she couldn't be involved. "And she didn't warn you about me?"

He frowned. "Why would she have?"

"Because she and Beth have had a few run-ins before," Mathi said, amused. "But she's also a high-end broker of services—why on earth would she have recommended two very obviously middle-of-the-range felons?"

"Hey, we ain't no middle range—"

"Oh, you're right, forgive me," Mathi drawled. "Rank beginners could have done a better job than you did here today."

Both men swore at him, but could do little else given my orders.

"Did you note your employer's number when they rang?" Sgott asked.

"I'd be a fool not to."

"And it is...?"

"It's not like I fucking memorize that sort of stuff, is it now?" Raul seemed to be the mouthpiece of the two.

Sgott drew in a deeper breath. He might have the patience of a saint, but he was also getting a little annoyed. "Is it on your phone? Under what name?"

"Sunday Job."

I snorted. "Inventive."

"Hey, it works."

"What about a description of the man who hired you?" Sgott said. "Any visible scars? Anything that might set him apart?"

Raul hesitated. "We didn't actually meet him."

"But you saw him?"

Raul nodded. "He told us to park up on the sidewalk just up from twenty-seven. Saw this dapper-looking chap walking down the crossing, then slip into the house."

"It was odd," Jason piped up, "because he opened the front door but didn't go in. Turned around and went through the side gate instead."

Because as a Myrkálfar, he would have seen the spell haze. "Describe him."

Raul shrugged. "Myrkálfar, but on the youngish end; well-dressed, nice shoes."

I snorted. "Of all the damn things to notice—"

"Hey," he cut in, "they were Loake Bedales, you know? Got a pair very similar to them."

I glanced at Mathi, my eyebrows raised in question.

"Loake are considered one of the finest men's shoe-makers in the UK," he immediately said, "and have been around since 1880."

"Meaning they might have a record of his purchase?"

"Should have, yes."

"Anything else you noticed?" Sgott asked our prisoners.

"His left hand," Jason said. "It was deformed."

"Deformed how?" I asked.

"Missing a couple of fingers."

I hadn't noticed that either time I'd seen him, but then, it wasn't like I'd had a whole lot of time for any sort of in-depth examination.

"Yeah, he was," Raul confirmed. "Fairly recent too. The scarring was pinkish."

"That it?" Sgott asked. "Nothing else you remember?"

Both men shook their head. Sgott turned to the officer who'd been recording the entire conversation. "Accompany them both to the hospital. If they get chatty, take a record of it."

He nodded, tucked his phone away, then stepped back so we could all exit.

"Hey," Jason called after us. "What about removing the damn pixie shit from us?"

I glanced at Sgott, my eyebrows once again raised in question. He smiled. "Leave it for the time being. We'll consider its removal once we've finished questioning them."

I nodded, watched as the medic closed the ambulance's rear door, and then said, "When did Kaitlyn get released from the hospital?"

"Yesterday. She's currently working out of a secondary office outside the old city." He glanced at me, amusement playing across his lips. "And I'll be questioning her, young lady, not you."

"She owes me a favor—I saved her life, remember."

"And destroyed her home and her main business building in the process. She's not happy, let me tell you that."

"Then when you talk to her, tell her next time something untoward threatens her, she can look elsewhere for help."

"She knows that is not in your nature, just as it wasn't in your mother's."

"Thing is, there's a lot more of my father in me than

either Mom or I had realized." It was bleakly said, and Sgott frowned at me.

"Meaning what?"

I waved the comment away. "Nothing. Do you need a statement from us?"

"Yes, but we can get it in the morning—"

"We're off to Wales relic hunting for the council tomorrow morning," Mathi said, "and are likely to be gone all day."

"Ah, well then." Sgott motioned another of his people over. "James here will take your statements now then. And please, if you have any other insights about our thief, inform me before you take any action on it. And that includes you, Mathi."

"As you are no doubt well aware," he replied evenly, "my father has cut my access to the IIT systems, so I am bereft of meaningful 'insights' and informational avenues."

"You are many things, Mathi Dhār-Val, but you will never be bereft of insights, information, or indeed integrity."

Mathi bowed slightly. "I shall take that as a compliment."

"You should. I would not say the same about your father." Sgott touched my arm, a gesture that was both affectionate and a warning to stay out of trouble, then moved away, heading toward the still-smoking ruins of the house. James took our statements and then asked if we needed a lift anywhere.

Mathi politely declined and then touched the small of my back, guiding me down the street to the worse-for-wear Merc. A couple of cops were squatting near the front end, one appearing to scrape paint samples into specimen containers while the other took photos. Henrick stood nearby, watching proceedings, but glanced around as we approached. There was a briefcase in one hand, and over his shoulders were several leather bags, including my purse. He handed me the latter when I was close enough, and I nodded my thanks.

"I called Marc, sir. He awaits just beyond the roundabout."

"Excellent. And the Mercedes?"

"Will be out of action for repairs for at least a week, once the IIT have released it. I've already arranged a replacement."

"Excellent work, Henrick. Thank you."

Henrick nodded, then turned and led us down the street, turning left at the roundabout and striding toward the silver Mercedes—a carbon copy of the vehicle he drove —parked a little farther down. He opened the rear door, ushered us inside, then climbed into the front passenger seat.

"Home, sir?" Marc said.

"We'll drop Ms. Aodhán off first, thanks, Marc."

"Very good, sir."

The privacy screen rolled up, and the vehicle pulled smoothly away. It was a Sunday night, so the traffic was light, and it didn't take us all that long to reach the end of the lane.

"What time tomorrow morning?" I said as I undid my belt.

"I've made arrangements for a private plane—it'll be more efficient than driving all that way—so about seven?"

"You'll let Lugh know?"

"Indeed."

"Thanks." I climbed out, waited on the footpath while they left, then ran across the road and down the lane. After checking everything was okay with Ingrid, I ran upstairs, dumped my stuff, and went straight into the shower. The wind might have deflected most of the dust and debris, but I nevertheless felt caked in it. After redressing in sweats, I ordered a meal from downstairs, made myself a pot of tea, then threw more logs onto the fire. Once my steak, chips, and vegetables had arrived, I settled down on the sofa to eat, then slowly made my way through the other box of records.

I was only half done when the Bruadar came to life. Excitement pulsed through me, and my heart danced almost as fiercely as those stars. I took a deeper breath in a vague effort to calm down, then placed my tea mug on the coffee table and said, "Call accepted."

For a second, nothing happened, then the stars flared even brighter, and the kaleidoscope once again swept me away. This time, when I arrived in that cool darkness, I was not alone. He was once again wearing jeans, but had added a black sweater that sadly hid his washboard abs while emphasizing the width of his shoulders and arms. His feet were bare, and his dark hair looked damp, suggesting he'd had a shower before calling me here.

His gaze met mine, and everything just seemed to stop. The twin beating of our hearts echoed and merged, and just for one precious second in time, we were one being rather than two.

Meant to be, instinct whispered.

Get a grip, the saner half replied.

He half reached out to me, a seemingly instinctive move that he stopped almost immediately. I hated that. Hated the distance, the reluctance, that hovered between us. Because of me. Because of what I'd said to him earlier. And while I'd never regret being honest about my feelings and fears, I nevertheless needed to fix the divide it had caused. If I really did only have nine months of life left, then I'd be damned if I was going to spend it resisting the insanely heated attraction that lay between us.

"Evening," he said, his expression composed but his eyes anything but. "I hope I didn't interrupt anything vital."

"Well, if you consider sipping a cup of tea while going through Mom's old records vital, then yes, you did. I take it you have some news to share?"

He nodded. "Although in truth, it's simply an excuse to see you. I do miss you, you know."

"And I you." I wanted to say so much more—wanted to do so much more—than simply stand here. And yet, despite the resolution I'd made only a few seconds ago, I resisted, torn between my desire for him and the lingering need not to get hurt. "Shall I start?"

"As I've said before, I do like a woman unafraid to take control."

A smile teased my lips. "And used it in a completely different context."

"Whether in the bedroom or in conversation matters not. Both are ultimately sexy."

"There are many who would disagree with that."

"There are many who are fools."

My smile grew. "Says the man who always gets the girl, be she outspoken or not."

"And yet, before me stands one who will not allow herself to be caught."

"The problem is not catching her, Cynwrig, it's the fact that your people won't let you marry her without you stepping away from everything you hold dear."

"And if there was a way around that problem?"

I ignored the leap of hope and raised my eyebrows. "Is there?"

"It's a theoretical question."

Of course it was, because there was no way around it. Still... "Then theoretically, yes, she would be willing to marry, even if she's only known the man for a short period of time."

As Darby had noted, some leaps of faith were worth it.

"That is good to know."

I couldn't help but laugh. "Even if, as far as she and you are concerned, it is never going to happen?"

"'Never' is not a word within my vocabulary."

I rolled my eyes, saw the answering flash of annoyance in his. And yet, surely he could understand my reluctance to take a theoretical marriage seriously. "Can we step out of the twilight zone now and concentrate on real matters?"

"If you insist." He paused. "I would prefer to discuss said matters seated, however. Standing here will get uncomfortable in the long run."

Once again, a smile tugged at my lips. "Are we talking chair comfortable or bed comfortable?"

"A sofa or two chairs would be safer. My control should we share a bed would be severely tested."

"A Myrkálfar admitting to a lack of control? Shocking."

"Almost as shocking as the depths of my desire for you."

It was dryly said and yet edged with a deeper emotion that had my pulse soaring. "And yet, here we stand, neither of us acting on those desires."

"Do you wish there to be action on said desires?"

"Despite the fears that still rage, yes, I believe I do."

"Then I am ecstatic to comply."

I laughed, and he caught my hand, tugging me into his embrace. His body was hard against mine, his flesh heated, and his erection fierce. The man really did *want*. He didn't say anything, however; he just kissed me. And oh, what a kiss. It was soft and passionate, demanding and yet not. It made promises the man couldn't possibly keep, and yet there was more than a small part of me that wanted to believe. Wanted to trust that, against impossible odds, it would somehow work out for us.

After what seemed forever, he pulled back, though thankfully not far. His breathing was harsh and heated against my kiss-swollen lips, and his lust was a thick cloud that smothered, making it even harder to breathe.

"Consider me convinced about the depths of your desire," I murmured, my voice breathy and almost inaudible. "I believe we should reconsider the option to take this to bed."

"Taking it to bed rather than talking is part of our whole problem," he replied. "Do not get me wrong. I want nothing more than to bury myself in your flesh right now, but—"

I didn't let him finish. I grabbed his shirt, pulled him close again, and kissed him with all the fervent desire that burned through me. Talking wasn't going to solve the problems that lay between us. Neither would sex, but it at least held the promise of a satisfying ending.

He groaned softly against my lips, then his arms went around me again, and our kiss deepened, became hot and hungry and desperate. His fingers slid under my sweatshirt, sending delicious tingles of desire skittering across my flesh as his touch slowly—agonizingly slowly—moved up toward my breasts. When he caught and gently squeezed one puckered nipple, I gasped and arched into him, pressing my mound against him, feeling his instinctive reaction even through the weight of his jeans.

He chuckled softly. "You win. Let's take this to bed."

"And how do we bring said bed to life in this place?"

"Imagine what you want, and it will be."

"I want you naked and in me, and that isn't happening."

His laugh was a soft and decidedly wicked sound. "Imagine the bed, Bethany. Once it becomes a reality, me losing myself in your magnificence will definitely follow."

Somewhat impulsively, I imagined a big four-poster bed with lots of impractical pillows and a thick and luscious comforter. The air vibrated briefly, and Cynwrig once again laughed. "Well, that is certainly a little grander than what I was expecting."

I turned. Grand was an understatement. Aside from the fact it was huge, it was heavily carved with vines and leaves that ran through the range of autumn colors. It wasn't painted—it was in fact living wood, however impossible that might be—and its song ran rich and wild through the air and my body, fueling those inner fires to even greater heights. Pillows lined the bedhead, layers of red and gold velvet, while the comforter was also velvet, but a deep green that reminded me of a thick carpet of grass.

"It is a little over the top, isn't it?" I replied, amused.

"It is, but this place does tend to take ideas and run them to the extreme end." He caught my hand and led me over. "Shall we undress each other?"

"As long as it doesn't take forever. I might spontaneously combust if it does."

"Impatience. I like it." He caught the ends of my sweater and lifted it up and over my head. Then he cupped my breasts in his big, powerful hands and began to lick and kiss and tease, until I really could take no more and growled for him to keep moving down.

He did so, slowly slipping my sweatpants and knickers

down my body. I kicked them off, then gasped as his fingers slipped between my legs, finding my clit, sliding through the wetness, teasing me, taunting me, bringing me to the very edge, then pulling away again.

"Oh," I growled softly, "you're going to pay for that."

"Looking forward to it," he said with that wicked grin.

I arched an eyebrow and slipped my hands under his sweater, doing nothing more than exploring the hard planes of his stomach, reveling in the pleasure of simply touching him. Then I tugged his sweater free, let it drop to the floor, and once again explored the magnificence on show, this time with tongue and lips rather than just touch, following the happy trail of hair until I reached the barrier of his jeans. I undid the button, slid down the zip, and then dropped to my knees, letting my tongue play across his erection until his body was trembling and I was tasting precum.

He made a low sound in the back of his throat, dragged me upright, then picked me up and threw me onto the bed. I laughed and scrambled under the comforter, watching as he hastily stripped off his remaining clothes.

"Prepare to be ravished, wench," he growled, and climbed in beside me.

"Looking forward to it," I murmured.

His lips once again claimed mine, and from that moment on, there was no talking. I explored every inch of him, touching and tasting, refamiliarizing myself with all his muscular magnificence. He returned the exploration in kind, making me shake and shudder and ache, until the delicious pressure had me so tightly wound, it felt as if I would surely shatter. Then he entered me, and everything did shatter, my orgasm so fierce I was little more than a leaf tossed on the tempest of a storm, lost to everything but the sheer power of the forces flowing through me. A few seconds later, he joined me in that joyous oblivion, his deep groan echoing through the shadows that still haunted the area beyond the bed.

For several seconds, neither of us moved. Then he pushed up on his elbows, holding his weight off my body as his gaze caught and held mine. While a multitude of emotions flitted through the glorious silver depths, it was fierce determination that gleamed the brightest. This man was not going to let me escape him, no matter what it took.

And while that made my heart dance, not even the might of the Myrkálfar could defeat death himself.

I opened my mouth to tell him and then closed it again. While the reluctance was based mainly on nothing more than the cowardly need not to spoil the perfection of this moment, I really did want to explore all the possible avenues of salvation before I admitted the inevitability of death to either him or my brother.

Besides, if I got the tracer as Darby demanded, surely them knowing the truth of my future held less importance?

No, it did not. Not when there were powerful emotions at play, his as much as mine.

I dropped my gaze from his, and he shifted to my side. "Would you like something to drink and eat while we talk?"

My eyebrows rose. "I thought you said there was no food or water in this place?"

"There isn't, unless, of course, you bring it in with you. Which I did."

"Then I will certainly partake in said food and drink."

He rolled off the bed and disappeared briefly into the darkness. I pushed upright and tugged the velvet cloud of cushions behind my back to brace it. He reappeared a few seconds later, carrying a basket containing a bottle of red—

Cuvée du Vatican Châteauneuf-du-Pape, which wasn't the most expensive of wines but was still one of my favorites—two glasses, and a small platter of cheese, fruits, and crackers.

"The man comes prepared for seduction."

"A good red never goes astray, be it for seduction purposes or simple enjoyment."

"I was speaking more of the cheese and crackers. They are a weakness."

He placed the basket beside me and then climbed onto the bed, crossing his legs and facing me. "I thought chocolate was your weakness."

"No, chocolate is one of the five essential food groups."

He laughed softly. After opening the bottle, he poured the wine, handed me a glass, then placed the bottle back into the basket and raised his glass. "To a continuation of our relationship."

"For as long as time and Fate give us." I tapped my glass lightly against his and took a drink, tasting notes of black fruits, spices, and smooth tannins. The aroma—jam, cherries, and wood smoke—was also lovely. "Now, as I said before, shall I begin the conversation?"

"Please do."

I took another drink, then jumped in feet first. "What do you know about the Eljin Lavigne pictured in the article Treasa sent me, and how is he related to our Eljin?"

A smile tugged at his lips, but his gaze became wary rather than warm. "I feel obliged not to answer that question, given we are courting the heart of the same woman."

"Given one of you will never have my heart and the other can't take it even if he wanted to, that's not an acceptable reply."

Something flared through the wariness. Something that

was almost... victorious? Propriety? "That is an answer that leads me to hope that you and Eljin are no longer an item."

"Let's just say that he and I will no longer be spending any alone time together."

While I tried to keep my voice even, anger must have seeped through, because his gaze narrowed dangerously. "Why? What has he done? Is he the reason your chin is scraped and bruised?"

"My chin is bruised because I hit the ground a bit too hard escaping an explosion. As for Eljin, we're in the process of dealing with the matter, but it would be handy if we knew more about him. Mathi's lost access to the IIT system, and I don't want to involve Sgott. Not yet, anyway."

"What did he do, Bethany?"

I hesitated. "No retaliation. Promise that."

His eyes gleamed dangerously. "I can't and won't promise that. I can, however, promise I won't do anything until we know who he works for. Good enough?"

"Good enough."

"Then what did he do?"

"He's been drugging me for information."

The surge of his anger was so damn fierce that for a moment I couldn't breathe.

"How?" he growled. "Through food? Alcohol?"

"Uncertain." I hesitated. "Darby said it was a combination of Devil's Breath, which causes sleepiness and memory loss, and Damiana, which increases sexual interest and desire."

"So, the bastard was fucking the hell out of you and then memory scanning?"

"It would appear so." I paused but couldn't help mischievously adding, if only to ease the fierce blanket of his anger, "But at least it was *good* fucking. I would have been even more pissed had it been bad."

He did *not* look amused. "I take it, given he's obviously still alive, you have not mentioned this to Lugh yet?"

"No. But I did tell Mathi, and he currently has a friend doing a background search on both Eljin and the woman he went to London to see—Eljin claims it was his sister, but I'm not entirely convinced right now."

"The Eljin in that photo had no sisters," Cynwrig said.

Meaning he and Treasa *had* done some research before they'd handed it to me. "Yeah, but he's also a lot older. We thought it possible our Eljin was a grandson or something."

"No, because the older man died without issue."

"Huh." I picked up the cheese knife, cut a triangle of the brie, then popped it on a cracker and munched on it contemplatively. "Is he a relation of some kind?"

"Not as far as we could ascertain after a thorough search through the birth records. No other Eljin appears in the older man's family tree. Ours appears to have manifested some three years ago, and much of his work history has been manufactured."

I frowned. "How is that possible? Rogan would have done a thorough background on him before employing him at the museum."

"Rogan might have had his own reasons for not doing a complete background."

True enough, I supposed, given the man was hellbent on retrieving the claws, whatever the cost. I took another drink. "If you knew all this, why not tell me sooner?"

He hesitated. "In truth, while I suspected he was not who he said he was, there was no evidence of criminal behavior or ill intent toward you."

"You still could have mentioned it."

He raised his eyebrows. "Would you have believed me? Or would you have thought it nothing more than the ramblings of a jealous man?"

"Do Myrkálfar even do jealousy?"

"Touch our women, and we do far more than mere jealousy."

That came out darkly menacing, and I couldn't help but grin. "I feel the need to remind you that I am not a possession, and will probably never be yours—at least in the way that statement intended."

"And I concur with the first part of that statement."

I took another drink and wondered what the hell he was planning. He was *definitely* planning something—a change of Myrkálfar law, perhaps, that would allow him to marry as he wished? And yet, if that were the case, why ask for Geitha's Tears to be retrieved, given the goddess's artifact was the one responsible for partner choosing? Why not let it stay lost?

Whatever the answers to those questions might be, it was pretty evident he had no intention of telling me just yet.

"It does makes me wonder why," I said, after a moment, "given your suspicions, you did not take steps to remove him from my life."

"There are plenty of reasons a man or woman might manufacture a false past, Bethany, and some of them are legit. Until we knew otherwise, I thought it best to watch."

"And hope that I made a sensible decision when it came to the men in my life?"

"Indeed. Although I daresay you consider me far from sensible."

"Ain't that a truth." I grinned and ate some more cheese. "In other news, I met my father the other day."

Surprise flitted through his expression. "And did he have any wisdom or information to impart?"

I quickly updated him on everything except the whole death thing, then added, "He also said you were placed in my life to cause utter havoc."

"And instead, you cause utter havoc in mine."

His voice was dry, and I laughed again. "He did say that this game had a limited time frame, and my subsequent dream said it would end in nine months."

"At least that gives us a time frame to work with."

"Yes, though there's still the matter of the missing relics and the council's edict I find them all." I took another drink. "Which reminds me, has Mathi contacted you about us needing the services of a dark elf tomorrow?"

He nodded. "I've assigned Bodhrán. I trust him to keep you all safe."

Keep me safe, he actually meant. "He a relation?"

Cynwrig shook his head. "We grew up together—our parents were at one point close friends."

"At one point? What happened?"

"My mother died, and my father—" He paused and shrugged. "He basically lost interest in almost everything except running the kingdom and ensuring his children were more than capable of taking over 'the family business,' as he liked to call it."

I picked up a chocolate-covered strawberry and ate it. "How did you go working up a list of suspects from those who attended Jarvil Maehdon's funeral?"

"We have a number of possibilities, but we've yet to interview those from the immediate family."

I frowned. "Why not?"

"A Myrkálfar mourning period cannot legally be interrupted without good reason."

"You're in a mourning period, and yet you still have to deal with all the outside shit that comes with being heir."

"Because of the very fact I'm heir to the throne. There are separate rules for us."

Such as the "no fornicating" thing with those outside the Myrkálfar race—a rule a long-ago heir had very quickly found a way around. Cynwrig picked up the bottle of wine and raised an eyebrow in question. I held out my glass.

"Are any of Maehdon's family—immediate or otherwise—missing a finger on his left hand?"

"I have no idea, but that is easy enough to uncover. Why?"

"Because one of the two men our thief hired to stop me and Mathi chasing after him today claimed that he was missing a pinky."

"That certainly gives me reason to break the mourning period. I shall arrange a meeting in the morn."

"If you find him, I need to talk to him."

"Why?"

"Because it's possible he might have information about a blade we think is being used by Carla to force council members and others to obey her will and extract information."

"Who told you this? Your father?"

"No, Beira, so if you get rid of our thief before we get our answers, she will not be happy. She's already unhappy enough with me because apparently I am taking too long for her liking."

He laughed softly. "Gods and patience are rarely companions."

"Yeah, so I'm discovering." I helped myself to more walnut cheese. It really was quite lovely. "How did Maehdon die?"

"Natural causes, according to the coroner's report."

"And you believe that?"

He hesitated. "Maehdon had been in good health *and* good spirits when I'd seen him the week before. While death can sneak up on any of us, I do not believe that was the case here."

"Meaning you think someone might have bought off the coroner?"

He half smiled. "That's generally a hard thing to do."

"Speaking from experience, are we?"

The smile grew. "Not personal experience."

Meaning he might not have tried, but someone close to him certainly had. "Were there any witnesses to make you believe it was something other than a twist of fate?"

"His grandson—who found the body—claimed to have seen a woman leaving the house as he arrived, but no one matching the description he gave has been found in either the IIT's database or indeed in the Driver and Vehicle Licensing Agency records."

I took a drink, eyeing him for a second. "Did Jarvil happen to have any dealings with Carla Wilson before she went to ground?"

"I honestly don't know, but it is certainly an option, given what you said about the knife."

"Well, she does appear to have her claws in multiple men." I reached for another strawberry. "What about his sons?"

"What about them?"

"Well, could one of them be reacting to the IIT's dismissal of the grandson's story by playing lone wolf?"

"Unlikely. They are not the lone wolf type."

"They're Myrkálfar—it goes without saying that vengeance is built into their genes."

"None of Maehdon's sons are overly endowed with the vengeance gene."

"And yet, you investigate them."

"It is never wise to leave any stone unturned, however unlikely."

"How many sons does he have?"

"Five."

"Five?" My eyebrows rose. "The Maehdon line is a productive lot, obviously."

Cynwrig grinned. "You forget that the Myrkálfar generally do not have the reproduction issues that plague the Ljósálfar, though we are, of course, nowhere near as fertile as humans or indeed pixies."

"And how many little Cynwrigs are you planning to have tumbling around the feet of your throne?" I couldn't help but ask.

He sliced the brie and ate it, his eyes not wavering from mine, his expression intent. Nerve janglingly so. "That is a decision that can only be decided after serious discussion with my wife-to-be."

"Theoretically, presuming your wife was here with you now, how would you answer?"

"Theoretically, I would say two to four. Big families do run in my line, but I am of a mind to spend my time with the woman I love rather than running after a full gaggle of children." The intensity in his gaze increased, and I resisted the urge to rub my arms. "What of yourself?"

"Still speaking theoretically, I would say my branch of the Aodhán line has never been overly blessed with fertility, thanks to gifts the gods gave us, so if I conceived more than one, I would consider it a win." I quickly finished my wine, though it did little to ease the sudden dryness in my throat, then added with forced lightness, "But it's pointless me worrying about such things, because my continuing lack of good judgement when it comes to men suggests that's an option that might never be on the table for me."

And definitely *wouldn't* be if the gods had their way and the current game did end with my death.

"Perhaps your luck is changing," he mused lightly. "The gods did throw me in your path, after all."

"To cause chaos," I replied, "not babies."

He laughed. "A truth I cannot dispute. But, speaking of babies, or at least, the practice of making them—" He gulped down the remainder of his red, plucked my glass from my hand, placed both in the basket, then moved it to the floor. "—we should make the most of our limited time together tonight before sleep steals us away."

"Meaning we cannot sleep in this place?"

"No. The magic requires awareness. If we sleep, it will automatically return us to whence we came and shut down until required again."

"That's damnably inconvenient."

"Consider it similar to a power-saving feature."

He slipped under the blankets and then tugged me on top of him. I wriggled to make myself comfortable and felt his instinctive response.

"Are you sure we're not pushing your virility right now? Because that's a pretty lackluster response—"

The rest was lost in a yelp of surprise as he flipped our positions and, over the course of the next few hours, proceeded to prove just how virile a Myrkálfar heir could be.

～

MATHI PICKED me up at seven as promised, and I yawned all the way across to the private airfield.

"Hard night?" he asked as we both climbed out of the car.

Henrick collected my overnight bag containing a spare set of clothes from the trunk. I nodded my thanks and said, "Could say that. I hope there's coffee on board."

"Coffee *and* cake. No bacon butties, I'm afraid."

"I'm devastated."

My voice was dry, and he chuckled softly, pressing a hand against my spine and guiding me over to the small plane. "Anyone I know? Or should I mind my own business?"

"I bet you can guess the answer to *that* question."

"Oh, I bet I *can*—Cynwrig?"

My gaze shot to his. "He's in mourning—"

"And you're wearing a Bruadar."

My eyebrows rose. "When did you see it?"

"Saw the base of it when you absently pushed your sleeves up the other day. They're very distinctive."

"Yeah, well," I muttered, "it's a good way to communicate—"

"Is that what we're calling it now?" he cut in dryly. "'Communication'?"

I nudged him. "Idiot."

A pretty stewardess waited at the base of the stairs and welcomed us both warmly before adding, "Your three other guests are already aboard, sir."

Meaning Lugh had *not* been successful in convincing Darby to stay home; maybe he hadn't even tried. A wise man did know a losing hand when he saw one.

I clambered up the stairs and entered the plane. The cabin was spacious, with eight well-spaced, plushly comfortable chairs in an area that could have easily handled double that. There was a bar and food heating area up the front, and two toilets at the rear. Darby and Lugh were sitting to the immediate left of the door, in chairs that faced each other, and Bodhrán was at the back.

"Morning, Mathi. Ms. Aodhán," he said with a nod.

"Bethany, please. We don't stand on formalities in this outfit."

"Especially when our relic-hunting escapades have a habit of leading us into life-and-death situations," Mathi drawled. "Formalities do tend to get in the way in such times."

"I was warned you had a habit of finding problems." Amusement twitched Bodhrán's lips. "But the research I've undertaken suggests our destination is not an area known for earth-related problems."

"It's not the earth-related problems we have to worry about," Lugh said. "It's the godly ones."

"And will there be such problems?" he asked.

"Hard to say." I walked over to the window seat midway down the plane and sat down. "But there is a lake with live things wiggling about in it."

"Did anyone think to bring a boat?" Bodhrán asked. "Or are we just going in, all guns blazing? Figuratively speaking, of course."

"That approach works more often than you'd think," Lugh said with a grin. "But I have sourced a couple of inflatable rafts. We just have to swing by the store and pick them up on the way through."

"Easily enough done." Mathi took the chair opposite me. "Janis, please tell the pilot we're ready to go."

The stewardess nodded and did so. The plane's engines

fired up, and the ramp was withdrawn. A few minutes later, we were on our way.

I undid the belt when I was allowed and turned to face my brother. "I don't suppose you happened to work on those scrolls for a few hours last night?"

"He did indeed," Darby said, voice dry. "In fact, he used them as an excuse to get out of doing the dishes."

"As excuses go, I do find that an acceptable one," Mathi commented.

"Says the man who has never picked up a tea towel in his life."

"You lie, Bethany Aodhán. I have, in fact, picked one up at least half a dozen times in my life."

"No doubt when the servants were off on holidays," Darby mused. "Or perhaps when Beth threatened to nut you if you didn't."

"One of those comments might be accurate, but can we please concentrate on the matter at hand? Lugh, please do continue."

"It appears," he replied, the amusement dancing around his eyes fading to seriousness, "that what we have is a list of those attending a meeting, dating back decades. Doesn't say what sort of meeting, of course, because that would make things far too easy."

"Could it be related to the Ninkilim meetings?" I asked. "And could they, perhaps, even be the damn scrolls Mom stole and we could find no trace of?"

"That would depend on whether Carla—or one of her identities—really does own the house," he replied. "Right now, we can't take it for granted, despite your visions."

"There is one person who might know," Mathi said. "Loudon—he was the secretary for the Ninkilim, and responsible for all their meeting records."

Loudon Fitzgerald was an elf dealer of antiquities who was also a collector of ancient scrolls. He'd also been a friend of Mom's and at one point—before Sgott—her lover, but that hadn't stopped Mom breaking into his vault and stealing a number of scrolls. From the little we knew, they hadn't contained anything vital, but that might have Loudon attempting to cover his ass. And with good reason, given his partner in crime had been murdered not long after we'd visited Loudon.

"Hasn't he gone to ground?" Lugh asked.

"No," Mathi said. "He's currently in IIT protective custody. I'm not sure where, but it should be easy enough to find out."

"Might be better if we personally ask either your father or Sgott," I said. "Aside from your current lack of access, any search through the IIT system will likely raise alarms."

"He probably isn't on the system anyway," Mathi replied. "Not given the suspicion that the organization has been infiltrated by the Ninkilim."

"Then I'll talk to Sgott when we get home."

"And *I* will continue working on the translation," Lugh said. "It will take time, though, so do not expect immediate miracles."

"Miracles in a non-immediate manner will do just fine," I commented, amusement twitching my lips.

Lugh snorted but otherwise didn't say anything. Janis came around to take our orders for tea, coffee, and cake—the latter being a choice of plain old chocolate, lemon drizzle, or banana and walnut. I chose the latter because it at least had some fruit and nut in it, and was therefore the closest option to "healthy" breakfast cake.

By the time we'd finished, we were coming into land at Cardiff Airport. Once we'd deplaned, we found the Land

Cruiser Mathi had rented and headed out, detouring to the camping store to collect the rafts and paddles Lugh had ordered. The wasn't much traffic on the road, and it only took us a little over half an hour to reach Bridgend; from there, it was another ten minutes to the castle. Mathi pulled into the small parking area, and we all climbed out. The day had turned bitterly cold, and the sky dark and threatening. Thunder rumbled in the distance; a few seconds later, lightning flashed, briefly crawling across the base of the heavy skies.

It was a power I could call if trouble struck.

And strike it will....

I rubbed my arms and did my best to ignore the premonition. Lugh walked around to the Cruiser's trunk, dragged out all his gear, then tossed protective overalls, climbing harnesses, and head lamps to all of us. I tugged mine on, then strapped my knives over the top of my overalls. I briefly thought about tucking my phone into a pocket, but there was unlikely to be any signal once we got deeper underground anyway, so even if we did strike trouble, it wasn't going to be much use. I shoved it into my handbag, then tossed both into the trunk before Lugh slammed it closed. Darby was remaining close by, so there was little chance of anyone breaking into it without her noticing them lurking about.

Lugh swung the packs containing the ropes, anchors, and the two lashed-together inflatables over his shoulders, handed the smaller third pack containing water and snacks to Bodhrán, then motioned me to take the lead. I headed through the gate, my gaze on the ruins that dominated the hilltop. Like most fortified castles of this era, there really wasn't all that much left of it—just a few walls and what looked like the remains of a keep in the inner ward, and, in the outer, an almost complete hall sans its roof, lots of mounds, and several more well-constructed stone walls. In the middle of the stone wall that spanned the ditch surrounding the inner ward was a semicircular sluice gate, though it was missing the actual gate. The little I'd read about this place said it had been designed to allow defenders to flood the ditch with water, thereby providing the inner ward extra protection. It wasn't, however, the gate we were after. That lay on the far side of the castle. I walked around the end of the hall and past the raised wooden walkway that gave easy entry into the inner ward, then half slid down the well-grassed slope into the ditch's base. The other ditch wall was also in good condition, and although the gate remained in place here, it had been grassed over and was not likely useable. A steep embankment rose high behind it.

I scanned the stone wall carefully and, after a couple of moments, spotted the vaguely cross-shaped luminous white stone. I walked over and gave it a twist. For several heartbeats, nothing happened. Then, with a ponderous groan, a door-sized section of the stone to the right of the cross dropped away, revealing a narrow tunnel into deeper darkness. I turned on the headlamp and pointed the beam into the entrance. It wasn't doing a whole lot to raise the shadows haunting deeper within, but the little I could see suggested that while it appeared very narrow, the tunnel remained in fairly good condition.

Which, as far as these things went, wasn't always the case.

Mathi stopped beside me then glanced over at Bodhrán. "You want to check if there's anything dangerous lurking in the tunnel's depths?"

Bodhrán immediately moved past us and squatted in

front of the newly opened entrance. He placed a hand on the ground, his gaze narrowing in concentration; a second later, the faint wisp of energy spun around me. His magic, reading earth and stone.

After a few minutes, he rose and brushed the grit from his fingers. "The tunnel appears to be stable, but it's unnaturally steep in places."

"What about the lake?" I asked. "How far down is it?"

"About a kilometer, though I can't tell you much more than that. There appears to be an odd deadness in the ground surrounding that entire area."

"Unfortunately, odd dead areas and godly relics do appear to go together," Lugh said. "Can you take the lead? Beth will follow you in, and hopefully between the two of you, we'll catch any earthly or magical traps that might await."

"How long you going to be in there?" Darby asked. She was studying the tunnel's opening dubiously, though it was practically pristine compared to some of those we'd entered in the past. "Just so I've an idea when to call in the cavalry."

"An hour each way and maybe an hour at the relic site," Lugh said. "But allow four, just to be safe."

"What if some curious kids come by and decide to head in?" she asked. "Or hell, some National Trust bods?"

"If the entrance doesn't close by itself, I'll create a temp one," Bodhrán said.

Darby nodded and rubbed her arms, watching as, one by one, we all went in. Lugh was barely through when the door silently closed.

I tugged the lamp over my head and looked around. The air was damp and slightly musty, and the walls were a flecked, dark gray granite that had streaks of quartz running through it. In the bright light of the lamps, they almost looked like rivers of moonlight. Perhaps the altar I'd seen in the vision was made of quartz, although the fact it had been glowing without the caress of light suggested there might be some sort of godly or magical enhancement present.

"Ready to move out when you are," Lugh said.

I glanced at him. The tunnel was tall enough that he wasn't having to hunker down awkwardly, but there was little room either side of his shoulders. If the tunnel got any narrower deeper in, he'd be losing skin.

Bodhrán brushed his fingers lightly against the granite, 'listening' for any possible problems that he hadn't noticed earlier. We all followed in single file and, slowly but surely, the incline increased and the air grew hotter, staler. Moisture pricked the walls and gathered in small puddles on the floor, increasing the chances of a misstep, especially as the steepness of the slope increased. We were probably halfway through the tunnel when Bodhrán stopped so abruptly I almost ran into him.

"What?" I immediately said. The knives weren't reacting in any way, so whatever he'd seen or sensed wasn't magic based.

"There are ghosts ahead."

"Ghosts?" I cocked my head and listened intently. After a moment, I caught it—a low-range hum of sorrow and anger.

"Could they be related to the castle?" Mathi asked. "Prisoners who died, perhaps?"

"I don't think it ever had dungeons," Lugh said, "although I believe it was used in the eighteenth or nineteenth century as a prison."

"If the song of these ghosts is anything to go by,"

Bodhrán said, "they were sacrifices to the gods and thrown into a crevice."

"Wouldn't be the first time we've come across either in a relic hunt," Lugh said. "Can you tell how wide the crevice is?"

Bodhrán flattened his hand against the stone. "Ten feet. There appears to be a bridge over it though."

"Yeah, I wouldn't be trusting that," Mathi said. "Especially given the journey down this tunnel has been entirely too easy so far."

I scowled at him. "And *you* should know better than to put a comment like *that* out in the ether."

Amusement lurked around his lips, but he didn't otherwise reply.

"The bridge is solid as far as I can ascertain," Bodhrán said. "The problem will be the slope—it becomes close to vertical about twenty feet this side of the crevice and, with the increasing flow of water at our feet, it will be treacherous."

"Which is why we have the climbing gear," Lugh said. "Stop again just before that incline, and you can hammer in an anchor so we can abseil down."

"Will do," Bodhrán said.

We continued on, though our pace was by necessity slower now, thanks to the narrow but constant flow of water down the center of the tunnel's floor and the green slime that lined it on either side. I had good grippy boots on, but even so, kept my gaze down and watched where I was placing my feet.

Five minutes later, we stopped again. Lugh swung off his pack, retrieved an anchoring pin, and handed it to Bodhrán. Once he'd wrapped stone around it, Lugh tied a rope onto the loop at the end, tested the connection by throwing his weight back against it, then tossed the end to Bodhrán. The dark elf tied himself on, then turned and disappeared over the edge.

It really *was* steep.

"Okay," he said, a few seconds later. "I'm on the other side of the crevice and the bridge is safe."

"What of the ghosts?" I asked.

"Tried to grab me with filmy hands, but they have no power to pull you over the edge. You'll be fine."

I knew I'd be fine. It was more the thought of them touching me, sharing their misery and anger in that brief moment of connection, that I didn't want. But it wasn't like I had a choice, given that, no matter what else happened either in the tunnel or the cavern, I was the only one who could actually retrieve the harp. I tied myself onto the rope and repeated Bodhrán's movements, turning around and slowly lowering myself over the edge. The tunnel's floor wasn't vertical, but it was close enough to it. I rappelled down without problem, then crept along the crevice's narrow edge to the bridge—which was little more than a stone slab three feet wide—and hurried across, keeping my gaze on Bodhrán rather than what lay below. Ghostly fingers nevertheless rose, grabbing at my feet and calves. But it wasn't their sorrow that washed through me; it was their dread.

They weren't trying to pull us into the crevice; they were trying to warn us.

I reached the other side and sucked in a deeper breath. "The ghosts don't want us going any further."

"No, they do not." His reply was grim. "But go on we will, won't we?"

"We've no choice."

"According to Cynwrig, it wouldn't matter if you did."

I half smiled. "I am not as reckless as he makes out."

"Reckless is not a word he has used to describe you."

He helped me undo the rope, and then called out to Mathi to come down. I raised my eyebrows. "And what words has he used?"

Amusement tugged at his features. "When a friend tells you something in confidence, you do not betray it."

"Well, that's just annoying."

"Now that *is* a word he has used."

I laughed, a sound that echoed sharply around us. In the distance, something stirred. Something that felt dark and dangerous. I shivered and crossed my arms, watching as Mathi, and then Lugh, came down the rope and ran the gauntlet of those ghostly fingers.

"The slope shallows out from here," Bodhrán said. "The cavern containing the lake lies about two hundred and fifty meters further on."

"There's no more problems?" I asked

"The earth from here to there is solid, but, as I said, I cannot vouch for what awaits once we enter."

"Given it's likely that what awaits in the cavern isn't likely to be friendly, I'd better take the lead from here."

He briefly hesitated, suggesting that he, like Mathi, had been ordered to take care of me. Which was both heart-warming and annoying. I liked—loved?—Cynwrig, despite the short nature of our relationship, but I was also more than capable of looking after myself.

I drew a knife, more to feel the weight in my hand than any sense of immediate danger, and walked on, the light from the headlamp dancing across the walls, catching the quartz, making those rivers gleam and shimmer.

But the closer we got to the lake, the more those luminous rivers took on a bloody hue, and the greater the sense of danger became.

And yet, the knives and the Eye remained mute. Whatever I was sensing, it was a physical threat more than a magical one.

Up ahead, gleaming with an unearthly glow in the headlamp's bright beam, were what looked to be two Corinthian columns supporting a highly decorated lintel—or architrave, to give it its proper name. And amongst the leaves and trees carved into what I presumed was quartz, were ellul—eel-like beings with a human face and razor-sharp teeth.

Which was, no doubt, a warning of what lay waiting for us inside the cavern.

My knuckles were almost white with the force of my grip on the knife. It was tempting, so damn tempting, to simply turn around and look for another means of finding the pectoral, but time was of the essence. Not only for both of my current searches, but for me overall. I couldn't let fear waste precious seconds searching for other options when there was a perfectly good one on the table.

I forced my feet on, my gaze on the darkness beyond the gateway—a darkness that didn't lift despite the strength of the beam and my growing closeness.

And that could mean only one thing—some sort of barrier lay between the two columns.

So why weren't the knives reacting?

Did it mean the barrier, whatever it was, posed no threat to me? Most likely. But if that were the case, then the next question had to be—would it pose a problem for everyone else? Given the way these things generally worked, I was guessing the answer would be a definite yes.

I stopped a few feet away. This close, the barrier was

very evident—a thick black slab that stretched from one column to the other. No air stirred through it, and no sound crept past it.

But the ellul were waiting for me. I was sure of that, if nothing else.

I shivered and again had to fight the urge to turn around and get the hell out of here.

Bodhrán stopped beside me, his hands on his hips and his expression puzzled. "Whatever that wall is, it isn't natural."

"No, but I don't think it's magic, either. Or at least, not human magic."

"Which makes sense, given it's a godly cavern." Mathi stopped behind me. "Will your knives slip through it?"

"They should, given we haven't yet met a substance or magic that they couldn't." Even so, I raised my knife and pressed it forward. It slid into the thick darkness without effort or reaction. I hesitated, then stepped forward and pressed my arm into it. Again, no reaction, though the air beyond the slab of black crawled across my skin with a thick heaviness. Trepidation stirred anew. I quickly withdrew my arm and then the blade, and glanced at Bodhrán. "You want to give it a try?"

He reached out with his right hand, but before he could actually touch it, the wall rippled, and a thin stream of black whipped out and snapped at his fingers.

"Well," Lugh said, stopping just behind Bodhrán. "I'm guess that means the rest of us aren't getting in."

"Perhaps whatever shields this entrance simply didn't like me," Bodhrán commented.

"Unlikely, but—"

Mathi stepped past Bodhrán and reached out. Another

whip appeared, snapping with ghostly teeth at his fingers. He barely jerked them back in time.

"I guess that means I *am* going in alone." I glanced at Lugh. "You'd better show me how to inflate a raft."

He swung off his pack and began untying the rafts. "You may have to do this solo, but you will be roped to me, and you will *not* undo said rope, no matter what happens. Clear?"

"Clear," I said mildly. "Though it's not like I untied the last time we found ourselves in this sort of situation."

"Cutting is the same as untying, Beth, and ellul are not Annwfyn. They don't have limbs or claws for a start."

"No, but they've got big fucking teeth and a taste for human flesh. I can tell you now, if it's a choice between slicing the rope and letting those bastards get me, I'm slicing."

Lugh scowled but otherwise didn't comment. After handing me the small retractable plastic paddle, he ran through the details on inflating the raft, then pulled the second rope from his pack and tied it onto my harness.

"Be careful in there," he warned, with big-brother sternness. "Don't take any risks."

"It's not me you have to worry about," I replied. "It's the gods and whatever damn tricks they have up their sleeves."

"Well, if things get bad, shout and we'll haul you back."

"The wall may well cut sound, so we'll use the rope signals again."

Which was what we'd used when the Annwfyn had attacked, and for much the same reason. Those signals had saved my life, though I did still bear the scar on my foot where one of the bastards had stuck a claw through my boot. He'd lost his arm and then his life when Cynwrig had smothered him with liquid stone.

"You remember them?" he asked.

I nodded. "One tug, I'm okay; two, I'm on my way back; three, get me the fuck out of here."

"Here's hoping the latter is *not* required this time."

"From your lips to the gods' ears," I muttered, and slung the raft over my shoulder.

Then, after taking a deeper breath that did absolutely nothing to calm the growing sense of danger, I stepped through the barrier. It was thick and gelatinous, and it flowed across my body like plastic. *Liquid* plastic. My breath caught in my throat; I didn't dare breathe, lest I sucked the goo into my lungs. It seemed to take forever to get through it, which made me think that this gateway, like at least one other that we'd come across, was warping either time or distance or maybe even both.

Eventually the goo retreated from my flesh, and I was almost pushed out into a black but oddly airy-feeling space. The headlamp's light puddled on the ground at my feet but had no impact overall on the veil of night holding court. I couldn't even see the ellul, though I could hear their splashing, could feel the undercurrent of their electricity, a sensation not unlike muted lightning.

I shivered and tugged on the rope to let Lugh know I was through and safe, then dug the Eye from under my protective suit. The fact that neither it nor the knife were currently pulsing with life suggested no harmful magic lay in this place, but there was obviously something here. Otherwise, the headlamp would not be so ineffectual.

The Eye pulsed at my touch, and I briefly closed my eyes, imagining the darkness as a thick wall of magic and the knife's light slicing through it, shattering it. I had no idea if it would work, but I was now using the triune in ways none of my ancestors ever had. Besides, I had nothing to lose by trying.

The Eye pulsed again, and this time, the knife responded. Just as I'd envisaged, bright, blue-white light shot down the blade and leapt from its tip; it hit the black screen a few feet in front of me and crawled across its blanket. Everywhere it touched, it burned. A low hum began to fill the air and then, with a soft boom, the blanket exploded. As black soot began to rain around me, the lightning retreated back into the blade, and the headlamp finally revealed what really lay ahead. The cavern was high and wide, with a forest of stalactites hanging from the ceiling. There were stalagmites here, too, but they ringed the small island that lay at the very heart of the cavern and provided an almost impregnable fence—one perhaps designed to keep the ellul out. The altar sat proudly on the island's crest, gleaming like moonlight in the wash of the headlamp's light. I couldn't see the harp from where I stood but I could hear it. Its music was sharp and unpleasant and seemed to rise and fall in time with the electric hum of the eels.

Did the fact it was active mean Carla was currently using the blade? From what Beira had said, that seemed likely.

The dark span of water between me and that island practically seethed with the bastards. Right now, their movements were so damn fierce that waves lapped the shore of both the island and the small strip of rock on which I stood.

I really, *really*, did not want to get into the water. Aside from the fact there were so damn many of the sharp-faced fucking things, their teeth were long enough—sharp enough—to puncture the raft. I doubted I'd be able to oar across quickly enough to reach the island if that did happen, so maybe I needed to call on a little extra help....

I'd used the air to get myself out of trouble more than once already, so there was no real reason why I couldn't use it here to get me across to that island. I reached out with my free hand and tried to create a leash of thick air.

Except, it didn't respond.

Didn't do anything more than stir sluggishly around my fingertips.

I swore softly. Why couldn't things be fucking easy for a change?

Because there would be no godly fun to be had if they were...

Fuck the gods and their fucking games.

I angrily tugged the raft from my shoulder and followed Lugh's instructions. Once it was inflated, I placed it in the water, then carefully stepped into it. The ellul immediately swarmed, snapping and tearing at the PVC, ripping into the material with their teeth. Soft hissing began to fill the air. I swore again, shoved my knife into its sheath, then unfolded the oar and paddled as fast as I could.

It wasn't enough. It was never going to be enough.

The elluls' movements became frantic, the water a mass of rolling, writhing bodies that climbed over each other in their desperation to get at me. One leapt out of the water and came straight at me, its mouth agape, teeth gleaming sharply. I whacked it away with the oar, but more were now leaping, both into the boat and straight at me. I drew a knife and plunged it into the head of the eel tearing into my boot, then lashed backward as another savaged my shoulder. More ellul flopped into the now sinking raft, and the island remained a good twenty feet away. I needed to do something, and now.

Before I could, the raft tipped over, plunging me into the thick, bitterly cold water.

CHAPTER

NINE

They swarmed me, tearing at my clothes, my skin, my hair, as I sank like a stone into the soup. I dropped the oar I was still holding, then drew my other knife and kicked toward the surface. The headlamp's light gleamed off the slick black bodies that slithered and roiled around me, shining into red eyes lit with hunger and desperation. Panic surged, but I did my best to contain it and broke the surface, gasping for air. The ellul had formed an impregnable fortress of teeth and determination around me. I spun in the water, slashing with my knives, trying to keep the bastards at bay, but they were also underneath me, biting me, tearing at my boots and down into flesh.

If I didn't get out of this water, I was dead.

But with the air refusing to answer my call, I either had to try to force my way through the writhing wall of flesh that surrounded me or call to the storm that now raged in the outside world. A storm I could feel even in this place of deadness. I had no idea if it would or could answer; no idea if it would even be able to breach the defenses of this place, wherever this place actually was. As a general rule, light-

224

ning couldn't strike deep into the heart of the earth, instead discharging along the surface of the ground. At best, it vaporized moisture from the ground, causing small craters or even explosions. A kilometer deep into the earth might well be beyond a god's power, let alone a godling's....

In desperation, I reached for the stream of energy that danced through the skies high above.

It answered, and with such power that it smashed a hole through the cavern roof, sending a smoldering rain of burning rock blasting through the cavern as it punched down into the water, close to where I bobbed. Fiery fingers of deadly light spread out from the impact point, a net of power that surrounded me, not touching me, but sizzling everything within a twenty-foot radius.

A sea of dead ellul floated to the surface, their red eyes staring unseeingly up at the cavern's ceiling and the stink of burned fish coating the air and my throat. But there were more beyond that protective circle, more that slid through the deeper portions of the water, where the lightning couldn't reach. Waiting, watching, ready to attack.

As the fingers of fiery heat began to dissipate, I sheathed my knives and swam, as fast as I could, for the shore. Thankfully, the ring of energy moved with me, protecting me even as it retracted closer and closer to my body. The ellul weren't attacking me yet, but the wash of their movements was once again increasing. They weren't stupid; they were waiting for the ring to fade before they started tearing into me again.

My fingers scraped stone. Relief surged, but I wasn't clear yet. I pushed upright and ran on, lifting my knees high above the water in a vague effort to increase my pace, my eyes on the stalagmites that lined the shore and the promise of protection beyond them.

Something snapped at my leg; the lightning flickered, and the eel screamed, a sharp sound that was swiftly silenced. The ring might be close to extinction now, but what remained still held power. I drew my knives again and ran on. The water fell from my knees to my calves, then my ankles, and then I was racing up the stone shore toward the stalagmites.

The lightning didn't follow. I was on my own.

Water splashed behind me, then a sleek body hit the stones to my left and slithered toward me. I didn't stop. I ran on. I was close now, so close, to safety....

More bodies slapped onto stone. Desperation spurted through me, and I leapt high over the barrier, landing awkwardly on the other side and stumbling forward for several steps before finding my balance and turning around.

The ellul were slithering along the stalagmites, looking for a way in and not finding it.

The relief that surged was so damn fierce, my legs went from underneath me. I dropped to the ground, sobbing and shaking, all the while knowing it was not over yet. I would have to do it all over again to get out of here.

That's when I remembered the rope. My gaze darted down; it was still attached, but did it remain in one piece? I rose, grabbed the rope, and reeled it in. Slowly, ever so slowly, it rose from the depths of the dark water. Despite everything, it remained intact. Hope of survival remained... if Lugh could reel in the rope fast enough, and if I was able to call down the lightning one more time.

While the force of it hadn't flowed through me this time —I think for the very first time—weariness still ate at me. I tugged on the rope once to let my brother know I was okay —or as okay as you could be when you were bleeding from a dozen different bites—and then let it fall back into the water. The ellul ignored it. Maybe they only wanted flesh.

I shivered, spun on my heel, and walked up the rest of the hill to the altar. It was pretty basic in construction: a square stone base that bore no inscriptions, with a top—or mensa, I thought its official name was—that was a single piece of thick stone. Both were made of a quartz-like material that flooded the immediate area with its gently luminescent light. The harp lay in a nook in the base of the mensa, its strings still and its music no longer crawling through the air. Whether that was in response to my presence or an indication that our thief wasn't currently using the pectoral, I couldn't really say.

I walked around the altar's base, looking for anything that might set off a secondary trap. Nothing. Both the knives and the Eye remained silent, but that wasn't a guarantee the area was problem free, given they'd basically been mute throughout this whole fucking ordeal.

After a slight hesitation, I drew the blade and placed it flat onto the surface of the mensa. Again, no reaction. I walked around to the rear and squatted in front of the small, and surprisingly simple, golden harp. I warily touched it with the knife's tip. Another big fat nothing.

Could it really be this damn easy?

I doubted it. I really did. But maybe Aamon figured if you survived the ellul, you were probably deserving of a prize. Or maybe it was something simpler—with the pectoral thrown into the gaming ring by its god, the magic protecting this place was no longer active.

I'd find out soon enough which one was true.

I sheathed one knife, then, after a rather long hesitation, carefully brushed the top of the harp with my fingers. Its strings briefly rippled, though no music sounded. I glanced up sharply, scanning the shadows and the ellul that still milled beyond the stalagmite fence. No magic stirred. No new threat appeared.

Which was really disconcerting.

I picked up the harp, then rose, my gaze darting around, still awaiting a response, my tension ramping rather than easing when nothing came. But maybe Aamon didn't think it necessary when there was still the swarm of ellul to get through.

I unzipped my protective suit, tucked the harp underneath my sweater, then did up the suit again. Now all I had to do was get out of here.

I took another of those deep breaths that did absolutely nothing to ease my tension or the rising tide of fear and slowly walked back down the hill, the rope a wet snake that trailed behind me. The closer I got to the stalagmite fence, the more frantic the ellul became, but they didn't try to leap over it. Which, considering the height some of them had gained leaping out of the water, was surprising. Maybe there was more to the fence line than what I was seeing.

I stopped close, wound up the rope, and clipped it onto my harness. The last thing I needed when Lugh was hauling me back to safety was the trailing ends getting caught in the damn rocks.

With all that done, I raised my face to the ceiling I'd shattered and once again reached for the power that still raged in the world beyond. As lightning punched through the ceiling, I tugged three times on the rope, quickly leapt onto the nearest stalagmite, and then jumped toward the water. The rope snapped taut, and I was pulled forward hard, body slamming into the black soup, and instinctively gasped in shock. Water rushed into my mouth, leaving me coughing and spluttering and barely able to keep my face and shoulders above the water. I swore and turned onto my left side so I could breathe a little easier. The ellul swarmed, but lightning now lit the water around me, striking at the bastards as they tried to reach me. A stinking trail of half-cindered ellul filled my wake. Then I was being pulled up the rocky shore and back through the thick black wall.

This time the plastic seemed all too happy to let me pass unhindered, and I slid to a halt at my brother's feet.

"Fucking hell, Beth, what happened in there?" He knelt beside me, gaze scanning me frantically, concern deepening. "You're wet and covered in blood."

"It's not as bad as it looks."

"I rather suspect that's another of your understatements." Mathi's voice was dry. "Especially since you're missing a boot, and your foot looks a mess."

"It is? It does?"

I pushed up into a sitting position; Lugh immediately pressed a leg against my back, preventing me from falling back. The bottom half of my boot was indeed missing, but all my toes were where they should be, and while there were a couple of deepish cuts, they obviously hadn't hit anything vital, given I could still wiggle everything.

"Well," I said, "at least this time there isn't a claw sticking out of it."

"I take it that happened in the past?" Bodhrán asked, his expression a mix of amusement and disbelief.

"She does have a habit of getting a little too close to pointy deadly things," Mathi said. "Did you at least find the harp?"

"I did. It's tucked under the suit."

"Good. Then I suggest we get out of here, just in case those ellul or whatever other magic protects that place decides it really needs the harp back." Mathi hesitated, his gaze skimming down to my foot again. "You able to walk?"

I nodded. In truth, my feet—and the rest of me—were so damn cold I really wasn't feeling much in the way of pain. The coverall should have protected me to some extent from my plunge into the lake, but multiple teeth tearing into it, trying to get at my flesh, meant I was more than a little wet underneath it.

"No walking until I at least treat your foot," Lugh growled, then swung off his pack and retrieved a small medical kit.

I patiently waited while he washed, cleaned, and bandaged my foot before inspecting the various other bite sites and treating the worst of them. Once that was done, he and Mathi caught my elbows and helped me rise. I tentatively put weight onto my foot; pain slithered up my limb, but it was manageable.

Whether I'd still think that by the time I got out of here was another matter entirely.

Lugh untied the rope, wound it up and stashed it back into his pack, then motioned Bodhrán to take the lead again, with me sandwiched between Mathi and Lugh. We made it back to the bridge without incident, and while the field of ghostly fingers reappeared, their murmurings were filled with relief—which only made me wonder how many people had come seeking the pectoral in the past and failed. If the ghosts knew, they weren't saying.

Bodhrán and Mathi went up the steep incline first, then Lugh roped me on, and the two men hauled me up. Which was good, because weariness now pulsed through me, and I really doubted I would have had the strength to physically haul my ass anywhere right now. It was becoming an effort to even walk.

Thankfully, the journey to the surface didn't really take all that long. As the door once again opened, triggered by who knew what, we stripped off our overalls and climbing harnesses and handed them back to Lugh. Once he'd stuffed them into the packs, we headed out.

Darby waited in the rain on the other side of the tunnel's entrance, her coat drawn tightly around her body and face, and thick gloves on hands that held a takeout cup. My stomach rumbled a reminder that I hadn't had anything to eat that morning aside from cake, and that was probably half the reason why I felt so weary.

Darby straightened as I limped out, her relief turning to consternation. "What the hell have you done to yourself? And why are you the only one who is not only wet but injured?"

"I was the only one who got into the cavern. There were ellul with sharp teeth."

"Of course there were, because why fucking not?" She shook her head and rose. "Let's get you out of this rain so I can patch you up."

I nodded and limped after her. Mathi and Lugh basically carried me up the embankment, but by the time we reached the car, I was shivering. A delayed reaction to what had happened more than the bitterness in the air, I suspected.

Mathi opened the Cruiser's tailgate, and I sat down, then eased back on my butt so that my feet weren't dangling close to the ground, making it easier for Darby to treat them.

"Here," she said, handing me the coffee. "Drink the rest of that—it'll help with the shakes until I can chase the chill from your skin. Lugh and Mathi can go grab us all a fresh cup."

"And food. *Hot* food," I said. "I am starving."

"It is indeed a miracle you're still functioning," Darby commented. "It usually takes several bacon butties and a number of chocolate bars to get you through something *that* intense."

She wasn't talking about the expedition. She was talking about me, Cynwrig, and last night. I might not have said anything, but she'd obviously been picking up some telltale vibes.

"Bacon butties and plane kitchens are never a good combination," Mathi said, his voice dry but bedevilment dancing in his eyes. "And if you had indeed spent less time in—"

"Never going to happen," I cut in evenly. "I tried. Sadly, I am not that strong."

"Oh, you are, as evidenced by the fact you've been resisting my magnificence for months now."

I rolled my eyes, and Darby snorted.

"I once again have the strangest feeling I'm missing a vital part of the conversation here," Lugh said, his gaze darting between the three of us. "And it's getting very annoying."

Darby patted his arm. "I'll explain later. Right now, you need to get our girl food and tea, or she will be unbearably cranky on the way home."

"That is a truth I cannot deny," I said solemnly.

Lugh rolled his eyes. "Fine. We go. Bodhrán, keep an eye out, just in case there's a belated response from the gods to our theft."

The dark elf nodded and moved to the front of the Cruiser, where the ground was higher.

Darby pressed her hands against my temples, closing her eyes as her magic surged through and around me. After a few minutes, she grunted, and I both saw and felt her relief.

"Most of the bites are fairly minor. Your foot and your overall tiredness are probably the worst of it."

"Despite what you're thinking, most of the weariness comes from calling lightning into the cavern."

"I did wonder if those sudden cracks of lightning were you, but I still doubt they're the entire reason for said weariness." Amusement danced through her gaze. "So tell me, does the liminal space live up to its reputation?"

"I think it would depend on the man or woman you were with but... yes indeed."

"Ha. Excellent. Though I would suggest next time you leave a little more time to sleep."

"Not going to happen. Not until we prove that dream wrong." My foot began to tingle as her healing heat ran down to it. "Have you had any luck tracking down drugs that can help extend brain survival?"

"Have you had any luck getting a tracker?" she countered.

I half smiled. "Haven't exactly had the time."

"Then do so, because if I can't find something suitable, then finding you in time becomes even more urgent."

"Fine. I will."

She grumbled a soft, "You'd better," then added in a more normal tone, "Now, climb out of those wet things before the men get back and you get a chill. I take it you did bring fresh clothes, given you were more than aware there was water involved in this hunt."

I smiled and reached for my overnight bag. "I did indeed."

"Good. What about the harp? Did you get it?"

"I did." I unzipped my coat and tugged it out from under my sweater. "It's plainer than what I expected."

"What is?" she said with a frown. "Because I'm not seeing anything."

"Really?" I frowned at the harp that was plain as day for me. "It's right here. Look—"

I grabbed her hand and pressed it against the harp. Her fingers went straight through it.

"Well, fuck," I said. "That's inconvenient."

"Not really," she said. "If no one but a god or a godling can see it, then no one but a god or godling can steal it."

Aasym had told me that humanity could not take what is little more than air, but I hadn't realized it'd meant it literally. "It's still damn annoying."

"Well, I daresay that comes with the territory when dealing with the gods."

That was a truth I could not deny. I placed the harp beside me, quickly stripped off my clothes, and then redressed. When Lugh and Mathi had returned with coffee and toasties for us all, I repeated the process with the harp. None of them could see or touch it. Lugh tossed me a small drawstring bag to put it in, and then, once Mathi had rung his pilot to tell him to ready the plane and file the flight details, we climbed into the Cruiser and headed back to the airport. There was a slight delay in boarding, but we were in the air within the hour and back in Deva by midafternoon.

Mathi dropped me off at the lane, but I'd barely gotten through the back door when the Eye burned to life. Once again, there was a vision to be had.

I hurried down the corridor, greeting the bar staff as I passed them, and raced up the stairs. Ingrid was talking to someone in the office, but I didn't stop, hurrying on up to my floor, then over to the loft ladder. I pressed the button to unfold it, paced as I waited for it to come down, and then clambered up. I tossed my purse and the bag containing the harp onto the sofa, then ran down to the end of the room to retrieve the Codex. Once I was comfortable, I placed the knives and the Eye onto the Codex and said, "Show me."

Instantly, I was swept away.

You've done the inventory? came the all too familiar voice of the Ninkilim leader.

Indeed, I have, Carla replied. *It is not good news.*

I thought you had nothing of import stored there.

I forgot the scrolls were there.

What scrolls? It was flatly said, and yet his fury was almost smothering.

The ones the witch's mother stole.

I guessed *that* answered the question as to whether the scrolls were the ones Mom had stolen, but how had *they* retrieved them from her? Had they forced the location out of her before they'd brought a fucking tunnel down on top of her? Or had some sort of magical tracker been placed on them? The latter would certainly explain the puff of smoke I'd seen when I'd touched them with the knife.

Why in the gods' names would you store them there? came the snapped reply.

With the witch's spawn wandering about finding relics willy-nilly, it was as safe as anywhere else. She paused. *Any progress on our thief? I doubt it's a coincidence he is hitting all of my residences, be they old or new.*

His identity remains unknown, but the dark elves are currently tracking down the whereabouts of Jarvil Maehdon's immediate kin, which leads me to suspect one of them might be involved. You should not have killed the man.

It was an accident.

You plunged your knife into his heart. The man's voice was dry. *That can hardly be called an accident.*

He moved, she replied, with absolutely no concern or remorse evident. *It matters not, because his death was listed as natural. There were no witnesses to gainsay that.*

Except for his grandson—he saw you coming out of the house, remember.

That kid? She snorted. *Even Jarvil didn't have a very high opinion of him.*

It is never wise to misjudge a Myrkálfar, Brídín, even one so young.

Trust me, they are no different to any man, be he Ljósálfar, shifter, or human. You are all led by your cocks rather than your brains.

Not all of us.

Another snort, this time sharper. *You may believe that if you wish, but we both know it is my ability to appease needs that would horrify your more genteel lovers that you value above all else.*

Indeed, but as I have said, do not ever believe I won't destroy you if it comes down to it.

How can I forget when your insurance lies in my head?

A statement that explained her comment in an earlier vision that capture would mean her death. He'd obviously implanted something. If we ever *did* find her, we'd have to work damn fast before she was neutralized.

To bring this conversation back on point, she added, *neither he nor anyone else will find me. I wasn't wearing my true form—or indeed, a form anyone from the council would recognize.*

Then how is our thief so successfully targeting all that you own?

Perhaps Jarvil left an "open in case of death" letter. He was the type.

Didn't you order him to say nothing about your presence in his life?

Of course, but it is impossible to cover every scenario. Even godly artifacts do have their limitations, you know. Besides, the blade's effectiveness does wane over time.

You should have dealt with the man before he was able to leave a message, if that is indeed what has happened.

I was dealing with him, she retorted. *He moved, as I said. But none of this would have been a problem if your lot did their fucking job and tracked the bastard down.*

You cannot expect the IIT to achieve what even the Myrkálfar cannot in this situation. Our connections pale in comparison to their network.

Inner alarms started to ring. That statement suggested we weren't dealing with just one or two moles in the organization, but rather someone much higher up in the ranks.

Carla sniffed. It was an unimpressed sound. *Have you placed a tracer on the witch and Mathi?*

Mathi has pulled the tracers out of his vehicles, but our inside source remains on the witch.

Inside source indeed. Anger surged, and while it was mostly aimed at Eljin for the betrayal, I could not deny the fact that, had I trusted the Eye's judgement rather than allowing my hormones to hold sway, I would not have gotten myself into this situation in the first place.

And she remains unaware?

He suspects not, given the manner of her sudden retreat at their last meeting.

Then perhaps he needs to play it cautiously for the next few days.

He could play it as cautiously as he wanted, because he

was *not* going to get any further chances to drug me. The next time he saw me, it would be with the full backup of my brother and Mathi, and he *would* tell us who'd employed him, or he *would* pay the price.

I might not want to unleash the inner darkness, but I was willing to make an exception in his case.

Or we can just get rid of her. Easier by far.

We dare not. Not until we have located the Harpē.

She becomes more dangerous by the day. I think it best—

You're not paid to think, dearest Brídín, and you will—

The rest of his statement was lost as the Eye pulsed sharply and ripped me from the vision. A heartbeat later, I realized why.

The building's bright song had darkened. Eljin was in the building, making his way up the first set of stairs.

I had a couple of minutes, if that, to get the hell out of here. Because if I saw him, he would know I suspected him. I wasn't a good liar—that had been proven time and again —and while I was more than capable of defending myself from him, I didn't want to do so until I was ready.

After shoving everything but the Codex into my purse, I jumped up and ran down to the skylight at the far end of the room. With Eljin now on the second floor and making his way around to the stairs leading up to the living area, I really didn't have time to retract the loft ladder—it was too damn slow and wasn't exactly quiet. If I wanted to avoid him, I really only had one option.

Well, two if I used the Bruadar bracelet, but I wasn't about to risk Cynwrig being busy and unable to accept the call.

The skylight's lock had been broken for years now, and while I kept meaning to fix it, I hadn't, so it remained held in place by a long but sturdy piece of wire. Once I'd tucked the Codex back into its hidey-hole, I undid the wire, then stepped onto the footstool and pushed the skylight all the way open. Cool air rushed in, thick with the warning to hurry—a warning the building's song echoed. I quickly grabbed the sides of the skylight and half jumped, half wiggled my ass onto the roof.

He was in my living space, making his way toward the loft ladder.

I carefully shifted my position on the roof, trying not to make much in the way of sound, then dragged up the rest of the wire and closed the skylight. He'd reached the ladder....

"Bethany?" he called up. "You up there?"

Yes, I am, but you won't fucking find me if I can at all help it.

I found a slightly raised copper slate nail, wound the wire around it a couple of times, then pulled it back across the window and found another raised nail. The wire barely reached it, but it only needed to hold for a few minutes. Eljin had never been into the loft, so in all likelihood he wouldn't even question the wire's presence. The other skylights were locked, and the key was on the keyring in my purse.

I cautiously slid back toward the ridgeline to ensure I was out of sight even if he did step onto the footstool, then pulled out my phone. After turning the sound all the way down, I sent an urgent text to Mathi.

Can you get back here ASAP? Eljin is here, looking for me.

The building's music warned he was now in the loft, but pausing under each skylight. Checking them, obviously. But why he'd do that when— I stopped. If he'd been mining my memories via the drug, he'd be aware that I'd climbed out on the rooftop more than once. And if he was checking them, it basically confirmed what Carla had said in the vision. The bit that confused me was the fact that, as a Tàileach pixie, he only had to connect to the building's song, and it would tell him where I was. So why hadn't he done that? It certainly would have been my first move had our positions been reversed.

A message flashed up onto the phone's screen. *Running down the lane now. Where are you?*

If he was in the lane, it meant he'd already been on his way back here. But why? What had happened now?

On the roof, I sent back.

I'll shout out when he's contained.

Contained, not dead, I sent back.

A dead man can tell no tales, he replied. He had to be using voice command to reply, because while Mathi had many talents, running and texting wasn't one of them. *And we need him to be very verbose right now.*

I can pixie him.

He's likely protected against that. In building now, coming up.

And Eljin was now standing under the broken skylight. It opened fractionally, and I tensed. The skylight briefly lowered, then was hit again, this time with greater force. The wire slipped fractionally; it wouldn't take too much more effort to break either it or the skylight.

He obviously knew I was up here, even though I hadn't felt him slip into the building's song. Although in truth, he probably didn't need to, given how loudly it was vibrating with Mathi's presence. If I didn't know better, I would have said she was urging him on.

But why was Eljin so determined to open the skylight? For all Mathi knew, I'd given Eljin permission to be in my loft. Was it confirmation that Carla had won her boss over and they now wanted to be rid of me? Or had she gone against his orders, and told Eljin to come here and deal with me?

Or was he here for an entirely different reason altogether?

I'd theorized—even hoped, if only because it meant that my judgement of men had at least improved a little over the years—that he'd been working under the influence of Carla and the blade. But if he was here without her knowledge or orders, then that hope was well and truly stomped on.

A third blow hit the skylight, and it crashed open, making a godawful noise in the process. The upper half of his body appeared, his shoulder muscles straining the limitations of his shirt as he hauled himself up onto the roof. Any second now, he would turn and see me; I had no idea what he intended and no desire to find out. The urge to run was fierce, the urge to grab him with the wind and fling him far, far away was even fiercer, but I resisted both and called to a knife instead. As he turned toward me, I flipped the knife over and hit him hard. The knife's sharp blade caused me no damage, but the hilt hit with a satisfying thud. He slumped back, and an audible grunt rose from below. Mathi had obviously caught him before he could hit the floor.

The inner bitch couldn't help but whisper, *Shame, that.*

"You got anything around here to bind the bastard with?" Mathi asked.

"Only the wire attached to the skylight."

"That'll do."

I slid carefully down, unwound the wire from both nails, then checked both Mathi and Eljin were clear before dropping through the skylight. After pulling it closed, I sliced the wire away from the latch and walked down to

Mathi, who now stood midway down the room. Eljin lay face down at his feet.

"Thanks for the rescue." I handed him the wire. "But how come you were already on your way back?"

"Got a message from Dawson. The woman Eljin met was not his sister."

The anger that swept through me was so fierce, lightning rolled down the knife's blade and struck angrily at the unconscious man. I pulled it back quickly enough that it didn't physically touch him, but the anger remained within, a festering darkness that wanted satisfaction.

I stuck the knife back into my purse and rubbed my arms. "Then who is she? Do we think it was Carla in disguise?"

"It wasn't Carla. Her name is Camille Allard, and she's married to one René Allard. They have no children, and she's definitely not a decorator."

I stared at him for a second, not quite understanding. "Where does Eljin fit in, then? Are they having an affair?"

Amusement stirred through his expression. "Is tea or chocolate deprivation affecting your thought processes right now? Eljin here is René."

"But—" I waved a hand. "How? Even if he did usurp the identity of the Eljin in that article, the age difference is vast. How the hell could he have gotten around that?"

"Dawson's still digging, but it's easy enough to alter records if you have the money and the right forgery contacts."

"Speaking from experience, are we?"

"Not personal experience, no."

He roughly pulled Eljin's—I really couldn't think of him as René right now—arms behind his back, and quickly bound his thumbs together. When that was done, he rolled him onto his side, bent him in the middle, and used the remaining length of wire to bind his thumbs to his ankles. Eljin wasn't going anywhere without our help.

"Is the wife aware of what he's doing?" I asked. "Did Dawson speak to her?"

"He spoke to people in the know over there. René and Camille run a discreet but very profitable information collecting service."

"But..." I repeated, my mind refusing to compute the whole situation. "What woman in their right mind allows their husband to long-term fuck another?"

"One who understands it's nothing but business. Apparently, sex is their preferred means of mining information, because both René and Camille are dream thieves."

I nodded. "He did tell me he could get a sense of a person's past, their dreams, and their motivations, but I just hadn't followed it through to a logical conclusion. He did say he found me extremely difficult to read."

"Which is no doubt why they resorted to drugging you."

"No doubt." I paused. "I take it their fees are rather high?"

"According to Dawson, their fees start out steep and rise to exorbitant, depending on engagement time and the information required."

While I was well aware that sex had been used as a means of stealing information for centuries, I'd never expected it to be used against *me*. Fury stirred anew, and lightning danced across my fingertips; it was all I could do *not* to unleash. Although, given he remained unconscious, unleashing now wouldn't have been half as much fun.

I sucked in a breath and fought for calm. "I'm obviously

a long-term target, which means we're dealing with someone with very deep pockets."

"I think it more likely we're dealing with an overall body of someones, especially if, as we suspect, his employers are connected to the Ninkilim." He rose and met my gaze. "I contacted Cynwrig. He's sending Bodhrán here to pick up Eljin once we have finished questioning him."

"I'm not sure *that* is the best option right now. Not given Cynwrig's penchant for disappearing people."

Mathi smiled. "Then you had best talk to him, because the man is, rather understandably, furious on your behalf."

"*I'm* furious on my behalf, but that doesn't mean I get to kill the bastard." I lightly toed the still unconscious man and saw his muscles tense slightly. He was waking.

"Oh, Cynwrig doesn't intend to kill him." Mathi paused. "Well, I don't think he does. But tucking the man deep underground for a century or two? More than possible."

I snorted but didn't reply as Eljin continued to wake. Though his eyes didn't open, the small movements of hands and legs suggested he was testing the strength of his bindings.

"You're bound with wire," I said. "You won't be getting free unless I release you."

"And you can certainly forget the idea of any sort of freedom in the mid to long term," Mathi added.

"What the hell is going on, Beth?" He tried to roll onto his back—which would have been very uncomfortable, given how he was tied—but Mathi planted a foot in the middle of his spine and kept him still. "Why have you bound me like this? I've done nothing—"

"Nothing except lie about who you really are and why you're really here." I stepped forward and touched his neck.

The lightning sparking from my fingertips brushed the skin, and he tensed briefly. Though it was tempting to let that lightning dance across his body, I once again resisted and reached for my pixie magic instead. "You will answer every question we ask, you will not shout for help, and you will make no attempt to escape."

The magic surged through me, then stopped dead at the point where my fingers touched his skin. It didn't run into him; it certainly didn't command him.

Either he was wearing some sort of protection against my magic, as Mathi had suggested, or there was elf in his background somewhere. "Where is it, Eljin?"

"Where is what?" His confusion looked real, but then, this was a man for whom deceit was apparently second nature. "Beth, this prank is really getting out of hand. Please, just—"

"*René*," I cut in. "The game is up. You have one chance, and one chance only, to come clean with us. Where is the charm protecting you from my magic?"

"There is no charm. I'm quarter elf." Amusement touched his lips, though his eyes were cold. Calculating. "If you don't release me, I *will* yell for help."

"Feel free," I said. "I pay the wages of those downstairs, so they'll be more inclined to listen to me than you. Besides, we both know that if you *were* taken into IIT custody, you wouldn't hold on to life for very long. Your employers aren't going to risk any sort of useful information leaving your lips, and Carla is very adept at killing those held in high security, having already killed four prisoners."

His gaze narrowed. "You lie."

"The one thing Beth cannot do is lie successfully," Mathi said. "We not only know your identity, René, but we also know the woman you met in London this weekend is in fact your wife rather than your sister. We know the business you both run. What we don't know is who employed you to steal Bethany's memories."

"If you've hurt Camille—"

"You'll what? Hurt us? Kill us?" I snorted. "In case it's escaped your notice, you're trussed up tighter than a duck's ass. You can't help yourself, let alone her. Now answer the goddamn question."

"Or what? You'll kill me?" he echoed. "As you've already noted, that's probably my fate anyway."

"At least with us, you have a chance of life after imprisonment, depending, of course, on what happens when Lugh gets wind of the situation. He's rather protective of his little sister, in case you never realized it."

He didn't immediately reply, his gaze sweeping the two of us. There was little in his expression to give away his thoughts. "Carla hired me."

"Carla is a general, not the leader. We want *his* name."

"Well, I can't give it to you."

"Can't? Or won't?" I asked.

"Both."

The fury rose again, and before I realized what I was doing, the wind swept him up from the floor and flung him back against the wall with enough force to send plaster dust spiraling through the air. I wanted to do more. I wanted to rip the air from his lungs and leave him gasping. Wanted to... I sucked in a breath and forced the black tide back down.

This wasn't who I was, even if it was who my father wanted me to be. Although it did make me wonder, if I ever *did* go down that path, would the pixie blood curse still apply? Maybe I needed to ask someone, just in case temptation ever overwhelmed restraint.

I eased the wind's pressure a fraction but didn't actually release him, leaving him dangling halfway up the wall, head facing down. The man *had* been drugging me, after all. He deserved a little discomfort.

"In case you have forgotten," I said, my voice surprisingly even, "I can control the air—the same air that you're currently breathing. If you want to keep on doing so, you might want to start answering questions."

"I can't tell what I don't know, Bethany, however much you might wish otherwise. I never know the identity of my employer. It is safer for them; safer for me."

"What about Camille?" Mathi's voice was flat, which—to anyone who really knew him—was Mathi at his most dangerous. "If she handles the invoicing while you are out on contract, she must have access to detailed financial and identity records."

Eljin snorted. "You, more than anyone, Mathi, should know how these types of transactions run—burner phones, payments diverted through various shell companies, no direct contact with the contractor."

I crossed my arms, not believing him for a second. "Every high-priced whore has a pimp who—"

"I'm *not* a whore," he cut in angrily.

"Well, the definition of a whore is someone who engages in sex for payment," I drawled. "Is that not what you were doing with me?"

"A whore is someone who engages in temporary liaisons. I am more a professional escort—"

"Who uses sex if necessary to get the information." I snorted. "How do you and Carla interact, then? I know she was the one who arranged to have the drug you were using on me made."

"Carla made the initial contract approach and provides my orders, but I've never met her, either in France or here in the UK."

"Then how were you giving her the information you dragged from my mind?"

"I wasn't—"

"Just give me a straight fucking answer," I cut in, that fierce wave of anger sweeping through me again. "Or gods help me, I will force it from you."

He didn't answer. Not immediately. Then Mathi lightly touched my arm, and I realized I was dragging the air away from Eljin—my brain was currently refusing to think of him as René—making it impossible for him to breathe, let alone speak.

I swore, pushed the anger down, and released him. He took several great gulping gasps of air and looked pale. Frightened, even, if only very briefly.

Satisfaction slipped through me, a small snake I needed to be very, very wary of.

"Jarvil," he eventually gasped. "It was all done through Jarvil Maehdon."

My gaze shot to Mathi's. "Jarvil was a *broker*?"

"Of antiquities, yes. I was unaware he also brokered services."

"He doesn't," Eljin said, still battling for air. "I purchased small antiquities from him that contained either instructions or the drug. I have no idea if *his* contact was Carla, so if you want answers, you need to talk to him. Now, please, can you put me right way up? It's becoming rather uncomfortable."

"Good," was my only response to his plea. "How, then, were you sending the information you stole?"

"Same method, basically. I simply returned the item for a refund."

I glanced at Mathi, my eyebrows raised in silent question.

"An old but reliable method," he said. "Especially in an age where everything is done on the phone or online."

I returned my gaze to Eljin. "I take it that box you were shoving into your bedside drawer when I arrived at your place the other day was one of your so-called purchases?"

"Yes—"

"Then you must have gotten it from someone else—Carla killed Jarvil at least a week ago."

He blinked. "Why would she do that? She was fucking the man."

"An interesting comment, given you claim never to have met the woman in the UK," Mathi commented.

"No, but I did meet Jarvil on a regular basis at his shop and scanned him on several occasions." He smiled, though it held little warmth. "It always pays to uncover what you can about your employer's minions, just in case things go ass up."

"Does that mean you saw Carla's true form via his thoughts?" Mathi asked.

"No. I only know the form she presented to Jarvil."

"And that was?"

"Carla Wilson."

Surprise flitted through me. For some reason, I'd been expecting her to use a different surname with Jarvil, especially given there were multiple arrest warrants out for that identity. But maybe Jarvil had valued sex with her more than he had the law. He was a dark elf, after all, and while they were generally far more law abiding than Ljósálfar elves, they did basically own the black market.

Or was I being unfair to a dead man? Carla possessed a blade that allowed her to control the actions of anyone whose flesh it tasted, so maybe she *wasn't* as busy in the bedroom as we were all presuming. Maybe her "conquests" were fed the belief of sex rather than the actuality.

A sudden change in the building's song caught my attention. I slipped into the golden rivers and studied the approaching movement; it was light, and spoke of earth and stone.

I glanced at Mathi. "I think Bodhrán is here."

"I'll go get him."

As Mathi turned and strode toward the loft ladder, Eljin said, "Who is Bodhrán?"

"The Myrkálfar coming to collect your ass." I approached him, stopping when only a few feet separated us. "You really should have broken the contract and walked away the minute you discovered who Cynwrig was, Eljin."

He snorted. "Why? Do you honestly think you are more than a plaything to him?"

"I'd rather be a plaything than an assignment. At least with Cynwrig, I knew where I stood. Whereas with you—"

"Oh, do not try to tell me that I hurt your feelings, Bethany, because I've been in your head and your dreams and know the truth." His tone was harsh. Derisive. "Your feelings were never engaged when it came to me. Even if I hadn't been paid to fuck you, you would never have chosen me. You want what you cannot have; you and I never stood a chance."

I opened my mouth to deny it, then closed it again. As he'd said, he'd been in my head, and he *knew*. "Truth or not, it does not negate what I said. Cynwrig considers me part of his harem, and you do not mess with a Myrkálfar's ladies."

He didn't reply. His chest seemed to be rising at a more rapid rate, suggesting he was having trouble breathing. Which I guessed was logical, given that not only was he bent in half but upside down. All his organs and intestines would be squished together *and* pressing down on his lungs.

That small snake slipped through me again, whispering, *Who really cares?*

I flipped him upright. I was *not* going to be what my father wished.

Once his breathing had eased, he said, "You cannot give me to the dark elves. It is unconscionable."

"Unconscionable would be handing you over to the IIT and letting Carla kill you. The Myrkálfar will keep you safe."

"If you think that, you are a fool."

"I said safe. I didn't say comfortable. I believe there is a very deep, dark hole with your name on it, Eljin. I hope the money was worth it."

With that, I turned and walked away before the anger got to me again and I did something stupid.

"Bethany, please, you cannot do this," he called after me.

I kept walking.

"They want you controlled, Bethany."

I stopped cold and turned, hands clenched against the rage that was once again rising. "And how do you know this if you're not in direct contact with Carla?"

"An antiquity with new directions arrived this afternoon. It's why I came here this evening."

"To kidnap me? Or kill me?"

"I am many things, but a killer? No."

"Love to believe that, but sadly, I cannot." Overhead, thunder rumbled, the noise so loud, so close, the building shook with its fury. *My* fury.

"Look, I came here to invite you to dinner—"

"During which I would once again be plied with a drug, one that would this time knock me out, and then handed over to the lovely Carla, who would attempt to make me compliant to her wishes."

He hesitated. "Yes."

"Luckily for me, then, that I was already aware of your duplicity."

I turned and started down the stairs.

"They will kill you if they can't control you, Bethany."

"They wouldn't be the first to try, and they probably won't be the last, given the game is afoot."

"You can't do this, Bethany."

"Watch me."

I continued down. He kept calling my name, but he didn't call for help. Perhaps he knew that of his two options, the Myrkálfar were likely the best. I dumped my purse onto the sofa, then walked over to the kitchenette and put on the kettle. Bodhrán and Mathi appeared on the stairs, neither making much sound but their presence echoing heavily through the building's song.

"Is he still upstairs? Or have you thrown him out through one of the skylights?" Mathi said, the amusement crinkling his eyes belying the seriousness in his tone.

"I was tempted to do the latter, but resisted." I glanced at Bodhrán. "How do you intend to get him out without attracting attention?"

"What can't be seen can't attract," he said.

"A light shield? How'd you get one of those at such short notice?"

The dark elf grinned. "You'd be surprised at the range of magical implements that are available within a five-minute walk of this tavern."

"Really?" I paused. "I don't suppose one of those goodies would be a long-distance type of magical tracker, would it?"

"Most likely—why?"

"Because I have a bad habit of getting kidnapped, and I promised a friend I would get one."

"If you ask my opinion—"

"And I'm really not," I cut in, amused.

"—I'm thinking it's probably unnecessary, given the circumstances."

The circumstances no doubt being Cynwrig's ability to track my weight on the earth. "But you'll get one for me anyway?"

"Indeed, I will." He glanced at Mathi. "Where is our prisoner?"

"This way. Beth, you want to release him?"

I did so. A heavy thump rumbled through the flooring as he hit harder than he normally would have from that height. I may or may not have had something to do with that.

I flicked on the lights, made my tea, then grabbed a block of chocolate from the fridge and moved over to the sofa. The fire was out, and by the time I had it burning again, Mathi and Bodhrán were on their way back down.

Not that I could see Bodhrán—despite the growing darkness that haunted this upper floor, the light shield encompassed him completely, allowing him to move between the patches of light and shadows without the usual giveaway shimmer—and that generally meant expensive.

"I'll just make sure he gets out without incident," Mathi said. "Be back in five."

"You want a coffee?"

"Are we talking instant, or will you drag the maker out of the cupboard?"

"I haven't the energy to drag."

"Then no, thank you."

I snorted, sat back on the sofa, and broke open the chocolate. When he returned, I said, "I think Eljin has a stash of the drug he was using on me in his bedside drawer —is there any chance we could use it to trace the herbalist responsible for it?"

"Perhaps. If you give me the alarm code, I'll stop by his place on my way home and collect it." He paused. "Are you okay?"

"I'm fine. Angry as all get out, but fine." I gave him the code, then bit into the chocolate. "I forgot to mention— when I was in the cavern, the harp started to sing, which likely means Carla was using the pectoral on someone. It might be worth contacting your father—"

"You might have more luck with Sgott. My father appears unusually determined to keep the system locked down right now."

Which remained unusual behavior when it came to his son, and it had me remembering the conversation I'd overheard. I hesitated, then said, "My most recent vision suggested someone high up in IIT has been compromised by Carla. Do you think your father, or even, gods forbid, Sgott, might be one of Carla's unwilling victims?"

"I seriously doubt Sgott is. Aside from the fact he's still grieving the loss of your mother, very few people would get close enough to that man with a blade and live to tell the tale. As for my father—" He grimaced. "We can't totally discount the possibility, but Carla isn't an elf. While I have never had any qualms about bedding a gorgeous woman no matter what the race, he is the exact opposite."

"He doesn't have to bed her to be stabbed by the blade."

"True, but the only time my father is alone outside his office within the IIT is in the Ljósálfar compound. She wouldn't get one step beyond the outer sanctum, let alone anywhere near the inner."

"That still leaves the possibility of it being someone close to either of them."

"Yes, but if we catch Carla and destroy the blade, it is a problem that becomes moot."

"Only as far as Carla controlling them. We already know they're willing to use drugs—you're evidence enough of that."

He grimaced again. "Yes, but regular drug testing has long been a feature in the IIT."

"But you'll still mention it to your father?" When he nodded, I leaned forward and picked up my tea mug. "What are your plans for this evening?"

"I've a date."

"With a prospect?"

"No."

I rolled my eyes. "How do you intend to know and understand the woman you'll eventually marry if you're off fucking around with random other women?"

"My lawyers are currently in contract negotiations with those representing the final three. Until that is all dealt with, I refuse to give any party unwarranted hope."

"It's all so clinical, Mathi. You deserve better than a 'good' deal. You deserve someone who cares."

"I have you."

I rolled my eyes. "That is not what I'm talking about."

"When it comes to matters of the heart, I am a desert." His voice was dry, but amusement danced in his blue eyes. "One emotionally close contact is all I have room for."

I snorted and chucked my purse at him. He caught it with a laugh.

As he did, the harp began to sing.

TEN

I swore and thrust upright, the movement so abrupt tea lapped the cup's edge and splashed over my jeans. I swore again, but placed the cup down on the coffee table and said, "Our thief is at it again."

"Well, there goes my date," he said, obviously unperturbed.

"*And* my much-needed soak in a bubbly bath. And no, we cannot combine the two later on."

I took my purse from him and tugged out the harp. As I touched it, the discordant tune sharpened, and the room briefly faded. What I saw instead was music, each note a visible entity that leapt from the strings and danced through the air, forming a conga line that slipped through the building's front windows and continued on unseen.

If we followed it, it would lead us to our thief.

"We need to go. *Now*."

I tossed my purse down but kept hold of the harp. I didn't even pick up my coat, keys, or phone. There simply wasn't time. He was close—*real* close, if the strength of the harp's off-tune song was anything to go by—but if we wasted so much as a minute, we would lose him.

Why I was certain of that, I couldn't say.

"Do we need the car?" Mathi asked as he chased me down the stairs.

"No. He's near."

I hit the ground floor, ran for the front door, and flung it open. Evening had settled in, the streetlights washing bright puddles of light across rain-darkened pavement. Overhead, thunder rumbled, a deeply ominous note through which an old goddess spoke, telling me to hurry the fuck up....

Imagination? Probably, though when it came to Beira, one could never be truly sure.

The stream of notes went right down Eastgate Street toward the Cross.

I ran after them, dodging pedestrians as the wind picked up and urged me on. The Cross's red sandstone gleamed in the warm light coming from the nearby shops, briefly bloodying the notes as they danced past it. They continued on into Watergate Steet, but a third of the way down, went right and disappeared through the windows of a blue-and-white-painted building that held no signage other than a small logo on the door that said Dusty Diamonds.

I slid to a halt, pressed a hand against the window to shield my eyes from the lights behind me, and peered in. As I did, a shadow darted up the stairs at the back of the room; the notes stilled and then faded. He'd stopped using the pectoral, meaning we were in danger of losing him again.

"We need to get inside, Mathi."

"Already on it."

He dragged his lockpick out of his wallet and did his

thing. A few seconds later, he opened the door and stepped inside. As I followed him in, something shattered on the floor above us.

I doubted it was a window—the glass sounded too fragile.

"You head upstairs," Mathi said softly. "I'll head around to the back of the building in the event he decides to clamber out on the roof or use the fire escape."

I nodded and, as he headed out, ran through the crowded room, trying my best to avoid the shiny bits and pieces that covered all the shelves and nearly all of the floor —the dusty diamonds the shop was named after, no doubt. None of it looked particularly expensive; in fact, while I was no expert, most of it seemed more aimed at tourists than any real collector. But maybe the expensive stuff was kept upstairs; many collectors did that to save themselves the worry of "window shoppers" breaking something valuable.

I grabbed the handrail and took the stairs two at a time. The wood was silent under my fingers, drowned under the weight of too much paint and too little care. Even the building's song was hushed to the point of being inaudible. The floorboards had been treated as badly as the handrail, and the building's network of golden rivers fractured by too many extensions. Neither was able to give me anything on our suspect's location.

At the top of the stairs was an open door, its lock smashed and the frame splintered. I called a knife to my hand and warily stepped through. Little in the way of light crept into the room, despite the windows on the street side of the building being uncovered and quite large, and the shadows were thick and heavy. I couldn't immediately see our thief—or anyone else for that matter—and there was no sound beyond the normal creaking of an old building. I had no sense that he or anyone else was up here. But unless he'd gone out a window—and the breakage I'd heard hadn't sounded like window glass—then he had to be.

I edged forward, keeping my back to the wall and the knife in front of me. The inner tension ratcheted up several notches with every step, and its force echoed through the knife, sending little jabs of lightning into the air. In the deeper reaches of the room, the shadows briefly stirred.

"I know you're there," I said softly. "You need to come out."

He didn't reply. No surprise there.

I took several more sideways steps and raised the knife. The lightning leaping from its tip caressed the stained glass pendant light almost directly above me and spun rainbows across the ceiling. It revealed that this section of the upper floor had been converted into a proper living space. Immediately in front of me was a living area, while to my right were two doorways—the one closest to the stairs being a bathroom while the other appeared to be a small bedroom. I continued on warily, the knife's dancing light slowly revealing the rest of the room. Beyond the living area was a tiny kitchenette, and beyond that, a number of bookcases and— The thought froze as a figure darted across the room and disappeared through a door down the far end.

My first instinct was to run after him, but with the building's song giving me almost no information as to whether he'd been up here alone, I wasn't about to take any undue risks, no matter how desperately we needed to catch the bastard. I continued on warily, sweeping the knife's light in front of me, seeing nothing beyond the glittering glass shards lying at the base of the cabinet he'd broken into and the dust that danced through the air. I paused at the door and cautiously peered around the frame, discovering a staircase leading up to the roof rather than another room. The steps were metal and didn't look particularly safe, but if our elf had gone up them, they should hold me. Of course, he was a young dark elf, and not only walked lighter, but probably weighed a whole lot less, too.

I moved up warily, my footsteps echoing softly and the knife's little flicks of lightning continuing to fold the shadows away. At the top was a rather ratty-looking metal door; at the base of it lay the remains of a padlock. If our thief had been responsible for the lock's destruction, it was unlikely the door held any other magical protections, but just to be sure, I touched the knife's tip to the handle. Lightning buzzed around it for a few seconds then danced away. The door itself held no threat; there was no guarantee the same could be said for whatever lay beyond it.

Again, the thunder rumbled. This time, Beira's voice was clearer and sharper. *You're letting him get away. Move.*

Don't you have something else to do? I snapped back in annoyance.

Yes, so hurry up so I can get to it.

I swore at her, heard the distant echo of laughter in the thunder, and kicked the door open with a little more force than necessary. It crashed back against the frame of a covered rooftop terrace—a very old one, if the rusted state of the metal framework and the amount of moss and mold covering the polycarbonate roof was anything to go by— sending sparks flying. The wind sharpened around me, whispering of movement. Our thief had just leapt over onto the next building. I swore, caught the wind, and cast it after him, then hurried after it. He swung around, eyeing me, his expression amused—arrogant—as he slapped a hand to his shoulder. The harp came to life, the notes once again forming their conga line as the thief's body began to dissolve.

The bastard was not going to get away from me. Not this time.

I split my leash, ordering one arm around his body and the other at the object he was gripping, ripping it out of his fingers. The notes died, and our thief solidified.

He swore—long and very colorfully—and tried to run. I tightened my leash around his waist, ripped him off the roof, into the air, and let him hang there for several seconds. The darkness within wanted to do far more; wanted to damage him as he'd tried to damage me, but I swallowed the urge and plucked the still-glowing pectoral from the wind's grip, shoving it into the back pocket of my jeans as I walked over to the edge of the roof.

"You down there, Mathi?"

"I am indeed." He appeared from under the awning covering the next building's back door. "I take it from all the bellowing that you've caught our thief?"

"Yep. I have the pectoral, too, so he can't escape. I'll lower him down to you."

"You able to keep him bound by the wind until Henrick gets here and we can contain him properly?"

"Sure." I paused. "You keep restraints in your car?"

"I keep many things in my car. Some of them would probably horrify you."

Of that, I had no doubt. I guided our thief over the rooftop and down into the laneway. He was still screaming, but with the air now whirling around him, keeping his voice contained, it didn't really matter. Once I'd placed him next to Mathi, I severed my direct connection to the wind while keeping our thief restrained, then turned and made my way back down the old metal stairs to investigate what he'd been doing in that room. The glass case he'd broken into was one of four sitting on the top of a wide display table, and the three he hadn't touched held rather ancient-looking leather books, meaning there was a fair chance that the one he'd broken into had held something similar. But how had he known which of the four... The thought stalled as the soft sound of wood creaking rose from the floor below.

Someone had just entered the shop. Slowly. Cautiously.

I had no idea if that someone was a thief taking advantage of the front door being open or one of the many police officers who did regular patrols around this area, but I wasn't about to chance being sidelined for hours explaining myself to a copper.

I quickly but carefully made my way back to the metal stairs and went up. After closing the upper door, I hurried over to the terrace's side, called to the wind, and asked it to lower me down. It did so with such vigor that it tore a gasp from my lips. I hit the ground a little too hard, heard Beira say, *Next time, order a soft landing,* as the wind whipped her presence away, and would have fallen had Mathi not grabbed my arm.

"Seriously?" he said. "We're now leaping off rooftops when there's a perfectly good fire escape not ten meters away?"

"I wasn't to know that, and it wasn't like I had time to look. Someone else was in the building."

"Then we had best move." He grabbed our thief and dragged him toward the parking area behind the Mediterranean restaurant a few doors down. Henrick waited near the Merc's trunk, several thin strips of plastic in his hands.

"The usual, sir?" he said.

"You have a 'usual'?" I glanced at Mathi, eyebrows

rising. "Just how often to you indulge in a little kidnapping?"

"Only when absolutely necessary."

"Which could mean anything from once a year to once a week."

My voice was dry, and amusement briefly warmed the seriousness from his eyes. "Indeed. Can you pull the wind back enough to reveal his wrists while the rest of him remains restrained?"

I did so. Henrick grabbed our thief's wrists; he resisted as much as he could, given his limited range of movement, but a glare from Henrick had him stilling. I couldn't really blame him, because that look had promised *serious* harm.

After we'd repeated the process with our thief's feet, Henrick gagged the man, then opened the trunk, shoved him inside, then slammed the lid down on his muffled protests.

Only then did I release the wind.

"Home now, sir?" Henrick asked.

"Yes, but detour down Watergate Street." Mathi glanced at me. "Might as well check who else went into that building."

Henrick opened the doors for us, then climbed into the driver's side and started the car. The engine's purr just about muffled the complaints coming from behind us.

A quick jaunt down Watergate did reveal it was a cop I'd heard, as there were now several patrol cars standing out the front and a number of officers going in and out. Lucky I'd heard him or her when I had, or I'd be explaining to Sgott why I'd broken into yet another property.

We continued on. The traffic wasn't too bad, considering the hour, and we made it over to Mathi's apartment in good time. Like many other highborns, he maintained a secondary residence outside the main Ljósálfar encampment; his lay in the Garden Terraces district, a beautiful and rather expensive area that was close to the canal and surrounded on two sides by community parks. He hadn't chosen the location for the greenery or indeed the water, but because it was close to the main commercial and shopping districts in East Deva and made commuting to work easier.

Henrick drove into the underground parking and skillfully wove through the various concrete pillars dividing the narrow spaces until we reached Mathi's parking allocation next to his express elevator.

Henrick stopped, opened our doors, and then hauled our captive out of the trunk. I hadn't really had much of a chance to take a good look at him, but in the garage's sallow light, he looked much older than he'd appeared in the vision. Perhaps his use of the pectoral had aged him—most godly relics did come with a price, after all. In every other way, however, he was standard issue Myrkálfar—dark skin, dark hair, and gray eyes, though he wasn't as muscular as many of them.

"Thanks, Henrick," Mathi said.

"Do you wish me to carry him up, sir?"

"No, go home for now. I'll likely call once we finish interrogating."

"Very good, sir." He gave me a polite nod, then climbed back into the car.

Mathi returned his attention to our captive. "Now, are you going to be a good lad and behave until we get to my apartment, or do I have to knock you out and carry you up?"

The dark elf scowled but nodded. Mathi grabbed his arm and forced him to bunny hop toward the elevator. He punched in the code to call it down and, a few seconds later, we were walking through the plushly carpeted, pale-green foyer to the penthouse's door.

I followed them in and couldn't help the odd feeling of coming home. I'd lived here off and on for a good part of the ten years we'd been together, and I'd loved the place—especially the kitchen and the living room, with their panoramic views over the gardens and the city. At night, with the glass dark, all you could see was a sea of twinkling lights, stretching out almost as far as the eye could see.

Mathi took the gag off our prisoner, then escorted him down the wide hall. "Beth, do you want to make us both a coffee while I make our guest comfortable?"

I nodded and walked through to the kitchen. It had received a makeover by Mariatta—the would-be wife who'd subsequently tried to neuter Mathi when he'd broken their contracted engagement—and was now all glossy white cabinetry and marble counters. One of those counters displayed Mathi's café-grade espresso machine. He might claim to be incapable of love, but that incapability did *not* extend to coffee.

"You two won't be so fucking comfortable once I report your actions to the IIT," the dark elf growled. His breathing was labored, and sweat beaded his forehead. Bunny hopping, it seemed, was giving his fitness a good workout. "What you're doing is tantamount to kidnapping, and you can be sure I'll be suing both your asses off."

And that right there was youth rather than experience speaking. "Do either of us look as if we actually care? Besides, given who you're targeting, the last thing you want is to land in IIT hands right now."

"How do you know who I'm targeting?" He scowled at me. "No one does—that's the whole fucking problem."

"Good on you for not denying the targeting," I replied, amused.

"What's the point? You obviously know who I am and what I'm doing."

"Actually, all we truly know is that you're one of Jarvil's sons or grandsons." Mathi shoved him into a plush leather armchair that rocked slightly under the dark elf's sudden weight. "So why don't we start with who you are and who you're looking for?"

"If you don't know, I'm not enlightening you. Not until you let me call my fucking lawyer—"

"That's not how these things generally work." Mathi's tone was more than a little condescending. "Now, be a good lad and answer the question, or I shall be forced to use chemical means."

While I'd never spotted said chemicals in my time living here, I had no doubt he did possess them. He wasn't one to make a threat like that without having the means of following through. Once upon a time, the knowledge would have appalled me, but I'd seen a lot—done a lot—in the last few months, and that had definitely broadened my horizons when it came to the gray areas between right and wrong.

"You can't do that. No matter what you think I've done, I have rights—"

"Rights don't matter a damn when you get on the wrong side of a Ljósálfar." I crossed my arms and leaned a hip on the counter while the machine did its thing. "Look, we believe you're going after the woman who killed Jarvil, and that means we're on the same side. So cut the crap and just answer our damn questions."

He glared at me. "Why should I believe you? You fucking kidnapped me—"

"The woman you're hunting," I cut in, not wanting to hear his tirade, "killed my mother, so believe me when I say I understand your need for revenge. But there's more at stake here than that. Help us, and we'll hand you over to Cynwrig Lùtair. Obstruct us, and we'll forcibly extract the information we need, then hand you over to the IIT and let you take your chances."

He snorted. "I like my chances more with the IIT than I do with you lot or Lùtair."

"Then you are a fool," Mathi said. "For your information, the woman you hunt successfully murdered four men in IIT's securest cells only a few weeks ago. You're obviously aware she's a face shifter, so do you really think she could not get to you if she wished?"

The young elf scowled at Mathi for a few seconds, then slumped back in the chair. "Fine. What do you want to know?"

"First up, your name." I walked over with the two coffees and handed Mathi one. "Are you one of Jarvil's sons or grandsons?"

"Macsen Maehdon. Grandson."

"And you worked with your grandfather?"

He nodded. "He was teaching me to take over the antique selling portion of his business. That's how I knew about that bitch, isn't it? Saw them together, but when I asked Pa about it, he acted like he didn't know what I was talking about. So I started keeping tabs on them, like, when she visited him."

If Jarvis was training him, he obviously wasn't as useless as Carla had seemed to think, even if he wasn't as worldly as some young Myrkálfar I'd come across in the past. "And on the day he was murdered? What did you see?"

"I didn't witness her attacking him, but I saw her go into his house and someone else come out. By the time I got in there, he was dead."

"Where were you when you saw all this?" Mathi asked.

"I was driving up to his place when I saw her enter— she must have had the security code, because she let herself in. I parked opposite and waited. She was there for fifteen minutes, if that."

I took another drink. "Who did you report his murder to?"

"The IIT, of course. Some wanker called Bryan Jonson. Didn't take me seriously at all. Hell, even the fucker in charge of the division didn't."

"The fucker in charge of the day division is my father," Mathi said mildly. "You will accord him due respect."

"Like he respected me?" Macsen snorted. "My pa was murdered, and he makes out like I'm an idiot?"

"I'm no fan of Ruadhán," I said, "but one thing he would never do is treat a witness like an idiot—"

"Even if he did think him one," Mathi murmured.

"—so it's possible you were misreading him." I frowned. "Why are you so positive it was Carla Wilson you saw, when she's a face shifter? Did your grandfather ever introduce you to her?"

"No, but he didn't need to. He left me an 'open in case of death' envelope that contained her image—which was a photograph taken from a person of interest report issued by the IIT—and the brooch you stole from me. Which I want back, by the way. It was my grandfather's and—"

"*It* was part of the Éadrom Hoard, which was stolen more than six months ago," Mathi said, even though he was aware the pectoral never had been. "Unless you want your whole family implicated in that theft, I would forget it ever existed if I were you."

Macsen's scowl deepened and, despite the seriousness of the situation, amusement twitched my lips. He might look close to forty or fifty in human terms, but he definitely had the mentality of a teenager. Maybe that was why Carla had thought him an idiot, even though no idiot could do what this young man had been doing so successfully.

"Did your grandfather leave any specific instructions with those items?" Mathi asked.

Macsen nodded. "Said if he died suddenly, or under mysterious circumstances, then the brooch would help me find his murderer, and the first place to start would be the box."

Meaning that while Jarvil had had no immediate memories of Carla, his long-term ones were working just fine.

"What did you find in the security box? Anything specific?"

He shrugged. "Not really. Found a bunch of property deeds, birth certificates, passports, and been working my way through them."

"And when you broke into her houses?" I asked. "Did you find anything enlightening?"

He hesitated, gaze narrowing fractionally. "If I say, will you let me go?"

"You've already been told your options. Full release is not one of them." Mathi's tone was flat, which meant his annoyance was rising. "What did you find?"

The kid sighed. It was a very put-upon sound. "Fine. I found a necklace that held her vibes. Thought I could hire a tracer and find her that way."

I frowned. "How do you know it held her resonance? Are you sensitive to that sort of thing?"

"I'm not, generally, but when I use the pectoral, it can see sounds and the like."

Did that mean me seeing the harp's notes wasn't due to my godly blood, but rather a quirk of the relic? "And this necklace—and all the other items you stole—are currently where?"

"In Dorcha Dearg, of course."

"How?" Mathi asked. "The Myrkálfar have a watch on all your family's residences and a 'find and detain' order out on your immediate family."

"It's not exactly hard to slip in and out of places when you can become invisible." Another shrug. "It's as safe there as anywhere."

"What about the book you stole this evening?" I asked. "Have you still got it on you, or did you stash it somewhere for retrieval later after you'd spotted me?"

"I didn't steal a book."

I rolled my eyes, handed Mathi my coffee, then stepped forward and patted him down. He wriggled and cursed, which delayed me finding it for all of two seconds. I pulled it from his pocket and discovered he *was* actually telling the truth—he hadn't taken a book, but rather a small wooden trinket box. It was simple in design but obviously well cared for, because its frail but gentle song spoke of happiness. I stepped back, found the latch, and opened it. Inside there was a lock of dark hair tied by a faded yellow ribbon and a collection of baby teeth.

My gaze jumped back to Macsen's. "These are hers?"

"The pectoral says they are. I'm not gainsaying it."

The pectoral was also a locator? The Codex's archives had said nothing about that, but given the pectoral's sudden resurfacing and the fact that its godly creator had now entered the ring, maybe it was a recent addition. Nothing was impossible when it came to the gods and their addiction to the game.

I glanced at Mathi. "You got any decent tracer contacts?"

He nodded. "I'll liaise with Cynwrig, though, just to be sure we get someone who is clean."

Clean in terms of being free from the rat god's influence. "I might also know someone, though I'm not sure if she's in Deva or not. She was planning to relocate last I heard."

Margaret Falconer—who'd worked with Loudon and his now dead partner Gannon running a magic shop—was an amplifier medium rather than a tracer, meaning she could talk to spirits and through that hear their resonances. From what she'd said, a maker's resonance always stuck to their creations, and it was that song she could trace if the item still existed in this world.

"Contact her, then, but we'll still work on a backup list, just in case."

I nodded. "Whichever way we go, it'll need it done quickly. If my last vision was anything to go by, Carla's getting a bit antsy about my presence."

"Define 'antsy,'" Mathi said, eyes narrowing dangerously.

"She wants to get rid of me. Her boss is saying they need to keep me around until the Harpē is found."

"Well, let's all hope he has her well and truly leashed."

"Indeed." And if there was one comfort about knowing my death had already been written into the game, it was the fact that it came at the hands of her boss rather than her. Of course, game plans could change—we were dealing with gods after all, and they were fickle beings at the best of times. Besides, while hers might not be the hand that ended me, she could certainly cause me serious harm. I wasn't about to say any of that to Mathi, however. "If what I heard is true, he literally holds her life in his hands."

Mathi's eyebrows rose. "Meaning?"

"Meaning, she has some sort of implant in her brain that will kill her."

"Don't suppose you know what can set it off, do you?" Macsen growled. "Because that would save us all a whole lot of time and trouble."

"While I agree wholeheartedly with that statement, I'm afraid your days of revenge seeking are over." Mathi returned his gaze to mine. "I'll ring Cynwrig, hand over our prisoner, and arrange a retrieval from the compound. You should go home."

I nodded. "Let me know when you have retrieved the rest of Macsen's loot?"

"Of course. Do you want a lift home?"

"I'll call an Uber on the way down. Henrick does deserve some downtime, you know. And yes, I'm aware he's very well paid to make up for the lack of said downtime."

A smile touched his lips. "Get some rest. And that bath."

"Is that a polite way of saying I stink?"

The smile widened. "I would never be so uncouth."

I laughed, drained the rest of my coffee, then popped the cup into the dishwasher. "Behave yourself, Macsen, or I'll make sure the wind not only comes a-visiting, but drops you from a great height."

His scowl didn't quite cover the flick of fear through his eyes. "That's murder."

"Some might think so. Others might think it good riddance to bad rubbish."

The fear in his eyes got stronger, but he didn't say anything. My gaze fell on the trinket box, and instinct stirred. I bent and picked it up. "Mathi, do you mind if I take this with me? I might try to do a scrying and see what it comes up with."

His eyebrows rose. "I didn't think you needed to resort to scrying these days?"

"I don't." Mainly because the triune was generally faster and easier. "I just feel the need to examine it a little more closely, that's all."

"Then who am I to gainsay instinct?"

I dropped a kiss on his cheek, then left, calling an Uber on the way down. The thunder had given way to heavy rain, and though the Uber had parked as close as it could to the entrance, I still got very wet. It dropped me off near the corner of St Werburgh and Eastgate Streets—as close to the tavern as they could get—but by then the rain had become so bad I could barely see three feet in front of me. I waited until the Uber had left, then ran across the street. The streetlights barely lifted the gloom, and Eastgate Street appeared utterly empty. The tavern's lights were as muted as the streetlights, but the warm chatter coming from the building cut through the storm, suggesting we had another good crowd in—always a good thing in the slower winter months.

I ran through the bollards and headed for the tavern. But as I passed the Italian restaurant a few doors up, the knife in my belt flared to life, pressing heat against my skin as it formed a shield around me.

A heartbeat later, a hand appeared out of the gloom; a dark-skinned hand holding a dagger that gleamed with silvery fire as it arced toward my heart with deadly speed.

CHAPTER
ELEVEN

The blade skittered across the shield's surface, sending angry sparks dancing through the rain. I grabbed the knife from my belt and thrust it out and around, but it sliced through nothing but air. Then something—some*one*—hit me hard from behind, sending me stumbling forward. I flailed my arms in an effort to keep balance, but my feet slipped on the wet pavement, and I crashed onto my knees. Again, the shield flared, and more angry sparks flew. I swore and swept the knife around behind me, my knees protesting the sudden movement.

Once again, I hit nothing.

Worse still, the shield was fading, suggesting my attacker had already fled. But just in case, I caught the air and formed several leashes, snapping them forward in multiple directions. They, like the knife, caught nothing. My attacker was obviously using either a shadow shield or the far more expensive invisibility one, but that shouldn't have prevented the wind from at least knocking her over.

Because it had been a woman who'd attacked me. Her hands had been long and slender, her skin smooth and flawless, and her long nails well manicured. Perhaps that meant she was a bird shifter, which would certainly explain her swift disappearance. I looked up, into the storm. The rain pelted my face and made seeing anything nigh on impossible, but the night was free of any sort of movement or anger. Whether or not my attacker had been a shifter, she was long gone.

I swore again, climbed to my feet, and continued on to the tavern, my knees protesting every damn movement. I wrenched the front door open and stepped into the small and *very* warm ground floor room. People greeted me loudly as I made my way toward the bar, many of them ribbing me about being so wet. I asked Ingrid to organize someone to clean up the puddles before anyone slipped on them, then quickly made my way upstairs. I dropped the harp and the knife onto the sofa, then stripped off and jumped into the shower to warm up. My knees were red and beginning to bruise, but at least I'd avoided broken skin and blood.

After ordering a meal from the kitchen—it was a steak, egg, and chips sort of evening—I rose and put the kettle on. By the time I'd had a pre-dinner snack of tea and chocolate, my meal was ready. I scrolled through social media as I ate, catching up on all the local news, then grabbed more chocolate and another cuppa. It was tempting, *so* damn tempting, to reach out to Cynwrig, not because I wanted some loving—although I definitely would *not* have said no to sex—but because I wanted to sleep with the warmth of his arms around me. Wanted to rest secure in the knowledge that he was there, protecting me against all those who wanted me dead. I was no wilting flower, and I certainly wasn't alone in this fight, but sometimes, I really wished I had someone to come home to at the end of the day.

But that was not to be my lot. Not if the gods had their way.

I sighed, picked up the trinket box, and examined it more carefully. I had no idea why I'd felt the need to bring it home with me, which was damnably frustrating. I carefully tipped the hair and the teeth onto the table, then lightly pressed my fingers against the latter. Gran had sometimes been able to get a feel for people with mere touch, but it had never been one of my gifts. Nor had it been Mom's, though both she and Gran could scry with the best of them and sometimes used personal items to help direct what they were seeing. Neither the hair nor the teeth caused any sort of response in me, however.

The box itself was a plain but gorgeous old thing, its song gentle and distant, a background caress more than anything stronger. I deepened the connection, and that's when I discovered it had a false bottom.

I pressed a finger around the inside of the box, but couldn't find any sort of lever or button. Frowning, I examined the exterior, once again running my fingers across the wood, listening to the gentle song, letting it guide me. A rear leg moved fractionally under pressure, and, inside the box, the false bottom popped up.

I carefully eased it away. Inside was a folded piece of yellowed paper. I put the box back on the table and then carefully unfolded the paper. On it, someone had written out the alphabet, and above each letter was some sort of strange squiggle.

It was a code, but what the hell did it decipher?

I had no idea.

I grabbed my phone, took a photo, then carefully tucked the paper back into its hidey-hole and placed the hair and the teeth back in. I needed somewhere safe to store the box

—somewhere it was unlikely anyone would think of looking. After a moment, I rose and walked into the bathroom, pulling out a drawer that still held all Mom's bits and pieces, hiding it right at the back. Then I did my teeth and went to bed.

The building's song woke me who knew how many hours later, warning me Mathi was in the building. I scrambled out of bed and hurriedly chucked on sweats and a hoodie.

"You up?" he called out as he ran lightly upstairs.

"Sadly, for you, yes I am. Is that bacon I smell?"

He laughed. "Your sense of smell is sharper than a bloodhound's."

"Only when it comes to bacon butties." I shoved on my slippers, then walked out. "Did you manage to get hold of Macsen's loot?"

"I certainly did." He placed a tray containing the butties and two coffee cups on the table, then tossed me a small backpack. "It's mainly property deeds, birth certificates, driver's licenses, and a couple of passports, but there was also an oddly large number of personal items."

"Jewelry?"

"No. Mainly hair and toothbrushes, some of them obviously ancient, and most of which came from the security box."

Confusion flitted through me. "Why on earth would she be holding on to things like that?"

He pulled the cups and the butties from the cardboard tray, then sat down opposite me. "While a multishifter can take on the form of anyone they touch for a reasonable amount of time, it's often necessary for them to have some form of their target's DNA if they wish to reflect that person's image for extended periods of time."

"Does us having her collection mean she'll have trouble maintaining some forms long term?"

He nodded. "We—or rather, the IIT—should also be able to use them to match any Jane Does they're holding in the morgues."

"Until we've actually neutralized the bitch, I'm thinking it's best not to give anything to the IIT right now." I opened the backpack and peered inside. "Did you also get the necklace?"

"Yes. It's at the bottom of the pack, in a leather pouch."

"Ah, good." I dropped the bag onto the table then reached for my butty. "I'll contact Margaret Falconer when I get the—"

"The woman who was working with Loudon and Gannon?" he cut in. "Do you think that wise, given they were both connected to the Ninkilim?"

"They were; she's not. I'm sure of that. They tried to kill her, remember."

He grunted. It wasn't a convinced sort of sound. "Cynwrig did give me the details of a tracer in Liverpool. Highly recommends her services."

"Yeah, I just bet he does."

Mathi's eyebrows rose. "Is that a bit of jealousy raising its ugly head?"

"Of course it isn't. He and I are not, and never will be, exclusive."

"A statement that does not void my question."

"Your question is irrelevant." I unwrapped the butty and bit into it. "By the way, someone tried to knife me last night."

"*What?* Why didn't—"

"The knife protected me. I'm fine, obviously."

"Do you think it was Carla?"

I grimaced. "The hand holding the knife was dark skinned, but given she's a multishifter—"

"The one thing body shifters *can't* do is alter their skin color."

I frowned. "Well, that makes no sense, especially given they can alter just about everything else."

"It has something to do with the skin being the largest organ in the body, with three layers that have different anatomical structures and functions." He shrugged. "Body shape and features take far less energy, although even then, they are restricted to those with similar heights."

"Which is rather odd when you consider their animal counterparts can switch from a human to something as small as a rat. I would think *that* more difficult than changing skin color."

"Different magics have different restrictions." He shrugged again. "If it *was* Carla, do you think she was attempting to bring you under control via Bia's Blade?"

"Who else could it be? I don't think I've pissed anyone else off of late. Besides, the visions I've had do suggest they're extremely annoyed at the time we're taking to find the Harpē, so maybe they've decided to exert a little more control over matters."

Mathi snorted. "If they want it found sooner, then perhaps they should throw a few clue scraps in our direction. Or simply order one of the councilors they have under their control to move the Harpē up the list."

"They can't do *that* without raising the suspicions of everyone else." I bit into the butty again and blissed out for a few seconds. "Was their anything useful in the rest of the stuff Macsen stole?"

"There was a recent building purchase I thought we

could check out once we've finished breakfast. It's the most likely to hold something of interest."

"And, therefore, more likely to be the most secure."

"No doubt, but I can get around most alarms."

"And if you can't?"

"I shall employ Locryn's services again."

We didn't have the time Locryn would need to tunnel… and I had no idea why I was so certain of that. I frowned. "I need to take the pectoral back to Liadon first."

"The council want it returned. They won't be happy if it's taken elsewhere."

"Do you care?"

A smile tugged at his lips. "No, but we are being employed to find and retrieve, not find and destroy."

"You're not being paid, and I'm there as a form of punishment. They're getting the service they're paying for." I finished my butty and licked the grease from my fingers. "Where is the building?"

"It's over in Sealand."

My eyebrows rose. "The industrial estate?"

He nodded and picked up his coffee, taking a sip. "It's a former church building, going by what Google says about it."

"Why would she be buying an old church? Especially one in an industrial estate? She can't live there unless she applies for change of usage, and I doubt that would be approved. Not for an area like that."

"Given we don't know what any of her other identities do, that is a question that cannot possibly be answered." His phone binged and he glanced down at it. "The council want an update within the hour. I'll do that while you drop in on Liadon."

"Sounds like a plan. I'll just go change—"

"Before you do, I need to inject a bio tracker in you."

Bio trackers were a type of miniaturized internal medical scanner adapted to use the body's natural electromagnetic field to fuel a constant, low-level but unique signal that could be tracked almost unerringly—something I knew because I'd had the things implanted in me previously. Once by Sgott so he could trace me on the off chance that a meeting with the idiot who'd kidnapped Mathi went wrong, and once by a foe who'd basically wanted me to find a relic for him.

My gaze narrowed. "How big is the needle?"

"It's absolutely tiny. You won't even feel it."

"Doctors say that all the time when they're injecting you. They lie."

He chuckled. "Perhaps. But this needs to be done, because none of us wants to go through the hell of having you going missing again."

"I don't particularly want to go through the hell of being kidnapped again, I can assure you of that." I started to roll up my left sleeve. "But okay, let's get it over with."

"Not your arm. Your belly."

"What? Why?"

"Most bio products are placed in either the arm or the back of the neck, just under the hairline. The belly is less obvious, but just as effective." He motioned toward my hoodie. "Up it goes."

I scowled at him, but nevertheless caught the hem of the hoodie and lifted it up, ensuring it was tucked under my braless boobs in the process.

"You spoil all my fun," he said with a put-upon sigh.

I rolled my eyes. "Will you just get on with it?"

He chuckled, pulled a small, well-wrapped container out of his pocket, broke the seal, then opened it up. Inside was a small syringe; inside the syringe was the metal bio tracker, which was no bigger than a freckle. Mathi took off its cap, ensured there was no air inside the syringe, then pinched my stomach fat and injected the tracker. It wasn't pain free—no damn needle ever was—but it was nowhere near as bad as having a tracker removed had been.

I tugged my sweater down then went into my bedroom and, after closing the door, quickly slipped on a bra and knickers, then jeans, boots, and a thick woolly jumper. After grabbing a waterproof jacket—it wasn't currently raining, but I could smell the promise of it in the wisp of wind sneaking in through the bedroom's open window—I walked across to the bathroom and grabbed the pectoral from the jeans that still lay in a wet heap on the floor there.

Once I'd tucked it into my purse, I called my knives to me, shoved them in as well, then picked up my coffee. "Lead the way, my friend."

We headed down the stairs and out the back. Henrick had parked at the end of the lane and, ten minutes later, we were outside the council's ugly building.

"I'll meet you in the foyer once you've finished," Mathi said as we climbed the stairs.

I nodded. He peeled off at the first floor, but I continued on until I reached Liadon's door. I pressed my hand against the metal, which always felt weirdly warm but also a little oily under my fingertips; the symbols immediately came to life, glowing with an odd green luminosity as heat rolled across my palm and fingers. Liadon's magic, scanning me.

The door slid silently open. Liadon's orb was waiting on the other side for me.

"This is an unexpected pleasure," she said through her creature. "I was not expecting to see you again so soon."

"I wasn't expecting to be back here so soon, but luck was on our side for a change."

"You have found the pectoral?"

"Yes, and apparently, Aamon does not wish it destroyed."

"Indeed, he does not. This way."

The orb spun and sped off into the heated darkness. I hurried after it. "You can't take it from me here?"

"There are some relics I cannot touch. Aamon's is one of them."

"Why?"

"Its gift is incompatible with what I am." The orb spun around briefly. "Only those who are fully human can touch it."

"I'm not fully human."

"No, but it is your humanity that allows you to touch such relics, while it is your divine bloodline that offers you protection from many of them."

"It didn't offer me much protection against Agrona's sword or the fallout from her ring's usage."

"It does depend on the artifact in question, of course." Her tone was filled with amusement. "And you do remain alive, so there is that."

"I'm thinking me being alive has more to do with the gods not wanting their game to be ended so soon."

"That is also true."

She led me into a small dark room that very much reminded me of a bank vault, complete with variously sized security boxes floating in almost straight lines against the walls. These boxes weren't made of metal, however. They weren't even made of the black stone that this place had been carved out of. Instead, they were gauzy and indistinct, their contents darkish shadows, some of which were extremely weird looking, including one that roiled around lazily, reminding me somewhat of a snake.

I shivered and stepped to the other side of the orb, well away from *that* particular box.

The orb made a chiming sound, and a small box little bigger than the pectoral slid out of its position and floated across to me. The lid slid open, and another chime sounded, this one more authoritative. I fished out the pectoral and carefully dropped it into the box. "What about the harp? It's not going to fit in there."

"Oh, it will."

I frowned doubtfully but nevertheless raised the harp to the small box. The harp immediately shrank to the appropriate size, enabling me to place it neatly beside the pectoral.

The lid closed and, with another soft chime, the box slid back into its position.

"Do these boxes just float about here until the god or goddess decides they need their artifact back in the world?"

"If the god remains active, yes," Liadon replied. "If they decided to move on, then the item is either permanently archived or allowed to be found and stored within the elvish hoards."

"Where they can be unleashed onto the unsuspecting population every now and again."

"The gods do like their chaos," she agreed. The orb spun around and led me out of the room. "I should have all the pertinent information on your mother's activities within a couple of weeks."

"You can't fast track that?"

"I shall let that comment slide, because you are obviously unaware just how many records have to be searched.

Your mother worked with the council off and on for centuries."

"Sorry, I didn't mean to be impertinent. I'm just—"

"Impatient for revenge," she finished. "Indeed. But beware, that is a dark path for one such as you."

"And yet it is a path my father wished me to tread."

"You may be your father's daughter, but your mother's bloodline is as strong, if not stronger. In the end, that may be your savior, not the darkness."

How could Mom's bloodline be stronger than a god's? "That is a statement that makes no sense, and a riddle I'm guessing you won't explain."

Her laughter ran through the darkness, soft and rather disconcerting. "I've been associated with the gods for a very long time. Some of their habits have worn off."

They certainly had—but I wasn't about to say that. The last thing I needed was to piss off a being who was not only vital in my quest to find my mother's killer, but likely also when it came to giving me information about the relics I was hunting. The Codex might hold whatever facts the gods had decided to impart about their artifacts, but the pectoral was proof that it wasn't the be-all and end-all when it came to information.

I followed her orb through the network of tunnels, gaze constantly scanning the patches of translucence, once again seeing the shadows of creatures that didn't resemble any form that humanity was familiar with—unless, of course, you counted the nightmares.

As we neared the door once again, the orb slipped to one side, allowing me to pass. "Be careful, young pixie. Darkness gathers this day."

I stopped and faced her orb. "Does that mean the opposition is about to make a new move?"

"I cannot answer that question. I can only warn you to be careful."

"For which I give thanks."

The orb bobbed, as if in appreciation, then scooted back into the darkness. I headed out the door and ran down the stairs, the scent of Liadon's domain—which was musky and unpleasant, vaguely reminding me of either rotten eggs or produce—clinging to my clothes. I hoped Mathi had air freshener in the car, because otherwise it could get rather unpleasant.

He was sitting on one of the foyer's visitor's chairs, doing something on his phone, but rose when I appeared. "The council wish to be informed *before* the event next time we're ordered to deliver items to Liadon."

"Why? It's not like they can gainsay her or the gods." I stopped several feet away. "How bad is the odor coming from my clothes?"

"Not as bad as previous trips into her underworld but I do have an odor neutralizer in the car."

"Of course you have."

"As I have said, I do try to cater for all eventualities."

The guard opened the door for us. I nodded my thanks and headed for the Merc, which was parked in the no-standing zone again. I waved a hand toward it. "One of these days, you're going to get booked for doing that, you know."

"I already have been, but convenience is more important than cost."

"Spoken like a true multimillionaire."

He glanced at me, eyebrows rising. "You're not exactly poor, dearest Bethany."

"*That* is beside the point."

He shook his head, asked Henrick to open the trunk,

and retrieved what looked to be a small medical kit. The neutralizing spray was inside. "Arms out."

I obeyed, doing a slow turn as he quickly and efficiently sprayed me. I wasn't sure what was in the damn stuff, but by the time I climbed into the car, the horrible scent was gone.

"Sealand next, sir?" Henrick asked.

"Yes, thank you."

As we smoothly pulled away from the curb and rejoined the traffic, I said, "What do we know about this place? Anything?"

"I called the real estate agent, but he couldn't tell me a whole lot about its current usage, other than the fact it had been rezoned several months ago for commercial purposes."

"Did you get a buyer's name?"

"It was rented, not purchased. The agent was reluctant to part with the rental information, but I convinced him."

"Threat or bribe?" I asked, amused.

"Cash generally opens more doors than threats. The renter's name was one Elise Andersen."

"I take it you've run a background on her?"

"I had someone run it for me. Hopefully that way, we'll delay any alerts being raised if they're watching everything I do."

"If the rat followers have infiltrated the IIT, then it's likely they'll also have alerts placed on particular names, too."

"It would depend on whether Carla's aliases are known by them." He paused. "Of course, it's also possible this whole thing is a trap."

My gaze darted to his. "What makes you say that?"

"The fact it was rented between Macsen's second and

third break-ins. Elise wanted immediate access and paid one year in advance."

Which wasn't suspicious in and of itself, but if Mathi's radar was twitching, I was going to listen. "How are we going to deal with the situation if it is?"

"Henrick will cruise past so we can check if there's anything untoward going on externally. If there's nothing obvious, then we'll approach from an unexpected angle."

"Unexpected meaning what, precisely?"

His smile flashed. "A roof or skylight is always a good option when they're expecting you to go through the front or back door."

"I hope there's a ladder, because this butt is not designed to be clambering up the side of a building."

"You don't need a ladder. Just order the wind to lift us both up there."

"We could both be taking our lives in our hands, you know that, don't you?"

My voice was dry, and he laughed. "I trust in the fact that you have no desire to depart this world until you've found your mother's killer *and* had your fill of Cynwrig. I suspect the latter could take a *long* time."

"He's expected to take a wife once he and his sister are crowned, and that gives me at most six months rather than years." And then there was the whole deal about my allotted time of death, which I couldn't mention to Mathi because he wasn't aware of that yet.

"Then all you have to do to delay his marriage is not find Geitha's Tears."

I cut him a sharp glance. "You know they've asked me to find that?"

"It was mentioned."

"By Cynwrig?"

"No."

I waited for him to elaborate, and frowned when he didn't. "Treasa? Bodhrán?"

"No."

"Mathi—"

He smiled. "It was your interfering old crone, if you must know. She seems to have taken an extraordinarily deep interest in you, and rather firmly passed on the 'suggestion' I ensure no harm comes to you."

But how had she known about— The thought stopped. I'd been wearing the Eye when Treasa had asked me to find the necklace, and also when I'd been questioning Cynwrig about it. The Eye was linked to the one the crones had, and while I wasn't exactly proficient at contacting them via it— as Mom obviously had been—it was a certainty that they did not have the same problem. Beira might be watching me on the wind, but for those times when the wind couldn't help her, she was just using the Eye.

I glanced out the window as we turned left into the industrial estate. I'd never actually been out this way before, and was surprised to see so many recognizable name-brand retail stores. Maybe I needed to come out this way more often.

"Mom had been working with them," I replied eventually. "Beira wants me to take her place, so it behooves their plans to take a deeper interest in me."

"Which suggests she's also planning for you surviving this game."

"As much as she can plan for that sort of thing, yes."

"I am relieved."

"I'm not. Not when it comes to the gods, no matter what the brand."

His gaze narrowed. "There was a disturbing degree of

fatalism in that statement—have you seen something you're not telling me?"

I hesitated. "No conclusive dreams, if that's what you mean."

"What about inconclusive?"

I waved a hand, and he scowled. "Bethany—"

"*Mathi*," I cut in, in the same annoyed tone. "Let's just concentrate on the task at hand. We can discuss the long-term probability of survival later."

"If you delay said discussion in the hope I will forget, you are wrong."

A smile touched my lips. "Because you only forget minor things—like agreeing to tell me when you took on another lover."

"*That* is different."

No, it really wasn't, but I let it go as Henrick swept us right into Sovereign Way, then slowed down. The screen between him and us slid down. "The building is just ahead, on the right, sir."

It was a weekday, so there were plenty of people, cars, and trucks about, moving in and out of the various buildings. Our building was one of the smaller ones, made of breeze blocks that had been painted half black, half white, with odd shaped—and oddly placed—windows along the front of the building. It appeared to have a flattish tin roof, which, unless it had skylights, was going to make getting through that way difficult. I could call up a storm and target the building with lightning, but that would take far more energy than I wanted to expend when we had no idea what we might be walking into.

"You see anything untoward, Henrick?" Mathi asked.

"No cameras at the front of the building." He paused,

glancing down the side driveway. "None to the side. Might be some at the rear."

"Isn't that unusual?" I asked. "Most modern churches these days have them."

"The real estate agent made no mention of them, and they usually do if pre-installed."

"Or perhaps they simply trusted their parishioners."

"It's not the parishioners these churches usually worry about," Henrick said. "Shall I continue on?"

"Do a U-turn at the Ford dealership. Given there's no movement and the place appears to be locked down, we might as well act like we're meant to be there and go in through the front door. But keep the motor running, just in case we need to leave in a hurry."

"Indeed, sir."

We turned around and headed back to the church. Henrick pulled into the driveway and then reversed into a parking spot. Mathi opened the center console and pressed a button; a drawer slid out from the bottom of the console, revealing a small gun.

"You really do have all manner of nasties hidden in this vehicle, don't you?"

"One can never be too careful when one has as many enemies as the Dhār-Vals do."

He tucked the weapon under his coat, then we climbed out and walked over to the small alcove covering the dark metal doors and the semi-circular windows above it. There was no camera in the alcove, no doorbell, and what looked to be a simple deadlock—simple when it came to someone of Mathi's picking skills, anyway.

"You know, this is all starting to seem a little too easy." I'd already pulled my knives out of my purse and strapped them on. The coat was long enough to hide their presence if anyone was watching the place, and it saved me the hassle of carrying my purse in.

"I agree," Mathi said, "but our only other option is to leave, and I do not believe that is a good idea. Not if we want answers."

"I'm not sure they'll be here to find, but what the hell." I motioned him to proceed, then stepped back and casually looked around, covering his movements from any of the cameras on the other buildings that might have a line of sight with this one.

In no time at all, he had the door open. The foyer beyond was small, with little more than six feet between the front door and the plaster wall that divided this area from the next. It didn't stretch all the way to the ceiling, which was mostly covered in those horrid foam ceiling tiles they'd used in suspended ceilings back in the eighties and nineties. The building itself was silent—the wall in front of us might be plaster, but its frame was metal, as were most of the other walls in this place, from what I could tell— which meant there was no song in this place to help me understand what might lie ahead.

I couldn't help thinking that might have been why it had been chosen.

Mathi stepped inside and to the right. I stopped beside him. There were two doors, one at either end of the plas- tered wall. The one to the right was open, so I sent the wind through it to investigate. It came back echoing of empti- ness. But light flickered down the knives' fullers, so there was danger here somewhere, be it in the form of magic or something else.

"The wind says there's no one in the room beyond the doors," I murmured. "But there's magic here somewhere, so I'll take the closed door, just in case a spell lies on it."

Though my comment was soft, something stirred through the air. Something that felt like anticipation. I shivered and drew a knife. There might be no immediate threat, but I still felt safer with its weight in my hand.

Mathi nodded and moved right. I went left and touched the blade's tip to the door handle; no light flickered down the fuller. Which didn't ease the tension in me, because if the magic didn't lie here, then it was waiting somewhere else. Somewhere less obvious, perhaps.

The room beyond was a vast empty space with a dais at the far end that stretched the entire width of the room. The windows above the dais were standard metal-framed ones, but so dirty the light bleeding in was basically brown. There was a small hall and a set of stairs on my side of the building, while on Mathi's, there was a solitary door. He indicated he was going to check it. I nodded and walked toward the hall, pressing my back against the main room's wall before peering around the corner. Three more doors—two on the left, one on the right.

Lightning now sparked from the tip of the knife I was holding, sending flickers of bright light dancing through the shadows. There was definitely magic in this building, even if I had no sense of anything untoward in the immediate area.

I carefully eased around the corner and approached the first door. After touching the knife's tip on the handle to ensure there was no magic, I warily pushed the door open. The room beyond had obviously been an office at some point, because in the section I could immediately see, there were a couple of old desks and a rather ratty-looking four-drawer filing cabinet. I whipped the wind around the door to check if anyone waited on the other side of the room, then quickly followed it in. Again, nothing more than a couple of old desks and more filing cabinets. I walked across to the nearest desk and brushed my fingers along the wood. Its song was faint and broken, and only spoke of the past. After getting a similar response from the other desks, I walked out, went to the next room and repeated the entry process. This room was empty, as was the one on the opposite side of the hall. I turned and retreated back to the main room, but as I walked in, the knife in my hand burned brighter, and the air began to pulse with the thick warmth of magic.

Whatever it was, its source was upstairs.

The inner tension ratcheted up several more degrees. Mathi reappeared from the room on the other side of the building. I raised the knife, sending jagged shards of lightning spearing into the gloom that held this place hostage.

He walked over, then leaned close and whispered, "Investigate or run?"

I hesitated, and in that moment, the decision was taken from me. Magic surged, and behind us, the front door slammed shut. The air that lightly stirred around me briefly whispered of movement—men, running toward us, making little sound—then the press of magic intensified, and the wind stilled. I reached for the air again, but it slid away from my touch. How that was possible, I had no idea, nor did I have the time to worry about it.

"It's a trap. There's a witch or a mage up there, along with a good dozen men."

"Then let's get out of here." He grabbed my free hand and pulled me into a run. "Can you punch one of the front windows out?"

"From inside? No. The air is being sucked away from me. I'll try from outside."

"Do it. I'll keep them off us."

When we reached the door into the foyer, he stopped and drew the gun from under his coat. I called to the wind that swirled with almost angry force around the outside of the building and punched it toward the nearest window. Glass shattered, and thick, deadly shards thudded into the plaster to the right of the door. But there was no escaping for us yet—the network of metal grilles that had held the eight panes of glass in place remained in the window. I swore, recalled the wind, and ripped them away.

"Right—"

The rest of my words were lost to the bark of Mathi's gun. A heartbeat later, he knocked me sideways. I hit the ground hard, and pain shuddered up my arm. I swore, heard something thud into the wall just above our heads, and quickly looked up.

Not bullets, as I'd presumed, but darts.

The sort of dart they used to bring animals down.

They weren't trying to kill us; they were trying to capture.

Mathi rolled away from me, his gun barking again. I scrambled upright and darted through the doorway. More darts followed my movement, thudding into the outside wall and dropping to the floor.

"Go, go," Mathi said urgently as he followed me through and slammed the door shut. It stopped the darts; it wouldn't stop the men. I might not be able to grab the air in this place, but I could still feel the vibration of movement, and they were coming at us fast.

I turned, took several quick steps, and leapt for the window. I gripped the sill, swearing again as the glass still caught in the putty tore into my skin. Mathi shoved me up the rest of the way, and I half fell, half jumped down to the concrete path on the other side, staggering forward several steps before I caught my balance.

As Mathi followed me through the window, the door into the foyer crashed open. I caught the wind and formed a barrier across the entire front of the building—just in time to catch the darts that chased him through.

"Go, go," he said as angry faces appeared at the window and the front door crashed open. They couldn't get much further thanks to my barrier, but still...

I ran for the car and jumped in. Mathi followed me through, landing heavily on my legs before I could pull them away. Henrick immediately took off, turning left so sharply we were both flung across the rear seat. Once Mathi had pushed back upright, I did the same and saw the men running from the side of the building. One of them was on the phone. This wasn't over yet.

"Henrick," Mathi said. "Get us to the fae hospital ASAP."

My gaze shot to him. He was pale and sweating, his skin holding a weird, almost waxy sheen. "What's happened? Were you shot?"

"A dart in the arm, I'm afraid."

Alarm surged, but before I could say anything, Henrick said, "Your assailants give chase, sir."

"Lose them."

I twisted around and looked through the rear window. There was a big black van behind us, and it was going every bit as fast as we were. The driver and his passenger were little more than pale blurs, but even so, I could see the latter was on the phone, no doubt calling up reinforcements. It was tempting to cast the wind their way, but there were too many other cars on the road now and I didn't want to risk causing an accident.

I turned, helped Mathi into his seatbelt, then pulled on

mine. He really did *not* look good. I had no idea what they'd used on the darts, but surely it couldn't be deadly. If they'd wanted us dead, they'd simply have used guns.

"Mathi?" I touched his cheek, trying to catch his attention.

His gaze slid to mine. "I feel... strange."

His words were slightly slurred, and the alarm strengthened. I'd seen many of these effects before, in both my brother and in Cynwrig. "I think you've been hit with Dahbree."

Dahbree was basically a rare but deadly truth serum, and if they were using that, then whoever was behind this assault wanted us to sing like birds before they got rid of us permanently.

Had Carla gone rogue, or was there someone else behind this? Macsen's family, perhaps?

The Merc turned right sharply, throwing me hard against the seatbelt. I swore and looked behind us again. The van wasn't losing any ground; whoever drove the thing appeared every bit as good as Henrick.

Another sharp turn. Horns blasted, and the squeal of tires filled the air. I twisted around again; one car had rear-ended another, while two others now faced in the wrong direction. The van swept around it all, briefly driving into the oncoming traffic, causing more chaos as drivers tried to evade him.

One vehicle, however, turned sharply and came straight at us.

It was another black van.

Henrick yanked the Merc left so hard she briefly went up on two wheels. We crashed up onto the pavement and into the parking area of a large warehouse. The vans followed, leaving more chaos behind them.

The man in the front seat of the first black van was still on the phone.

"Henrick, orders are being relayed via that van behind us."

"Are they now?" His gaze flicked to the rear vision mirror briefly. "Hold on tightly, because we're about to impact."

I swore and pushed back into the seat and headrest. A heartbeat later, the Merc came to an abrupt halt. Tires squealed, and black smoke swirled down either side of the car, then we were hit, hard. The car lurched forward sharply, momentum Henrick used; the Merc's engine roared as we pulled away to an accompanying symphony of tearing metal and breaking glass.

I looked behind us again. The entire front of the van had been pushed in; steam rose from the grille, and the bumper had been partially torn off. Their windshield had also shattered, so I couldn't see how the van's occupants had fared, but hoped like hell the guy with the phone had at least been taken out of action.

"Don't worry, Ms. Bethany," Henrick said calmly. "The car is reinforced to withstand that sort of impact."

"I'm not worried about the Merc; I'm worried about there being more of them."

"If there are, we shall deal with them."

I should have been reassured by his calm confidence. I wasn't.

I held tightly onto the grab handle and watched as Henrick sped around the back of the building, through a short weed-encrusted space, then into the parking area behind another warehouse. As we bumped out onto the road and accelerated away, I turned around again. There was no sign of the other van—just a line of buildings on one side and thick vegetation on the other. But just as my heartrate began to ease, it appeared.

I swore.

"Indeed," Henrick said. "They are very persistent."

"You want me to call in the IIT?"

He hesitated. "It might be wise. At the very least, they can escort us to the hospital."

I bent, grabbed my phone out of my purse, and called Sgott.

"I take it this is no social—"

"No," I cut in quickly. "We're in Mathi's car, being chased by black vans. Mathi's been darted, I think by Dahbree or something similar. We're currently on—" I paused, and Henrick immediately said, "Stadium Way."

I repeated that and added, "I have a tracker—"

I didn't finish the sentence. I didn't get a chance. Henrick's sudden, violent swearing had me looking around sharply. A black van—a different black van—was coming straight at us from out of a side street. The Merc slewed violently sideways, the tires and engine screaming, but this time, there was no avoiding the collision. The van punched hard into the side of the car, throwing us about like rag dolls and rocking the vehicle up on two wheels. The air bags exploded, filling the air with a thick smoky smell.

"Bethany?" I heard Sgott yelling. "Talk to me."

I wasn't holding the phone. I had no idea where it even was. But I nevertheless croaked, "We're hit, bad, help."

I had no time for anything else, not even to call the wind for help, because we were in the grass and rolling, over and over.

I hit my head, felt warmth trickling down my face, and a sudden twist of pain in my leg. The car settled upside down, and the groaning began, some of it mine, most of it the car's. For what seemed an eternity, that's all I heard. That, and the desperate, fear-filled pounding of my pulse.

Then, from somewhere close, a woman said, "Fuck, did you idiots hit the elf? You were told to leave him alone."

I didn't hear the reply. I did hear the distant wail of sirens. *Sgott*. He would save us. Save me.

"We've no fucking time for excuses," she growled. "Get the woman out and fast, before the fucking cops get here."

I knew that woman. Or, at least, knew her voice.

It was Carla.

The realization finally had me reaching past the haze of pain for the wind, but before I could direct it against her or anyone else, darkness surged and swept consciousness away.

CHAPTER
TWELVE

Waking was a slow and painful process. There were madmen armed with heavy picks digging their way through my head, desperately trying to get out, and a good portion of my body seemed to be joining in on the pain party, making it difficult to think.

For what seemed like forever, I didn't. I simply survived.

But as consciousness slowly sharpened, I became aware of the cold stone pressing against my back and the ropes that bound my wrists and ankles together. The air was cold and somewhat stale, and the silence was absolute. Nothing moved, either in this place or beyond it.

Eventually, I forced my eyes open, only to be met by utter darkness. The sort of darkness that came with deep underground caverns or perhaps even crypts.

Fear stirred through me, but I pushed it down and did a mental checklist of my situation. My knives were gone, but they had to be somewhere close, because I could feel the pulse of their energy. I called for them, but they didn't answer, which was no doubt due to the pulse of magic encasing the space I was in. While I couldn't be absolutely certain, I suspected it was the same magic that had stopped the air answering my call in the warehouse. I reached for it anyway, just to be sure. Heard the briefest howl of wind from some distance away, and the slight brush of air past my fingertips, but that was it.

I mentally swore and continued my silent checklist.

My boots were also missing, as was, oddly, one sock. Something heavy was wrapped tightly around my left calf —on the same leg that was missing its sock—but I could wiggle my toes without causing a screaming tide of agony, which suggested I hadn't broken anything. My coat was also gone, and moisture—blood?—coated the left side of my face, which felt swollen and bruised. My bottom lip was also swollen, so I ran my tongue around the inside of my mouth; all teeth accounted for and seemingly unbroken. My fingers moved as ordered, as did my arms—or at least, they moved as much as the rope hog-tying me would allow. I carefully rolled my neck from one side to the other and felt no stab of agony. All in all, it appeared I'd come out of the accident rather well.

I just had to hope Mathi and Henrick had....

I pushed away the concern that surged and jerked into a sitting position. A dozen new aches broke out across my body, and pain hissed from my lips.

Somewhere beyond the darkness that encased me came a squawk, then the soft tones of someone speaking. I couldn't hear what they were saying, so either my hearing was fucked or the magic that enclosed my prison was also muting any sounds that might otherwise seep inside. Perhaps it was also the reason it was so damn dark.

I carefully reached forward and examined my leg. The

inseam of my jeans had been cut open, and the thick bandage stretched from just above my ankle to just below my knee. If they'd taken the time to treat my leg, they obviously did not intend to kill me. That should have stirred relief but did the exact opposite.

I prodded my leg lightly and felt only the gentlest whisper of pain, which suggested whoever had bandaged the wound had also treated it with some sort of numbing salve. If that were true, then maybe, just maybe, the leg wouldn't hinder me too much if I got the chance to run. Of course, it also meant I wouldn't be aware of any additional damage I was causing, but I'd rather that than sit here and let them do whatever the hell they were intending to do.

I glanced around and tried to figure out where I was despite the darkness that blanketed the room. It felt small, and the walls I couldn't see exuded a chill that spoke of stone rather than wood. I drew my legs up slightly to provide some slack on the rope and felt along the edge of the stone I was sitting on. It was about two inches thick and a lid of some kind. I bent and skimmed my fingers down the base as much as I could. More stone. Perhaps my initial fuzzy thoughts had been right—I was not only in a crypt but sitting on a sarcophagus. There was no easy way out of this damn place, that was for sure.

Unless... I glanced down at my wrist. The Bruadar bracelet remained, so maybe I needed to use it—presuming, of course, that the magic that stopped my knives from answering didn't also restrict the Bruadar's magic. The urge to test it rose fiercely, but I battered it back down. Using the Bruadar might allow me to escape this situation, but it would also give Carla time to run and the time to form a new plan of attack. That was not going to happen. The bitch was not going to get the chance for further attempts on my life; one way or another, it was going to end here, tonight.

From outside came the sound of footsteps, then the rattle of a key in a lock. I tensed, my fingers twitching with the need to call my knives. I resisted. Until I knew where I was, why I had been taken—though I could pretty much guess that, given who'd I'd heard at the crash site—and just how many of them there were, it was better to hold my ace in check.

The door opened, and light speared into the room, the sudden brightness blinding. I looked away, blinking rapidly against the tears, but nevertheless caught the shadows of those who entered—three men, one woman. The man holding the light remained in the doorway, shining it directly onto my face.

I reached again for the air and the distant storm. This time, the latter was louder, closer. It was coming, but my ability to wield it was still being restricted by the damn magic protecting this place. I wondered what it would take to break it. Wondered if I had the time to find out.

"It won't work, you know," I said, my voice little more than a harsh rasp. "I know who you are, Carla. More importantly, Mathi and Cynwrig know who you are."

"You may know one name," she replied evenly. "You have no idea who I truly am or how to find me."

"Ah, but you're wrong. We have the information Macsen stole, and it will lead us to you." Only the faintest hint of anger crept into my tone, and that surprised me. I would have expected a whole lot more, given what this bitch had done. But perhaps the accident and the madmen banging away in my head were somehow divorcing me from my emotions.

She stopped in front of me, just out of kicking range,

and crossed her arms. With the light directly behind her, it was impossible to see her face, but her silhouette was tall and slender, and her hair was short. "While it is true that what Macsen stole will stop me from using several identities, it matters not, because you, my dear pixie, are out of time."

"Your boss doesn't want me dead, Carla. Or should I call you Brídín?"

Her shock ran through the air—and if I was feeling that, then the magic in this place was faltering. "How do you know that name?"

"Oh, I've been listening to your fucking conversations for weeks. Who is he, Carla? What position does he hold in the IIT?"

"Well, aren't you the enterprising little witch? Our relationship going forward could be more fruitful than either of us had anticipated. Hold her."

Before I could process the end part of that statement, the three men grabbed me—two gripping my arms and pulling them away at such an angle from my body that my shoulders burned and the ropes binding my wrists bit into my skin. The third man stepped between me and Carla, then dropped to his knees and pressed his bulk again my legs, pinning them against the sarcophagus.

It was only then I realized what her earlier statement had meant.

"Don't do this. Carla," I growled, trying to keep a grip on rising panic, and failing. "You *will* regret it."

"Oh, I regret many things in my life, but this will not be one of them."

She produced a blade from somewhere on her person. It was long and thin and glowed with a fierce and ruddy light. Bia's Blade, of that I had no doubt. I swore and fought the grip of the three men, throwing myself to one side and then back in a desperate attempt to get free. It didn't work. I reached for the wind, for my knives, for the Bruadar, and felt the tingle of their separate responses but also an odd restraint. The magic. It was still stopping them responding in any meaningful way.

Then Carla stepped forward and plunged her knife into my shoulder.

I screamed, the sound echoing through the silence. Somewhere in the distance the skies rumbled in fury, and the air in the crypt stirred. It wasn't enough. Not to pull the knife free, and not to blow the bitch and her people away from me.

I needed more time. I didn't have it. The knife's glow sharpened, its heat pulsing through me, a foul snake whose resonance crawled across every part of my inner being, trying to claim it for its own.

"Stop screaming," Carla said. "And stop moving."

The glow leaching from the knife's hilt intensified, and the song of its snake had my whole body vibrating in tune with it. The scream died on my lips, but not because the knife and its magic had me in its thrall and forced compliance, but because it *didn't*.

I stilled.

Liadon had said I was immune to some godly relics, and it certainly made sense that a weapon that could potentially control the opposition's main player would be one of them. But it was Beira who'd said the blade's resonance would allow me—or rather the wind—to find its location when in use.

Maybe, just maybe, I could use that to my advantage.

I called again for the storm, this time reaching for it through the foulness of the blade's music. Thunder rumbled, closer now, filled with fury and the need to destroy, but whatever magic had leashed my ability to call to the weather and my knives still vibrated through these walls. To use either, I first needed to destroy that magic.

And I had no idea where the spell was anchored.

"From this moment on," Carla was saying, satisfaction practically oozing from her skin, "you will obey my every order."

The knife flared, and once again its heat surged through me. Doing nothing, telling me nothing.

"You will report your relic-related movements and discoveries on a daily basis whenever you're undertaking a hunt. Understood?"

"Yes," I said, in a monotone voice.

Thunder cracked overhead, a sound that echoed through the stone around us.

Carla glanced up, her concern flicking through the air. "Are you doing that?"

"No," I responded.

Another deep rumble, and electricity began to build in the crypt, raising the hairs on the back of my neck. *Soon*, the storm seemed to whisper, *soon we will break through.*

Soon we will kill her.

But not before she'd fucking talked.

"What is your phone number?" she was saying.

I reeled it off. Again, the sky rumbled its fury, and power surged, striking at the building, sending a shock wave of electricity through its stone. Somewhere in the distance, glass exploded.

Carla looked over her shoulder, then added hastily, "Once you have written your daily report, place it in an envelope addressed to Pam, and then walk it down to Dusty Diamonds and give it to them. Understood?"

"Yes."

"You will not come after me. You will not attack or follow my men when they release you. You will remember nothing of our meeting or anything that has happened here. Understood?"

Another flat acknowledgement. She hastily pulled the knife free. The wound didn't heal, but she didn't seem to notice. She was too busy looking up at the ceiling and the thickening rain of stone dust. She shoved the knife away and gave me a smile that sent chills down my spine.

"I have a final gift for you, dear Bethany, before you utterly forget this event."

She stepped back, and a weird shimmer rolled over her body, concealing it from sight. When it retreated a few seconds later, I was looking at myself. Fury swept me, a fury so deep that something inside cracked. Outside, thunder rumbled, a long roll that promised revenge. Promised death.

She glanced up again, then returned her gaze to mine. "Sgott will feel the sweet enticement of the blade—"

I screamed and lunged for her; I didn't get close enough to do her any harm thanks to the men still gripping me, but her face nevertheless paled. Whatever she'd seen in my expression had scared the hell out of her.

And rightly so. She was a dead woman walking.

"Enjoy the memories you have of Sgott," she snapped, "because all he will see is you stabbing him, you betraying him. And he will ostracize you, never talking or seeing you again. And if you try to make it otherwise, I will destroy him."

With that hanging in the air, she turned and hurriedly left.

I screamed after her, but she didn't stop, and she didn't reply.

But the storm did.

The ceiling exploded, raining enormous slabs of stone and goddess only knew what else all around me. Carla's men swore and released me, stumbling for the door, trying to escape. The rain of destruction chased them, stopped them, but none of it touched me. I remained in a small bubble of calm while destruction fell on the men who'd held me prisoner.

As the last of them died, I called to my knives. They thudded into my hands, their fullers glowing brightly, their light breaking the veil of darkness, allowing me to see the hallway beyond the half destroyed door and the ceiling high, high above. There was no sound up there, no light, no panic. The place was empty. Empty except for me and the dead woman running.

I called to a thread of air, wrapped it around the hilt of one knife, and directed it to the ropes binding my wrists. Once they were cut away, I retrieved the blade, sliced through the leash binding my ankles, and carefully stood. Pain slithered up my leg and across various bits of my body, but they were all distant things and easily ignored.

Again, the thunder rumbled, a deeply furious sound bidding me to hurry. I picked my way through the destruction and scrambled over the stone half blocking the door. Dust hung heavily in the corridor beyond, making it impossible to see. I called to the electricity that danced through the air and forced it through the blades. Lightning shot out left and right, briefly illuminating the corridor and the destruction the storm had caused—was still causing. There were stairs to my left, and while there was no sign of Carla, the swirling wind brought me the sound of her steps. I could have ordered the wind to chase her, capture her. I didn't. The bitch was mine, and she would not escape me.

But just to be sure, I ordered the storm to unleash on whatever vehicles might wait beyond these walls.

Then I ran after her.

The dust caught in my throat, making me cough and causing the madmen in my head to renew their frenzied digging. Warmth flowed from my shoulder, soaking my sweater, but I didn't care, and I certainly wasn't going to stop.

She was not escaping me.

I reached the stairs and half ran, half limped up them as fast as I could. The wind was fiercer up here, the thunder closer. Lightning split the furious skies, hitting the side of the building to my right. Rocks and glass exploded in all directions, but the wind rose, directing it all away from me.

More lightning. In its fierce white glow, I saw my target.

I raised one knife, wrapped a sliver of wind around it, then flung it at her. Not to kill her, but to kill the magic that resided within her. The magic that allowed her to shift shape.

Thunder cracked once again, and the entire building shuddered. Lightning hit the still-intact portion of the roof above me, sending tiles and chunks of lovely old oak beams flying. The pixie in me mourned its destruction, but the darkness held sway right now, and it was fixated on the woman and revenge.

The knife hit her shoulder, slid deep into her flesh, and she stumbled, going down on hands and knees. I didn't know if she screamed and didn't really care. I slowed, weaving through the rain of stone and timber and tiles, untouched, uncaring, as the lightning crawled across Carla's body and she shuddered and shook, her nails digging into the stone and her flesh shaking and crawling and shifting.

Then she pushed up and staggered on, through the doors and out into the storm-held night. I caught the wind, retrieved my knife, followed her down the first few steps, then stopped.

Ahead of us lay more destruction—a black van and a silver Renault lay in smoking pieces. Last time I'd hit a car with lightning, I'd shorted the electrical system. This time, the tires and windows had exploded as well, rendering both useless.

Carla screamed and swung around, the knife in her hand pulsing furiously. Her face was pale, waxy, and nondescript, her eyes the same brown as her short hair. "What have you done to me?"

I smiled. It was not a pleasant smile. "I killed your magic. I stopped your ability to shift shape."

"You can't do that. It's impossible—"

"Unless you wield godly relics capable of not only protecting you against magic but killing it." I raised my knives. "Mom possessed such knives. Shame she wasn't wearing them the day you killed her."

"I didn't—"

"Then who did. Give me a name."

Her gaze narrowed, and the knife's intensity grew, its light spearing the darkness, lending it a bloody hue. "I order you to restore—"

"You can't order me to do anything, Carla," I cut in coldly. "You see, the thing about godly relics is, they don't always work on the gods themselves."

Anger ripped through her expression, and I could almost taste her desire to attack me, kill me. There was a part of me—a deep, dark, dangerous part—that wanted her to. Silently begged her to.

"You're no fucking god," she growled, and took a step forward.

I didn't move, didn't react. Though I wanted to. Gods only knew how much I wanted to. Not for what she had done to me, but for what she had threatened to do to Sgott.

"No, but I am a godling. My father was a god of storms and lightning, hence the show that happens above." She didn't look up, as I'd half expected her to. "Name, Carla, and you will live through this."

She snorted. "No, I won't. He'll kill me. He already has the means inside my head."

"Then tell me what you can."

"I can tell you nothing. He's been planning this for centuries, and he has left nothing to chance. The minute I attempt to say anything that could lead you to him, I die. The minute I land in IIT hands, I die. Kill me if you wish—in the end, you'll be doing me a favor."

I studied her for a second, my fingers clenching and unclenching around the hilt of the two knives. "Then what of the council?"

"What of them?"

"Give me the names of the councilors who have fallen victim to the power of Bia's Blade."

"No."

And with that, she attacked.

The move took me by surprise, and I lurched backward. Pain ripped up my leg, and I stumbled, falling down onto one knee, barely raising the knives in time to catch her blade in their center. She screamed and lashed out with one foot, the blow thudding into my side with surprising force. Something within broke, but it wasn't agony that rose, it was fury. The wind surged, screaming around us, but I resisted the urge to attack her with it. Instead, with Carla's blade still caught between my knives, I rose to my feet. She tried to withdraw her weapon but the lightning rolling between the two blades had it caged, and it wasn't going anywhere.

She swore again, released her knife, and then spun, aiming her boot at my gut. I jumped back, caught her leg with the wind, and pushed her, as hard as I could, away from me. She stumbled backward, flailing to keep her balance on the steps, and then fell in an ugly mess of arms and legs down to the bottom of the stairs.

I uncrossed my knives, releasing Bia's Blade, and then followed her down. The need for revenge pulsed through every bit of my being, a force that was almost a living thing. The skies above compounded the inner fury, filling my mind with whispers that begged me to give in to the darkness, to take the revenge I so desperately wanted. The urge was so damn strong that I actually knelt in front of her and raised the knife. The only thing that truly stopped me was the blood curse.

That, and the fear I saw in her eyes when she opened them.

She might as well have thrown cold water in my face. I pushed away from her, landing hard on my butt, my heart racing so hard it felt as if it were about to tear out of my chest.

No matter how deeply, how badly, I wanted to find my mother's killer, I could not follow the siren call of darkness and claim the life of a woman who'd already said she was not responsible for Mom's death. That may or may not be the truth, but if I did what the storm and the voices that raged within it wanted, if I killed her like this—when she was unarmed and broken—then that inner darkness would claim me, and I would become the warrior my father wanted me to be.

If I was going to emulate anyone, it would be my mother.

I shoved my knives back into their sheaths, then crossed my arms, my fingers clenched against the power that pulsed through them, through me, dangerous and demanding.

Carla groaned and tried to get up; a scream tore up her throat and echoed across the raging night. I had no idea what she'd broken—whether it be her back or her hip— and I didn't really care. I might not want to give in to the darkness, but that didn't mean I had sympathy for her current plight.

"Where is your phone, Carla?"

"Fuck off," she growled, though her voice held little strength, and her face was pale and sweaty.

I sighed, leashed her arms so she wasn't tempted to attack me, then leaned forward and patted her down. I found it in her jacket pocket. I hit the ON button, shoved it in front of her face to open it, then said, "Tell me where we are so I can call you an ambulance."

"And why would you fucking do that?"

"Oh, trust me, there's a large part of me that really doesn't want to, but I'm doing my best to be more like my mother than my father. Who, by the way, is screaming for your death because he believes it will hinder your boss's movements, at least until he can find a suitable replacement."

"I cannot be replaced."

"Everyone can be replaced, Carla. Where are we?"

She hawked and spat rather than reply. I went into the

settings on her phone, changed the access to me, then tucked it into my back pocket. The sound of sirens began to cut through the night, and I glanced up. In the distance, blue and red lights flashed, growing ever closer. Not one car, but multiple.

The tracker obviously worked.

I returned my attention to my captive. "If you can't tell me who killed my mother, then at least tell me why."

"Why should I?"

"Because the bastard who killed her will undoubtedly kill you, and this is perhaps your only means of getting a little posthumous revenge."

She considered me for a moment, her eyes narrow slits of anger and pain. After a moment, she said, "In my phone, you'll see a number for a Delores Collins. When I am dead, ring it, and tell her Brídín sent you."

"And what will she tell me?"

"Nothing, because she is not truly of this world and cannot speak. But she will give you the records I have been keeping for centuries. If you read them carefully enough, using the key you already have, you will find the man you are looking for. Kill him for me."

I opened my mouth to ask, "What key?", then remembered the code I'd found in the trinket box. "What do mean, she's not truly of this—"

I stopped. Carla's eyes had closed, and her body seemed to have collapsed in on itself. I reached forward and pressed two fingers against her neck. Her pulse was there—too thready, too fast—but there.

An odd mix of emotions ran through me, but I ignored them all and cast her blade—Bia's Blade—deep into the heart of the storm and quickly created a convergence that would keep it up there, and safe, until I was ready to deal with it.

Then I sat back and watched the red-and-blue lights draw ever closer. Unsurprisingly, Sgott was the first to arrive, and the first to come striding toward me.

"Lass, you look a goddamn mess—and is all that blood soaking the left side of your shirt yours?"

"Yeah, it is."

"And are you hurt anywhere else? Where is your shoe and sock?"

"Question of the hour, I'm afraid. As to the first part of that question, my head hurts like a bitch and there's a thick bandage around my calf, so I think it's likely gashed." I waved a hand to the woman in front of me. "Meet Carla Wilson; real name, Brídín, and no longer a shape shifter. My knife killed her inner magic."

"And did it kill her?" he asked sharply. Worriedly.

"No. She lives, although probably not for long given she's got what amounts to a kill-switch in her brain."

"And your knives? Their ability to kill magic doesn't affect the switch?"

"I honestly don't know, but if said switch is magic, then it's likely already dead, because I used the knives to kill her inner ability to shift shape."

"Ah. Good."

More cars and several ambulances stopped beside Sgott's vehicle. He glanced their way, motioned several offi-cers over, then knelt beside me. "Come on, my girl, let's get you to hospital."

"I'll be—"

"Fine, yeah I know, but humor an old man and just let me take care of you." He scooped me up in his arms and carefully lifted me, and the memories of him lifting me in the same manner when I was a kid and had fallen over and scraped my knees rose, making me blink back tears.

Making me glad I'd resisted the darkness.

I wanted to be someone *he* could be proud of, too.

I rested my head against his big chest, just as I had all those years ago, and felt safe and loved.

The darkness might remain, but I'd at least beaten it for now.

EPILOGUE

Mathi walked into my hospital room just as Lugh was leaving. The two of them—and Darby—were maintaining what amounted to a twenty-four-hour watch on me, just in case the opposition decided to make another kidnapping attempt. Sgott also had a man positioned out in the corridor.

I loved them all, but they were going a little overboard. Whoever Carla's boss was, I doubted he'd go down the kidnapping route again. Not now that Carla was dead. Her kill switch had been activated just as her ambulance had reached the hospital, and it had scrambled her brain. Not even the best surgeon or elven healer could repair the mess that remained.

Mathi rolled the tray table into place and placed coffee and chocolate on top of it. "I brought you rations, because apparently they want to keep you in for another twenty-four hours. They said your head wasn't right. I did claim it was normal, but..."

"Idiot," I said, swiping at him lazily. "Any news on the Carla front?"

"They're in the process of tracing all her aliases, using the information we got from Macsen."

"And the councilors she used the knife on?"

"With the blade out of action—"

"It's actually not. I threw it into the storm, where it still roams."

"But we are going to destroy it, right?"

"Ah, no. I've been ordered to return it to Bia. Or Liadon, so she can return it."

"The council will not be pleased."

"The council do not have to know. The blade wasn't a part of the hoard." I picked up the cup with my name on it, took a sip, and then reached for the chocolate and broke it open. "I don't suppose they've indicated when our next hunt might begin, have they?"

"Probably twenty-four hours after you're out the hospital, like they did last time." His gaze narrowed. "Why?"

I hesitated. "Carla told me to ring someone after she'd died, because this someone would give me all the records she'd been keeping over the centuries. Apparently if we read them carefully enough, we will find our puppet master."

"And did she give you the number of this someone?"

"No, but she did give me her name, and I have got Carla's phone."

"Have you now?" Amusement glimmered in his eyes. "That is evidence, you know."

"I know, but I've been hanging around you too long, and the need to bend the rules has rubbed off."

He laughed. "Then I shall ensure to impress upon them that you need more than a day's recovery."

"Good, because I still have to find Geitha's Tears, remember, and time is running out."

"There's still nearly six months before he has to marry, depending on how long they take to make the crowning arrangements—and I rather suspect Cynwrig will push the time frame out as much as he can."

"Even if he does, we're talking about an object that's been missing for centuries."

He hesitated. "It is also an object that will ultimately shatter you. I do not wish to see that."

I smiled and squeezed his fingers. "I'm not that fragile, Mathi."

"Even the strongest tree has a breaking point. I fear Cynwrig might be yours."

"He is Myrkálfar; I am not. I have always known he and I can never be."

No matter what my heart might say to the contrary. No matter how much he might ask me to trust him, believe in him.

Mathi smiled, but the concern in his eyes sharpened. "I may never personally experience love, Bethany, but I know it when I see it. I see it in you."

"It doesn't matter what you see, and it doesn't matter what I feel. It won't break me. I can promise you that."

He studied me for several long seconds, then nodded and pulled his hand from mine. "Whatever the future may bring, I will be here."

"I know. Thank you."

Bedevilment stirred through his expression. "Well, I can hardly afford to have my best—and probably only—true friend fall to pieces before she has completed the odious task of choosing me a wife."

I laughed. "Does that mean the contract situation has been sorted?"

"It does indeed. Let the games begin."

"May the best woman win."

I lightly tapped my cup against his and tried to ignore the stupid part of my heart—the part I'd sworn only seconds ago would not break—that wished, when it came to Cynwrig, *his* best woman could be me.

But even if, by some miracle, he did find a way around the restriction of tradition and expectations, the gods had spoken, and my death was slated.

And that meant heartbreak, even if it did happen, wouldn't last for long.

I guess *that* was something to look forward to.

ALSO BY KERI ARTHUR

The Black Lantern Series

Dark Secrets (July 2026)

Drakkon Kin Trilogy

Of Steel & Scale (Nov 2024)

Of Scale & Blood (May, 2025)

Of Blood & Fire (Sept, 2025)

Relic Hunters Series

Crown of Shadows (Feb 2022)

Sword of Darkness (Oct 2022)

Ring of Ruin (June 2023)

Shield of Fire (March 2024)

Horn of Winter (Jan 2025)

Bia's Blade (Jan 2026)

Geitha's Tears (Oct 2026)

Lizzie Grace Series

Blood Kissed (May 2017)

Hell's Bell (Feb 2018)

Hunter Hunted (Aug 2018)

Demon's Dance (Feb 2019)

Wicked Wings (Oct 2019)

Deadly Vows (Jun 2020)

Magic Misled (Feb 2021)

Broken Bonds (Oct 2021)

Sorrows Song (June 2022)

Wraith's Revenge (Feb 2023)

Killer's Kiss (Oct 2023)

Shadow's End (July 2024)

The Witch King's Crown Trilogy

Blackbird Rising (Feb 2020)

Blackbird Broken (Oct 2020)

Blackbird Crowned (June 2021)

Kingdoms of Earth & Air

Unlit (May 2018)

Cursed (Nov 2018)

Burn (June 2019)

The Outcast series

City of Light (Jan 2016)

Winter Halo (Nov 2016)

The Black Tide (Dec 2017)

Souls of Fire series

Fireborn (July 2014)

Wicked Embers (July 2015)

Flameout (July 2016)

Ashes Reborn (Sept 2017)

Dark Angels series

Darkness Unbound (Sept 27th 2011)

Darkness Rising (Oct 26th 2011)

Darkness Devours (July 5th 2012)

Darkness Hunts (Nov 6th 2012)

Darkness Unmasked (June 4 2013)

Darkness Splintered (Nov 2013)

Darkness Falls (Dec 2014)

Riley Jenson Guardian Series

Full Moon Rising (Dec 2006)

Kissing Sin (Jan 2007)

Tempting Evil (Feb 2007)

Dangerous Games (March 2007)

Embraced by Darkness (July 2007)

The Darkest Kiss (April 2008)

Deadly Desire (March 2009)

Bound to Shadows (Oct 2009)

Moon Sworn (May 2010)

Myth and Magic series

Destiny Kills (Oct 2008)

Mercy Burns (March 2011)

Nikki & Micheal series

Dancing with the Devil (March 2001 / Aug 2013)

Hearts in Darkness Dec (2001/ Sept 2013)

Chasing the Shadows Nov (2002/Oct 2013)

Kiss the Night Goodbye (March 2004/Nov 2013)

Damask Circle series

Circle of Fire (Aug 2010 / Feb 2014)

Circle of Death (July 2002/March 2014)

Circle of Desire (July 2003/April 2014)

Ripple Creek series

Beneath a Rising Moon (June 2003/July 2012)

Beneath a Darkening Moon (Dec 2004/Oct 2012)

Spook Squad series

Memory Zero (June 2004/26 Aug 2014)

Generation 18 (Sept 2004/30 Sept 2014)

Penumbra (Nov 2005/29 Oct 2014)

Stand Alone Novels

Who Needs Enemies (E-book only, Sept 1 2013)

Novella

Lifemate Connections (March 2007)

Anthology Short Stories

The Mammoth Book of Vampire Romance (2008)

Wolfbane and Mistletoe--2008

Hotter than Hell--2008

ABOUT THE AUTHOR

Keri Arthur, the author of the New York Times bestselling ***Riley Jenson Guardian series***, has written sixty novels—35 of them with traditional publishers Random House/Penguin/Piatkus—and is now fully self-published. She's won seven Australian Romance Readers Awards for Favourite Sci-Fi, Fantasy, or Futuristic Romance & the Romance Writers of Australia RBY Award for Speculative Fiction. Her Lizzie Grace series won ARRA's Fav Continuing Romance Series in 2022 and she has in the past won The Romantic Times Career Achievement Award for Urban Fantasy. When she's not at her computer writing the next book, she can be found somewhere in the Australian countryside taking photos.

for more information:
www.keriarthur.com
keriarthurauthor@gmail.com
Buy eBooks & Audiobooks directly from Keri & save:
www.payhip.com/KeriArthur

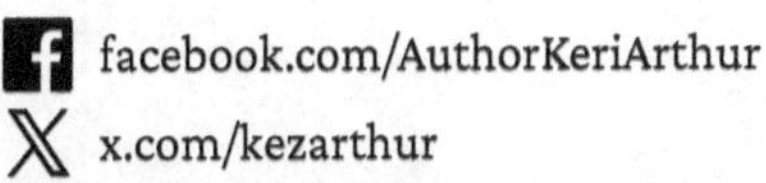